Sweet Love at Bayside

Sweet with Heat: Bayside Summers Series

Addison Cole

ISBN-13: 978-1-948004-90-9
ISBN-10: 1-948004-90-9

SWEET LOVE AT BAYSIDE

Cover Design: Elizabeth Mackey Designs
Cover Photography: Wander Pedro Aguiar

WORLD LITERARY PRESS
PRINTED IN THE UNITED STATES OF AMERICA

A Note to Readers

I'm thrilled to bring you another fun, flirty, and passionate series set in my favorite place on earth, Cape Cod. In *Sweet Love at Bayside* you'll meet several lovable, loyal characters, and we have many more to look forward to! And from time to time you'll see our Seaside characters in the Bayside series (they are neighbors, after all!). Be prepared for some wild, sweet and sexy fun!

Sweet with Heat novels are the sweet editions of the award-winning, steamy Love in Bloom big-family romance collection millions of fans have fallen in love with by *New York Times* bestselling author Melissa Foster. Addison Cole is Melissa's sweet-romance pen name, and *Sweet Love at Bayside* is the sweet edition of Melissa's steamy novel *Bayside Desires*. The storylines and characters remain the same as the original titles. Within the Sweet with Heat series you'll find flirty, emotional romances with all the passion two people in love convey but without any graphic love scenes and little or no harsh language (with the exception of an occasional "damn" or "hell"). Sweet with Heat features fiercely loyal heroes and smart, empowered women on their search for true love. They're flawed, funny, and passionate. Characters from each family appear in future series. Each book may be read as a stand-alone novel, or as part of the larger series.

Sign up for Addison's Sweet with Heat newsletter to be notified of the next release, sales, and special events.
www.Addisoncole.com/Newsletter

For more information on Sweet with Heat titles visit
www.AddisonCole.com

Chapter One

DESIREE CLEARY STOOD at the end of a jetty at Indian Neck Beach, watching three brawny guys race around Cape Cod Bay on Jet Skis while she FaceTimed with her best friend, Emery Andrews. She had known Emery since first grade, and she was the only person who would understand why, after driving for more than twelve hours, Desiree was standing on that jetty, pretending to be on vacation, instead of facing the woman who had summoned her to Wellfleet.

"I should have come with you," Emery insisted. "You're at the beach, and I'm stuck here teaching yoga and Pilates to people who go home and eat entire pizzas afterward. Not that I'm only thinking of *me*. I'm just saying. I could be your backbone when you see your mother. You know, make sure you don't wimp out on telling her how cruel it was to go months without any contact and then send you that email."

Emery had a right to be upset. She'd been there for Desiree for more than twenty years, picking up the pieces of Desiree's broken heart after short, awkward, visits with her mother. Lizza Vancroft had been breezing in and out of her life since Desiree was five years old. Desiree was used to hearing from her mother only once or twice a year, but her most recent email had taken the cake. She'd read the cryptic message dozens of times, as concerned as she was annoyed. *I need you to come to Wellfleet and run my art gallery for the summer. It might prolong my life.* She hadn't even known Lizza was ill, much less owned a gallery and had been living in the States.

"I'll be fine," she said, though she wasn't sure she believed it. After Desiree's parents had divorced, Lizza had taken off to teach overseas with Desiree's half sister, Violet, leaving Desiree to live with her father. Some small part of her was still waiting for her mother to make amends for leaving her behind. "I just need a few minutes to get my head on straight before facing her."

One of the Jet Skis headed directly for another, swerving at the last second to avoid a collision. "Holy cow. Someone is going to get killed. Look at these guys." She held up her phone to show Emery the crazy Jet Skiers. "Who does that? It's so dangerous."

"Hot Jet Skiing guys who thrive on danger. My kind of guys, and *your* perfect distraction." Emery waggled her brows.

"I don't need a distraction. Lizza is almost a stranger to me. It's like I'm waiting to get bad news from someone I met a few times but don't really know."

"I know. Your mother is as flighty as a fairy, and I'm sure right now you wish you were wired like her and Violet instead of being responsible and organized to the nth degree, like your father," Emery said. *Spot-on, as always.* "Then *you* could be the one who was living overseas working with one nonprofit or another without Internet or a care in the world, like Violet, instead of procrastinating the unleashing of a nest of demons you've spent years tamping down."

"You're so dramatic." Desiree smiled, thankful for Emery's

teasing.

She had no idea whether Violet would be there when she arrived. Though she and Violet had grown up on opposite sides of the world, they had spent a few weeks together at the Cape each summer with their grandmother. At least they had until they were teens and one or the other had found better things to do, most years whittling those weeks down to just a few days. They'd kept in touch only sporadically during college, and before their grandmother's funeral last winter, it had been more than three years since Desiree had seen Violet or their mother. But that didn't mean Desiree hadn't always wished for a relationship with her sister, despite how different they were.

"That's why you love me." Emery flashed a cheesy smile. "Seriously, though. You need to just go see Lizza and get it over with. And you should probably be glad I'm not there. Because as far as I'm concerned, her email was infuriating, unfair, and heartrending." Emery's eyes narrowed. "I'd like to give her a piece of my mind."

"So would I," Desiree admitted. "But I won't." A breeze swept off the bay, lifting the ends of her dress. She pushed it back down, catching a glimpse of one of the Jet Skiers slowing to watch her. As if she wasn't nervous enough today?

"I know. You've got the biggest heart on the planet. We need a plan. You do best with plans." Emery tucked her brown hair behind her ear and leaned closer to the screen, like she was sharing a secret. "Tonight, after you get your heart torn to shreds, since I'm not there to help heal your mama-wounds, *please* get yourself a nice bottle of wine and a big man. I promise that will help ease whatever pain she throws your way."

"Don't you mean a *big* bottle of wine and a *nice* man?" Desiree asked, as the Jet Skier who was watching her broke away from the others and sped past.

"Definitely not. You don't need a *nice* man. I know you *think* you want romance and all the mushy stuff like flowers, candy, and midnight walks." Emery flashed her don't-even-try-to-tell-me-otherwise scowl. "But trust me. You need a man who takes control, whose kisses turn you inside out and make you forget about your crazy mother."

She wrapped her arms around her middle, listening to the roar of the lone Jet Ski cutting tracks in front of her and wondering about kisses that turned a woman inside out. She had yet to experience anything like that, but Emery talked about them like she'd had enough to share. Maybe it *was* time to expand her horizons.

"*Hello?*" Emery said. "Think you can look at me and stop watching the hot Jet Skiers for two minutes?"

Desiree laughed. "Like you'd ever look at me instead of a guy? Besides, I'm only watching one, because *he's* watching *me*. The other two are long gone." She held up her phone again, showing her the hot guy with dark hair keeping time with her as she paced the jetty.

"You're so lucky. Go take hot Jet Ski guy for a *ride* and show up late to see Lizza." Emery waggled her brows. "For all you know, she's not even at your grandmother's house waiting for you."

That was true. Lizza and Violet still hadn't replied to her messages. But that didn't change the fact that Desiree wasn't a jump-in-the-sack-with-a-stranger kind of girl. "That's just what I need. A reckless adrenaline junkie before seeing Lizza. No thanks."

Emery turned away from the phone. "I have to go. My date is here."

"You have a date? With who?"

"One of the reckless, adrenaline-junky Jericho brothers. I'll let you try to figure out which one." She blew Desiree a kiss. "Listen, babe. Take my advice. Go for the Jet Ski guy; then you'll be nice and relaxed when you see Lizza. Call if you need me. Love you!"

Desiree ended the call, and the guy trailing her on the Jet Ski zoomed past. He made a sharp turn and headed back, eyes locked on her, making her heart race. Maybe letting loose for a night *was* just what she needed. One night of uninhibited *anything* would be a first. The Jet Ski turned again, taking another, faster pass, the hot guy's eyes still trained on her. Butterflies took flight in her stomach. He was obviously interested. *Maybe…*

He turned again and headed straight toward the jetty.

Straight for *her*.

Uh oh. How long had she been staring at him? *What was I thinking?*

She tried to act casual, looking at the boats, the sky, anywhere but at the man on the machine as she made her way along the rocks toward the beach. He fishtailed, spraying water in her direction. She shrieked and turned away as water rained down on her.

No, a reckless man was definitely *not* what she needed.

OH MAN! RICK Savage beached his craft, threw his life vest onto the sand, and ran after the woman he'd soaked. He'd been so captivated by the curvaceous blonde that when she'd started to leave, his first instinct had been to stop her. He'd clearly lost his mind. He knew better than to come that close to the jetty *or* to fishtail near people.

"I'm so sorry," he said, jogging over as she stepped off the rocks and onto the beach.

She turned, mouth gaping, strands of wet hair stuck to her cheeks, forehead, and shoulders. The most beautiful green eyes stared back at him in shock and horror. He felt like a total jerk.

"I'm sorry. I saw you watching me, and—" There was absolutely no excuse for what he'd done, so he went with the truth, no matter how bad it sounded. "I wanted to meet you before you took off."

"I wasn't watching you." Her eyes darted around them, as if someone else might hear her lying.

He cocked a brow.

"Okay, maybe I was for a second. But you were *stalking* me." She swiped at her sundress, which clung to her incredibly sexy body like a second skin.

He tried not to leer, but oh, man...

Forcing his eyes up, he said, "I wasn't stalking you—"

Her deadpan stare stopped him from telling his own lie.

"Okay, fine," he said with a laugh. "I was. You caught me. I'm sorry."

"Does this usually work for you? Drenching unsuspecting women?" she said with a hint of annoyance, and a smile, as she shook the water from her arms. "Not that I'm an expert on being hit on, but it doesn't seem like the best way to go about it."

"I'm sure you get hit on all the time, but this wasn't planned. It was a stupid mistake. It's actually illegal to go that fast near the jetty, so you can have me arrested if you'd like. I wasn't thinking. I was—"

She arched a brow, a slight smirk playing across her beautiful face as she tossed his mannerism right back at him.

He felt himself smiling. Man, this woman was as sweet as she was spunky. "What can I say? If you weren't so hot…"

"So, it's *my* fault?" She rolled her eyes. "You really do kind of suck at picking up women."

The caveman in him grunted, and he squared his shoulders. "I don't suck at it. I'm actually really good at it. A pro. A master. A *champion*."

She laughed. "Sorry, but…" She waved at her wet clothes. "Evidence proves otherwise."

And I'm about to prove that evidence wrong. "Let me buy you a sweatshirt and something warm to drink at Mac's so you don't freeze." Mac's was a walk-up restaurant by the Wellfleet Pier, a five-minute drive by car. Less by Jet Ski.

Her eyes rolled over his face, as if she were considering it. He'd never had anything close to a poker face, which meant she saw his remorse *and* his attraction. At six two, two thirty, he was a big dude, and he kept in prime shape with running and water sports. He was used to women ogling him and practically doing cartwheels to get his attention. She drew in a deep breath, her eyes dropping to his bare chest, and she bit her plump lower lip. "Sexy" didn't begin to describe the dichotomy of sweet and sultry this woman possessed. But she wasn't doing cartwheels. In fact, those hungry eyes shifted away from him.

"It's okay," she said. "I was getting ready to leave anyway."

She was blowing him off? There was no way he was letting her leave without doing something to make up for this debacle. Okay, maybe he also wanted to strip away those wet clothes and warm her up. But that was beside the point.

"Are you staying at a cottage on the beach? I can give you a ride on my Jet Ski."

"As tempting as that sounds, since I've never been on one, I have my car." She pointed to the parking lot with the hand that held her phone, and her smile faded. "Oh, *shoot*. My phone got wet."

"I can take care of that." He took it from her and dried it on his shorts. She watched his hands, his biceps, his pecs, his *shorts*, with laser focus. His fish wasn't off the line yet. "It should be okay now. Want me to put my number in your contacts? In case you change your mind about that drink?"

That brought a curious smile. He noticed the cutest dimple beside her mouth when she smiled. "Does *that* usually work?"

"No idea. I haven't had to use that line before."

He stepped closer, unable to resist brushing a lock of hair that was stuck to her cheek away from her face so he could see her better. Their eyes connected, and the temperature spiked. She must have felt it, too, because she was licking her lips like a hungry tigress. In the next breath, her eyes darted nervously around the beach, making her appear sweet and innocent. How did she do that in the blink of an eye? Rick was only at the Cape for a few more weeks, working on renovations at the resort before returning to his *real* life, and design-build business, in Washington, DC. The thoughts running through his mind were *not* sweet and innocent. He should let his apology ride, get on his Jet Ski, and drive away. But she had his rapt attention, and he was unable to walk away.

"You don't have to use my number," he said. "But you never know. Maybe when you're lying in bed tonight, unable to stop thinking about me, you'll wish you had it."

Her cheeks flushed, and those sparkling green eyes moved over his face and down his chest again, lingering long enough to send a stroke of heat to his core.

"Why not?" she said, surprising him. "Go ahead and put your number in my phone…?"

"Rick." He entered his contact information and handed it back, curling his fingers over hers and holding them for a beat.

Her eyes flicked up, dark and alluring. "I'm Desiree," she said a little breathlessly.

Oh yeah, you feel it, too.

"Desiree." Her name rolled off his tongue as if he'd said it a hundred times. "You sure I can't convince you to have a drink with me? We can go back to my place and build a bonfire."

"A bonfire…" She crossed her arms, rubbing at goose bumps, and her expression turned skeptical. "Just out of curiosity, why didn't you ask me for *my* number?"

The truth was, he had no idea. He just sensed he shouldn't be too aggressive with her, but he couldn't tell her that, so he went with, "I've got a sister. She got married last summer, but when she was single, I wouldn't want her giving her number to a guy she met like this."

Her lips curved up. "Um…?"

Great, now he sounded like a cretin and had to come clean. "Not buying it, huh?" He laughed. "The truth is, I was just trying to give you the choice instead of being one of those jerks who come on too strong. My brother and a buddy and I own Bayside Resort, here in Wellfleet. I'm pretty easy to track down. A safe bet. A good choice. The *best* choice." Her gaze warmed, and he tried again. "Bonfire?"

She inhaled a shaky breath. "I better not. It's been a crazy day, and I've got a complicated evening."

Complicated? He had a handful of questions about that, but before he could suggest they go somewhere to talk, she said,

"Sorry, but I'd better go. I have a lot to do tonight."

"I hope it's nothing too difficult." *Too difficult?* That was the best he could come up with? He was really out of practice. It had been a long time since he'd had to try to pick up a woman.

She smiled. "Actually, I don't know what it is yet."

He wondered if she was on the cusp of a breakup. That would explain her blowing him off. "You have my number. If things get rough, use it."

"Thanks, but I'm sure it'll be fine." She cocked her head to the side with a thoughtful expression. "You don't even know me. What if I'm a psycho?"

She was too cute. "If you were a psycho, you would have taken my head off when I sprayed you. Come on, I'll walk you to your car."

"I'm parked just over the dune. You don't need to."

"I'd like to."

Her eyes shifted over his shoulder toward the water. "But your Jet Ski…"

"It says 'Bayside Resort' on the side. No one's going to be stupid enough to steal it." He didn't care if they did. She intrigued him more than that machine ever had.

"You're persistent." A smile lifted her lips as he guided her up the sandy path with a hand on the small of her back.

"And you're beautiful."

"Does that usually work for—"

He stopped walking and drew her against him. The reins on his aggression were apparently short-lived. She sucked in a sharp breath, and when their eyes met, she let it out with a dreamy sigh. It was the sexiest sound he'd ever heard.

"You tell me, Desiree. Does it work for me?"

The unmistakable look of lust rose in her eyes. She licked

her full, pink lips, and he wondered how they'd feel pressed against his or searing a path down the center of his body.

"The verdict is still out," she said softly, but her unstoppable smile, and the fact that she was no longer shivering, told him all he needed to know.

Each time their sides brushed as they crossed the parking lot, she stole a quick glance. He had the urge to tell her she could brush against him, touch him, *taste* him all she wanted, but that underlying sweetness held him back.

"If you own Bayside Resort, then you probably have pretty women at your beck and call. Why go to the trouble of leaping off your Jet Ski to meet me?" She withdrew a single key with a tiny gold heart key chain from a pocket in her dress and unlocked the door of her MINI Cooper.

"You were gawking at me." He stepped closer, hoping to see that hungry look again. "It would have been rude of me not to."

A sexy smile lifted her lips.

"We'll have to take my car when we go out. There's no way I'll fit in this one."

A melodic laugh fell from her lips. "*When* we go out?"

"That's right." Holding her gaze, he ran his hands up her arms, from wrist to shoulder. Her skin was soft and cool, but it heated up quickly beneath his touch. "Warming up?"

"Mm-hm. You're very forward."

"Most people call me 'aggressive,' but I like your word better. I'd like to get to know you, Desiree. I hope I haven't scared you off." His hands dropped to her waist. She didn't move away, her body didn't tense up, and she held his steady gaze. *Game on?* He still wasn't sure.

"Like I said." Her eyes narrowed in speculation. "*Forward.*"

"You know what they say. If you're not moving forward,

you're going in the wrong direction."

"So, you're pretty sure getting women wet is the way to go?"

Maybe she wasn't as innocent as she seemed.

He drew her soft body against him, loving the way her breathing hitched. "Absolutely, and I'm pretty sure when we go out, you'll agree."

Her eyes widened with surprise. She was sending so many mixed messages he couldn't tell if she was toying with him or nervous. Or was she testing the waters? Dipping her toes in and pulling away when it got too hot? He wanted to take her in his arms and carry her to the volcanic side. But he feared he'd already pushed too hard, and went for a save.

"Get your mind out of the gutter, sweetheart." He leaned down and kissed her cheek. Her skin was soft as silk, and she smelled like the promise of a warm summer's night. She was watching him with that curious, lustful gaze again, and he brushed his thumb over her jaw. "I'm really sorry for soaking you with my Jet Ski, but I'm not sorry we met."

Chapter Two

DRENCHED AND TURNED on was not how Desiree imagined greeting her mother. But the lingering hum inside her from meeting Rick was a lot better than the awful feelings she'd been experiencing earlier. As she parked in front of the tall Victorian overlooking Cape Cod Bay, an army of emotions trampled through her, turning all that heat into discomfort. For decades, her grandparents had used the house and four cottages as a bed-and-breakfast called Summer House Inn. But now, the once-beautiful gardens were overgrown and wild. Weeds covered the patio near the cottages, giving the property a forgotten feel. Her mother had inherited the estate when they'd lost their grandmother, and it appeared she'd given the property about as much attention as she'd given Desiree.

She stepped from the car as the front door of the house swung open, and her mother stepped out onto the wide front porch carrying two big suitcases. Desiree froze. Lizza's hair was as wild and thick as a jungle, tumbling over her shoulders in natural waves, dozens of shades darker than Desiree's blond, but not as black as Violet's crow-colored hair. Her orange maxi dress shifted around her legs in the cool evening breeze, giving her a youthful appearance as she set the luggage down.

Orange. My favorite color. Did you remember, or is it a coincidence?

Apparently oblivious to her daughter standing in the driveway, Lizza walked to the far side of the porch and tipped her head up toward the sky, eyes closed. Desiree had seen her do that many times. She remembered mimicking the action when she was younger, hoping to feel whatever it was that brought a smile to her mother's face when she did it. But Desiree wasn't Lizza, and she'd never felt like anything but a little girl reaching for the impossible—a shred of her mother to hang on to.

As Desiree ascended the steps, her mother turned. Her Julia Roberts smile brought a rush of conflicting emotions.

"Desi," Lizza said. "Goodness. You were anxious to take a swim, weren't you?"

Not knowing how to explain why she was soaked, she said nothing at all.

After a brief, uncomfortable hug, Desiree assessed her mother's sparkling eyes and the healthy glow of her skin, which she hoped were positive signs.

"You look good. What's going on? Are you sick?"

"Oh my gosh. Am I *ever*. Thank goodness you came." Lizza's eyes trailed over Desiree's face. "You're troubled."

Seriously? "You sent me an email saying I needed to be here to prolong your life. Of course I'm troubled."

A motorcycle roared up the driveway and parked beside Desiree's car. A tall woman clad in all black climbed from the bike.

"Violet is here." Her mother picked up her suitcases and traipsed down the steps. "Come now, Desi. There's no time to waste."

Violet drives a motorcycle?

Violet took off her helmet and shook out her long black hair, eyeing Desiree with a curious expression as she embraced Lizza.

"Hey, Des. I came as quickly as I could. You okay? Why are you all wet?" She set her helmet on the bike and shrugged off her leather jacket, revealing colorful tattoos from her right shoulder to her wrist. She'd gotten more since their grandmother's funeral.

"Don't ask, and I'm as okay as you might expect me to be." They shared an awkward hug. "I tried to email you." She didn't know why she hadn't expected Violet to come. She was actually *close* to their mother.

"I've been traveling," Vi said, as if *traveling* were a universal excuse for being unresponsive. "Lizza said you needed me to be here this summer. Something about *prolonging your life?* Are you sick?"

"Not *my* life." Desiree waved toward their mother. "*Her* life."

"My two beautiful girls together again. I'm the happiest woman on the planet right now." Lizza hugged herself, inhaling deeply and tipping her face up toward the sky as she'd done earlier. "This is so right. So *perfect.* Can't you *feel* it? This is what we needed."

"If you mean feeling confused, I'm right there with you." Violet's lips puckered with annoyance. "Why *are* we here, Lizza?"

A cab pulled into the driveway, and their mother clapped her hands together. "Right on time."

"On time for what? Are we going somewhere?" Desiree couldn't hide the disbelief in her voice.

"Not *us*, honey. I'm going to an ashram for the summer."

Lizza carried her bags to the cab, and the driver hoisted them into the trunk. "I tried to stay to watch over the house, but staying in one place has nearly *killed* me. It's zapped me of all my creativity. I can't sleep. I can't think. I can't even sit still long enough to do yoga. I *need* this. I need to center myself, to rejuvenate my soul."

"Wait. What?" Violet crossed her arms, narrowing her cat-like green eyes, the only physical trait she and her sister shared. "What was all that bull about prolonging Desiree's life?"

Their mother grabbed one of each of their hands. There was no tension in her grip. Her expression was happy and relaxed, stoking the anger simmering in Desiree's stomach.

"Lizza," Desiree said in the calmest voice she could muster. "You're not sick? You're...*bored*? You tricked us into coming here to run your gallery? Why do you even have a gallery if you hate being here?"

"Oh, Desi. Negative energy is so unhealthy. This is a blessing, the two of you together again. There is no doubt that knowing you're together will prolong my life *and* yours. And, Vi, baby," Lizza said. "You're my solid girl. Desi needs you like the grass needs water."

A flash of jealousy tore through Desiree at the warm endearment her sister received, but her anger pushed it aside. "No, I don't. Do whatever you want, Vi. I'm going back to Virginia."

"Great. My life is going back to Bali." Violet strutted over to her motorcycle.

Lizza pressed both hands over her heart. "No, girls. Please, don't be selfish. You can't leave. Not unless you want to lose your grandmother's house."

"What?" they said in unison.

"The mortgage has to be paid. I have enough pieces in my

gallery and personal exploration shop to sell to cover the expenses well into the winter, but the bulk of the sales happen over the summer. If neither of you is here to run the gallery and shop, the mortgage will default and we'll lose the estate."

Personal exploration shop? This was just like their mother, expecting them to drop everything and clean up her mess. Wasn't that exactly what she'd done to Desiree's father when she'd decided she didn't want to raise her?

Desiree held up her hands. "Wait. Grandma's house has been paid off forever. That's how she was able to afford to shut down the inn after Grandpa died."

"It was," Lizza said. "But I had this idea to reopen the inn and make it into a retreat. A mini ashram with yoga and massage, and I needed money for renovations."

"Wait a second." Desiree's voice rose. "You can't strap us with a mortgage for your whimsical idea. We didn't ask for any of this."

Lizza's smile never faltered, which angered Desiree even more.

"You're absolutely right, Desi. You didn't ask for it. But the universe *heard you* anyway. You *need* this."

"I don't know what universe you live in, but clearly it's been smoking something funny," Desiree said. "Not only do I not *need* this, but I don't want it."

Violet stalked over to their mother, glaring at her in a way that sent a shiver down Desiree's spine.

"Lizza, give the money back to the bank." Violet's voice was dead calm, teetering on threatening.

Lizza wrinkled her nose. "I would if I had it, but the renovations are paid for. The cash is almost gone. But word of mouth has been great for the gallery. Talk it up every chance you get."

"Talk it up? How could you even *think* this was an option?" Desiree snapped. "I put my life on hold because you said my being here would prolong yours. As if you were *dying*."

"I *was* dying, and because you and Vi are here, I already feel better, healthier, *freer*." Lizza gave Desiree a hug despite her daughter's rigid stance.

"If being here made you feel like you were dying, then why did you borrow money to open an inn? You can't even stay in one place for more than a few months." Desiree's words came out harsh, but she was unable to temper them.

"The heart wants what it wants. I can't explain it. Things change," Lizza said with an infuriating smile.

Like your feelings for your daughter? The words were *right there*, hanging off the tip of her tongue.

Lizza stepped toward Violet, but Violet backed out of reach.

"Oh, girls. Cosmos brought you together. He always knows exactly who needs to meet and when. We *needed* this. All of us. I love you, and more importantly"—she opened the cab door and climbed inside—"I believe in you!"

Before either of them could say a word, the cab drove away.

"What the frick?" Violet yelled.

"Do you have to drop the F-bomb?"

Violet gave her a have-you-lost-your-mind look. "That is *not* the F-bomb, and it's about as careful as I intend to be, so get used to it."

Desiree paced, reeling as her life spun out of control. "She's obviously lost her mind. *Cosmos?*"

"If ever there was a time to say *frick* it's now. Frick, frick, frick!"

Desiree rolled her eyes. "Did that help? Because we're still in the same mess we were in before you said it."

"Well, I don't know about you, but I'm going to find a guy and a bottle of tequila, and have my way with both until this pissed-off feeling goes away."

Desiree flung her car door open and grabbed her phone. "You're staying? Taking over her shops to pay the mortgage? Did you have any idea this was what she was up to?"

"I haven't seen her since the funeral, and I had no idea she was cooking up any of this. But unless you have an extra few thousand bucks hanging around, I don't see how we can leave." Violet put on her leather jacket. "Will you be here when I get back?"

Desiree looked down at her soaking-wet clothes, wishing she'd taken Rick up on his offer to have a drink, because now she was too angry to see straight. She needed a hot bath and dry clothes. "I guess so. But you can't go out drinking and drive that death machine afterward."

Violet swung her leg over the bike. "I'm going to buy a bottle of tequila, pick up a guy, and drive home *before* I have my way with either. Okay, *Mom*?"

"Whatever." Violet was never going to change.

Violet's lips tipped up. "How about you get cleaned up and we take your car and go together? A little sisterly bonding. We've never gotten drunk or picked up guys together."

"There are hundreds of things we've never done together, and those are the ones you want to conquer? We are *so* different. Thanks, but I don't want to sleep with a stranger *or* drink until I pass out." Desiree pulled up her father's contact information on her phone. He was an international banker, and if anyone knew how to get out of this mess without losing their grandmother's house, it would be him.

"I can see you still haven't lightened up." Violet revved her engine. "I suppose you'll call *Daddy* and ask him what to do?"

Desiree lowered her phone, a wave of guilt and annoyance washing over her. While Desiree had seen her mother for only a few days every six months, Violet's father had taken off the day he'd found out Lizza was pregnant, and he'd never looked back. Vi had forever been spiteful that Desiree had a father to lean on, probably in much the same way Desiree felt about Vi having Lizza.

Pushing that uncomfortable thought away, she said, "He might be able to help figure out a way to get us out of this without losing Grandma's property. Obviously Lizza can't be counted on. Maybe we can say she's unstable and get the loan revoked."

"She's already spent the money," Violet pointed out. "Face it. We're stuck. But if you want to go back to your wonderful life in Virginia, I'll stay and do it on my own. I don't want to lose the family house because she made a stupid decision." She tugged on her helmet, revved her engine, and drove away.

Desiree groaned, clutching her phone and wishing she could throw it. But that would leave her in an even worse position. As she lugged her bags into the house, she wished she could be as bold as Violet for just one night. Maybe then she would have the guts to text that hunky Jet Skier.

Chapter Three

THE SUN BEAT down on Rick's shoulders as he neared the end of his five-mile run with his brother, Drake, and their business partner and friend Dean Masters early Tuesday morning. This was his favorite part of the day, catching up with the guys before real life took over and they had to deal with issues at the resort and get busy with renovations to the new recreation center. And today he'd needed the run more than ever. He hadn't heard from Desiree, and he couldn't stop thinking about her. She'd intrigued him with her conflicting cautious nature and lustful eyes. He wanted to peel back those careful layers and reveal all the secret seductive qualities she'd tried so hard to contain last night.

The run was good, but it didn't help. She was still front and center in his mind, and he was talking up a storm trying to distract himself.

"I'm catching that dog today if it kills me." Rick had been after a scruffy dog that had found its way into the pool several times over the past few weeks. It had outrun him twice already, disappearing between the shrubs at the edge of the property.

"We should set up a video camera to see how he's getting in," Dean said. "I haven't seen any holes since we filled those first few."

Rick and Drake had grown up with Dean and his brothers in Hyannis, about forty minutes from Wellfleet. When Rick and Drake had made the decision to purchase the resort, it was a no-brainer to bring Dean in on the deal. With Rick's building and investment expertise and Drake's business and marketing knowledge, Dean's skills as a landscape architect rounded out their team.

"I don't know, bro," Drake said, keeping pace with Rick. "You can't catch the dog. You got blown off last night, and still no booty call. I see a pattern here."

"I didn't get *blown off.* She'll get in touch, but it won't be for a booty call." Rick ground his teeth together, hoping Desiree wouldn't prove him wrong. There was no way he'd misread the sparks between them, and she definitely wasn't the type of woman who made booty calls, much less the type of woman a guy slept with and forgot. He'd spoken to her only once and she'd stuck like glue in his mind.

"Not a booty call, and you're still interested?" Dean arched a brow.

Rick ignored the comment. He wasn't a player, but he didn't feel the need to correct their misconception of his private life. He was busy with the resort, handling his own business remotely, and spending time with family. He knew they assumed he was into one-night stands because women hit on him often and he'd sometimes meet them for drinks, but he rarely slept with them. At thirty-one, he wasn't just out to get laid, and since he was set to return to DC when the renovations were complete, he also wasn't scouting for a girlfriend. There was no denying he'd spent more time than he'd like to admit thinking about what it would feel like to thread his fingers through Desiree's hair, to kiss her incredibly sexy lips and feel her gorgeous body beneath his. But he'd given equal time to wanting to know more about *her*, and it had been so long since someone had captivated him enough to slow down and think that way, it had taken him as much by surprise as it was taking Dean.

They slowed to a walk, pacing the beach in front of the resort as they cooled down.

"You saw what happened when I first noticed her," Rick finally answered. "I couldn't look away. It was insane. And she's even more beautiful up close, but it's not just that. She's sweet, and careful, but not weak or timid. She speaks her mind, but she's not witchy or snarky. She's just...*different.*"

"Sounds like the quintessential *girl next door*. Not exactly the type that goes for a bull in a china shop. Which explains why she didn't text you last night." Drake was a year and a half older than Rick, and calm as a stream, while Rick rolled more like white-water rapids. "If she's really that sweet, maybe you're barking up the wrong tree."

Rick dropped to the sand and pumped out a quick set of push-ups, then took a knee and squinted up at his brother. "I can't explain it, but she's the only tree I want to bark up, and for all I know, she's leaving town today. I was an idiot not to get her number."

"I have to admit," Dean said. "That got me when you said you gave her your phone number but didn't take hers. Where's the sense in that?"

Rick started another set of push-ups, and Dean dropped down beside him, matching his efforts. Dean had about twenty pounds of muscle on Rick, short brown hair, and serious eyes. He always looked like he was ready for a fight, but having been a trauma nurse for years before turning to landscape architecture, he was one of the most patient guys Rick knew.

"I don't know," Rick said. "I could kick myself for it, but I know she'll call."

Drake jogged up to the path, craning to look at something, which Rick guessed was probably Serena arriving at work. Serena Mallery had grown up with their younger sister, Mira, and she was the temporary manager of the resort. "When you get lonely because she doesn't, you can join us. Dean and Serena and I are going sailing tonight."

"No, thanks." Rick hadn't been on a sailboat since they'd lost their father in a sailing accident when Rick was fourteen. Drake had been riding his last nerve this summer, nudging him to get back on a sailboat. Give Rick a powerboat, water skis, a Jet Ski, or just about any other floatation device and he was fine. But he couldn't think about stepping foot on a sailboat without painful emotions bombarding him. It had almost caused him to refuse the opportunity to buy into the resort. Although Rick had followed in his father's footsteps as a high-end builder and investor, he'd escaped the painful memories of his father's death by starting his business in Washington, DC, and he hadn't been back for more than a few short visits each year. He had been on the fence about returning to the Cape for an extended period of time, but Drake had been persuasive, and Rick had never been one to pass on a solid business investment.

Drake's brows slanted in disappointment. "Then just remember, as an owner, you can't fraternize with the female guests."

Rick scoffed, wiped the sweat from his brow, and hiked a thumb at his brother. "Listen to this guy. He practically drools over Serena day in and day out and he's telling *me* not to fraternize?"

"She's not a guest." Drake flashed a cocky smile. "And I don't drool over her. She's a pain in my butt half the time." He took his shirt off, hung it over his shoulder, and headed toward the resort.

"That's why he's going straight to the office with his shirt off," Rick said as he and Dean pumped out one last set of push-ups.

"He lives above the office," Dean reminded him.

He gave Dean a *yeah, right* look.

"I'm just giving him the benefit of the doubt," Dean said as they headed up to the resort. "The same way I'm not giving you a hard time about going after the super-sweet girl."

"I *wish* I could go after her. I have no idea where to find her, but thanks for having my back."

They stopped to stretch on the lawn in front of the resort. Rick had built properties up and down the East Coast, and though Bayside Resort was less elegant than some, it was a spectacular sight. An array of cottages flanked the recreation center they were renovating, and the pool and tennis courts were just beyond, opposite the office.

"The rec center is coming along nicely," Dean said. "I finished the plans for the gardens around the patio, and the materials should be in soon."

Rick and Drake had almost finished the interior renovations, and with any luck, they'd have the entire project wrapped up in the next few weeks.

"You sure you still want to go back to DC next month?"

He'd asked himself the same question several times over the past few months. Somewhere on his path to success he'd gone from designing and building gorgeous homes to managing a multi-million-dollar business. It was a refreshing change to get his hands dirty again. In some ways, his time at the Cape had been a much-needed reprieve. Ever since one of his partners had gotten divorced, he'd been too sidetracked to bring in his share of the revenue, which meant Rick and their other partner had to double down their marketing efforts. Rick and Drake might not always see eye to eye, but their arguments were a piece of cake compared to the mounting discontent between his partners. Rick had little patience for drama, and every trip back to DC had brought him closer to the breaking point. The trouble was, being back on the Cape meant standing on the blade of a double-edged sword. He'd gotten a good dose of the family and friends he missed, but seeing them had stirred painful memories.

"Yup, still DC bound, as planned."

"That sucks. It's been great having you around." Dean elbowed him, nodding in the direction of the pool, where the soaking-wet dog Rick had been trying to catch was trotting toward the bushes. "Looks like your visitor is just leaving."

"He's *mine*. I'll be back." Rick took off running.

DESIREE SANK DOWN to the comfortable couch in the living room and tucked her feet up on the cushion beside her, talking with Violet about their conundrum and trying *not* to think about Rick. She had tossed and turned all night. Every time she'd closed her eyes, he was right there, luring her in until she'd picked up her cell phone, debated sending him a text, and chickened out. *Repeatedly.* She'd hoped to talk with Violet last night and make a plan about their mother's businesses, but by the time Desiree had realized Vi had come home, the sexy sounds coming from behind her sister's bedroom door had kept her from knocking.

"I don't see what the big deal is. It's a few weeks of your life, Des. Is that really too much to ask? You're a teacher, so you have summers off anyway." Violet sat cross-legged on the Oriental rug in the middle of the living room, her hands in praying position, head bent slightly forward, eyes closed. Her black tank top hung loosely off her heavily inked shoulder, her coal-black hair was tousled, and she still looked insanely sexy.

Vi was a vixen. A girl with no inhibitions. She did what she wanted, when she wanted to, without worrying about repercussions. *As long as I'm not hurting anyone else, why does it matter? That* was her moral compass. She was definitely their mother's daughter. Whereas Desiree was guided by right, wrong, and the firm decision *not* to become her mother.

And at the moment she was a little jealous of Vi's ability to let things like this roll off her back. How much easier would it be to live stress-free like her?

"The big deal is that she lied to us. I thought she was dying. Do you have any idea how hard it was to go forty-eight hours thinking the mother I hardly know might be terminally ill?" She didn't bother addressing her summer schedule. It was true that she didn't teach during the summers, but she liked to catch up with friends, visit her father in Connecticut, and come up with new ideas for the next school year.

Violet pushed to her feet and stretched her arms over her head. "I know exactly how that feels, only I had to live with it for *five* days before I got here. And it wasn't Lizza I was worried about."

A spark of guilt hit Desiree. She had been pleasantly surprised that her sister had rushed to the Cape for her, even if she had also been annoyed with their mother for using her as an excuse.

"Then why didn't you return my emails? Or call and ask me what was going on?" Desiree hated confrontations, especially when her feelings could get hurt. She escaped into the kitchen, spilling coffee on her tank top in her effort to try to outrun the uncomfortable emotions. She set the mug on the counter with a *clunk*, soaked a dish towel, and scrubbed at the stain.

"I was traveling." Violet leaned her butt against the counter.

"That is *not* a reason. It's...I don't know what it is. Is it easier to travel that distance and worry than to pick up a stupid phone? Seriously, Vi. One phone call is all it would have taken. It's like you don't see how you're just like her, or how frustrating it is for me to try to deal with you two."

"Don't be so high and mighty." She snatched the dish towel from Desiree's hand and added a spot of dish soap, surprising Desiree when she began scrubbing the stain. "You're like her, too."

"No, I'm not. I'm the antithesis of her."

Violet laughed. "Sometimes I forget that you really *don't* know her."

"And whose fault is that?" Desiree snapped.

Violet stopped scrubbing, her shoulders slumping. "We're fighting again. We're always fricking fighting."

Desiree shifted her eyes away. She hated when Violet used the F-word, even in its gentler form. "Is it any wonder? We don't know each other at *all*, we're nothing alike, and we're bonded by a mother who wanted nothing to do with me." Tears welled in her eyes, and she turned away. "It doesn't matter why you didn't call. What matters is that we're stuck, and I'm not dumping this place on you."

Violet set the dish towel on the counter. "I don't mind doing it myself. It's not like I have a great life to go back to." She crossed her arms, erecting the barrier she'd honed as a child. "I broke up with my boyfriend, which was why I didn't call. I wasn't exactly in a good mental place."

Guilt wound through Desiree. She set her hand on her sister's shoulder, fighting the urge to pull it away. She was an affectionate person by nature. She and Emery hugged all the time. How could it be so hard to touch her own sister?

Violet moved out of reach.

At least she wasn't alone in her discomfort.

"I didn't even know you had a boyfriend," Desiree said. She'd always assumed Violet wasn't into commitments of any kind, like their mother. "I'm sorry. Were the two of you serious?"

"As serious as I can get. I really liked the jerk."

"Then why did you sleep with that other guy last night?" Desiree had heard the guy leave at around four o'clock in the morning, when she'd been lying awake, still thinking about Rick.

Violet gave her an incredulous look. "To forget Andre, of course."

"I don't get that at all, but I'm not judging you. I just…" *Can't fathom doing it.* "I don't understand how having sex with someone else helps you to forget how much you like a person."

"No, little sister. I don't imagine you would," Violet said, full of snark and attitude, as she poured herself a cup of coffee.

"What's that supposed to mean?"

"You're *too* good. The proper preschool teacher, who always says and does the right thing." She shook her head and sipped her coffee.

"I'm not *too good* for anything," Desiree said angrily. "I curse, and I do the wrong thing."

Violet lifted her eyes. "Mm-hm."

"I do." She stormed across the kitchen. "I say 'damn' and 'hell' sometimes. And I say…" She couldn't get the damn F-word out of her mouth.

"Frick?" Violet offered.

"Yes, that one. *Exactly.*"

Violet laughed.

"And I do the wrong thing. Just last night I got a guy's phone number, and on the way to the Cape, I ran a red li—"

"Hold up!" Violet set down her coffee and held her hands up. "You got a guy's phone number? Like a stranger? For a hookup?"

"No, not for a hookup, and yes, a stranger. Well, he wasn't exactly a stranger after he told me his name. He was nice. A little pushy, but really hot, with linebacker shoulders and eyes like liquid fire. And he got me *so* wet." She sounded embarrassingly breathless.

Amusement rose in Violet's eyes. "Wow, you go, sis. He got you *so* wet, so you slept with him?"

"No! Geez, Vi. You have the filthiest mind." She felt her cheeks burning, but she was still reveling in the endearment. Violet had said it so easily, as if she'd called her sis her whole life. "He got me wet, as in he *splashed* me, or his Jet Ski did. You saw me last night. I was soaked. He's one of the owners of the Bayside Resort."

"Savage or Masters?" Vi asked.

"Um. Is that sex talk? Because I'm not into those things."

"Boy, do you and I need to spend some time together. *Last*

names. I met Drake Savage and Dean Masters at Undercover, that bar down the road, when we were here for Grandma's funeral. They were both smokin' hot, and nice. Pretty low-key. Your type of guys."

A knock sounded at the door.

"Are you expecting someone?" Desiree went to answer the door. "Why does everyone think I need a nice guy? I have no idea what his last name is, but he was hot." She pulled open the door and was greeted by the broad back of a shirtless man.

"Your mutt dog keeps—" The guy spun around with a scruffy wet dog in his arms, dirt on his knees, and daggers in his eyes, which quickly morphed to surprise and then something much darker.

Something that made Desiree's pulse skyrocket and her knees wobble.

Lust. Definitely lust.

"Rick?" She didn't usually care for sweat, but *wow.* He was even more staggeringly handsome than she remembered, angry eyes and all. And that layer of perspiration heightened the definition of his glistening muscles. With a body like that, the man should be bronzed.

IT TOOK RICK a second to grasp that he was staring into the beautiful eyes of the woman he'd been thinking about for hours and to get out from under the annoyance of chasing the dog. He'd had to get down on his hands and knees and make the *tsk-tsk-tsk* noises his father used to make to get their dog to come to him. He'd forgotten all about that noise until then. And now he'd forgotten why he was standing on Desiree's front porch, but he was glad he was.

"Desiree. You're staying here?"

She looked nervously at the pretty tatted-up brunette beside her, who was watching him with the same catlike green eyes as Desiree, only harder. Much harder. "Yes, for now." She fidgeted with the fringe on the hem of her white shorts. "Rick, this is my sister, Violet."

Violet lifted her chin. "How's it going?"

"Hi. It's nice to meet you."

"You seemed pretty angry." Violet crossed her arms. "Problem with the dog?"

He glanced at the dog. *Oh, right. The dog.* "Sorry. Your dog has been going into the pool at the resort. I've been chasing him for half an hour."

"We don't have a dog," Violet said flatly.

"You sure? His collar says he's yours." He leaned forward so Desiree could read the collar. She leaned right in, smiling and loving up the pup. If only he'd had a dog with him last night, maybe then she would have gone out for that drink. Her hair fell forward, covering one eye as she read the tag. His fingers itched to run through those long, silky golden locks. He tightened his grip on the pup to keep from doing so.

"He's not ours, but according to the tag, he lives here and his name is…" Desiree looked at Violet. "Cosmos."

Violet mumbled under her breath. "Of course it is. Cosmos brought us together?" She laughed, and Desiree covered her mouth, but her sweet laughter bubbled out anyway.

"What?" He was obviously missing out on something.

"Cosmos," Desiree said through her laughter, and doubled over at the waist. "She's so flipping crazy."

Violet laughed harder. "The *dog* brought us together?"

Rick couldn't help but laugh. "I'm totally confused."

"Join the party," Desiree said. "Oh, gosh." She shook her head, hiding her laughter behind her hand again. "I'm sorry. It's our mother. She's—" She pointed at her head, making circles with her index finger. "It must be her dog, but we didn't even know she *had* a dog."

She reached for Cosmos, and as he handed him over, he covered her hand with his. She blinked up at him through long, thick lashes, giving him that innocent look again, the look that made his stomach go squirrely.

"I'm sorry he went in your pool."

He couldn't take his eyes off her if he'd wanted to. "I'm not."

"Are you a Savage or a Masters?" Violet's serious tone severed their connection.

Rick felt himself grinning. "Savage. I'm not into BDSM." He caught Desiree blushing, and it made him want to tuck her up against him and cover her with kisses. *Kisses?* She really had gotten under his skin.

"I assumed differently, considering how pissed you were at the dog." Violet searched his face, openly assessing him.

"Violet," Desiree said under her breath.

Rick met Violet's serious gaze. "I've been chasing this dog for two weeks. It's wreaking havoc with our pool filter system. If I came across angry, I apologize, but that's why."

Her eyes slid to Desiree, then back to him. "We'll make sure he stays in the yard."

"Why are you suddenly so serious?" Desiree said to Violet. "You sound mean." She lifted her chin as the puppy licked it, bringing another sweet smile.

"She's not being mean." Rick understood where Violet was

coming from. If a guy had shown up to pick up Mira as angry as he'd been about the dog, he'd question him, too. "She's being protective."

"Of the dog?" Desiree petted the pup and looked questioningly at her sister. "Vi, I'll take care of him."

"So now you're staying?" Violet asked.

That caught Rick's attention. "Were you leaving?"

"I was considering it. It's complicated." She glanced at Violet. "But I still have some things to work out here."

A hint of a smile lifted Violet's lips, softening her hard edges, which Rick was glad to see. He'd wondered if Desiree's complications had to do with a boyfriend, and although he was relieved to see that it had to do with family, he was even more curious about the dynamics between her and Violet.

Violet reached for the dog. "Give me Trouble. I'll see if Lizza has food for him."

"Cosmos," Desiree said. After Violet went inside, she looked apologetically at Rick. "I'm sorry she acted like that."

"She was fine. She's just watching out for you."

She glanced at the door. "Is *that* what that was?"

"Oh, yeah. I've given the same tread-carefully vibe to plenty of guys who were hitting on my sister, Mira."

"And here I thought she was just being mean."

Her gaze fell to his chest as it had last night, and he remembered he was wearing only his running shorts. She licked her lips, heating him up from the inside out. Her eyes met his, and she had the guilty look of a kid who had been caught with her hand in the candy jar. And man, did that look good on her.

"Thanks for bringing the dog back," she said nervously. "I had no idea my mother had a dog, much less that he'd been running wild like that. I'll make sure he stays away from your pool."

He reached for her hand before she could flee. "I'm glad he was. You might never have called, and I'd be left searching for the gorgeous woman I drenched forever."

She laughed softly. "Somehow I think you'd find a replacement pretty darn fast."

"Oh, there'd be a line of women waiting. You can count on it. But I'd be too busy trying to figure out how to find you to notice." Her cheeks pinked up again, and it endeared him toward her even more. "Have dinner with me tonight."

"Dinner?"

"It's this thing people do where they share a meal and talk about their complicated lives."

She dropped her eyes, and he slid a finger beneath her chin and tilted her face up, leaving her no choice but to look at him.

"Say yes, Desiree. Don't leave me hanging again."

A playful smile reached all the way to her eyes. "Are you going to wear actual clothes, or should I expect you to be shirtless? Because it's a little distracting."

"That's not really an incentive for me to wear clothes, but I will." *I can't guarantee they'll stay on.* "However, you may go shirtless if you'd like, and I won't complain."

That earned another laugh. "Are you going to get me wet?"

"Only if I'm lucky," slipped out before he could stop it, and he loved the appreciative glimmer in her eyes. "I like you, Desiree. You mesmerize me."

She pressed her lips closed to suppress that unstoppable smile, failing miserably.

"I'll pick you up at seven."

"I didn't agree." She was still smiling.

"Yes, you did, just not verbally." He leaned in to kiss her

cheek, and she did that hold-her-breath-sigh thing that he'd replayed in his mind all night long. He pressed his lips to her cheek, and she closed her eyes as he whispered, "The line of women could wrap around the Cape, and not one of them would compare to you."

"Rick." She clutched his hand so tightly her nails dug into his skin.

"Hm?"

"That was an excellent line. Does it usually work?"

"I don't know, but just in case, maybe we should try this and seal my fate."

He framed her face with his hands and lowered his lips so close, her breath coasted over his lips, and her eyes fluttered closed. He wanted to stay in that prekiss moment for a thousand years, feeling her anticipation, his body thrumming with desire. He'd intended to give her a chaste kiss, but he knew he wouldn't want to stop after only one. And she was careful, hold-her-breath, complicated-life, steal-his-every-thought Desiree. He should take it slow so as not to overwhelm her, only Rick didn't know the meaning of the word "slow."

But for Desiree, he wanted to learn.

He brushed his lips over hers and kissed the corner of her mouth. "See you at seven, beautiful."

Chapter Four

DESIREE AND VIOLET found a leash for Cosmos in the pantry, along with a supply of dog food, treats, toys, and a dog bed, which was on a shelf with the tags still in place. They gave Cosmos a bath to wash the chlorine off him, and after discovering how much he liked the water, they took him to the beach, getting him dirty all over again. He was a little guy, with floppy ears, soft black-and-white fur on his body, tan around his paws and mouth, and the biggest brown eyes Desiree had ever seen. She'd never had a dog when she was young because her father was allergic, and as an adult, she worried that she was gone too much and a dog would get lonely. Cosmos was as nice of a surprise as the big, sexy man who had been carrying him, the man who had turned her insides to mush and then whipped all that mushy goodness into a torrent of hot, wicked desire. She'd been in the best mood, and anxiously awaiting their date, ever since.

Later that afternoon, Desiree and Violet headed down to the first cottage on the property, where their mother's gallery and shop were located. The pup trotted happily beside them.

"Why were you jerky to Rick?" she asked Violet.

"I wasn't *jerky*. But you saw how pissed he was when he got there. The last thing you need is a guy who loses his cool over every little thing." Violet shoved her hands in the pockets of her cutoffs, causing them to slip lower on her slim hips and revealing even more of the colorful tattoos on her side.

She wore only her shorts and a black bikini top and, Desiree noticed with a touch of jealousy, she was in amazing shape. Vi was tall and lean with an all-over tan that indicated she might have sunbathed nude, while Desiree had curvy hips, and though she wasn't a double D, her boobs would never fit in the tiny triangles Vi was sporting.

"He was fine once he saw it was me," Desiree pointed out.

"Uh-huh. And if it hadn't been you, but Lizza or me? Or anyone else? Would he have ripped them a new one because Cosmos had gone for a swim? He's a *dog*. They get into trouble. The guy needs to chill."

"I get what you're saying," Desiree said, a little annoyed by her sister's interpretation, which reminded her way too much of her mother's lackadaisical attitude toward other people's property. "But put yourself in his place. A dirty dog jumps into your pool, and his fur clogs the filter, the water gets mucky. It would be irritating."

Violet shrugged. "It's a dog. The guy should loosen up. And I don't want you getting hurt."

"So, you were worried about *me*?" She knew what Rick thought, but she wanted to hear it from Violet.

They walked across the brick patio in front of the cottages. It was even more overrun with weeds than Desiree had thought. She made a mental note to spend some time weeding. If she had to be there, at least she could make it pretty.

"I just don't like jerks."

Something in the way Violet said it told Desiree she was

being protective, as Rick had suggested. She wanted to tell Vi that worrying was nice, it was sisterly, and it warmed her to her core, but they didn't have that type of relationship. And she didn't want Violet thinking she needed protecting.

Instead, she said, "Thanks, but I'm a pretty good judge of character. I can handle myself."

"I'm sure you can." Violet smiled, and said, "*Rick?*" with a breathless lilt, hands pressed over her heart. "*Oh, broad-shouldered, shirtless god who got me wet, how did you find me?*"

"Ohmygosh." Desiree laughed. "I did *not* sound like that."

"Whatevs, sis. You totally got that take-me-every-which-way look, and if he's a jerk, you might be blinded by his take-me eyes and enormous…*muscles*." She waggled her brows.

"He does have incredibly sensual eyes, and nice muscles." Desiree turned her attention to the cute yellow cottage so her sister couldn't see the flush heating her cheeks as she thought about the *rest* of Rick's tempting body.

"I meant his enormous *trouser snake*," Vi said. "Come on. Let's see what good old Lizza has been up to."

Still reeling from her sister's dirty mind, Desiree tried to focus on the hand-painted vines of orange and purple flowers on the sign above the door, which read, DEVI'S DISCOVERIES. But now all she could think about was the feel of that part of his body against her belly this morning, when he'd held her like he was going to, as Emery had said, turn her inside out with his kisses.

She cleared her throat in a futile attempt to suppress the heat crawling up her thighs. Needing something to think about other than the way Rick's lips felt soft and hard at once on her cheek, and the way her body had ignited at his touch, she stared at the front of the cottage.

A small chalkboard hung beside the door, and read, HOURS: WHEN THE FEELING HITS, I'M HERE. So very Lizza. Desiree glanced up at the sign above the door again. "Does 'Devi' have a special meaning I don't know about?"

"Yeah. The mother of all goddesses. The *supreme* goddess," Violet said with a hint of sarcasm.

That was enough to slap Desiree back to reality. Did their mother think she was a goddess of everything? "Maybe she should have gone with a goddess of forgetfulness or travel." Desiree crouched to pet Cosmos, feeling a kinship to the abandoned pup.

A moment later, her nerves sprang to life when she stepped inside the cottage, feeling their mother's presence *everywhere.* Knotty hardwood floors were covered with speckles of paint and stuck-on clay. Yellow walls and white trim led up to exposed and painted rafters, all of which were in need of a fresh coat of paint. On the far wall, built-in bookshelves displayed clay vases, bowls, and pictures their mother had painted. A number of tables were covered with hand-painted cards, shells, and driftwood. Paintings hung from the walls and were set on easels scattered throughout the shop. Their mother's signature, *Lizza V*, with an overly scripted *L*, stood out in bold yellow in the lower right corner of each painting.

Desiree worked her way around the room, inspecting each of her mother's art pieces. The paintings were a bit abstract, but there was a consistent theme of women of all ages, and objects. One woman held a raggedy teddy bear, and in another painting, a little girl was crouched beside a tree, playing with a black ant the size of a cat. It was a little creepy, and strangely sweet. "Do you really think she sells anything?"

"I went into the den and looked over her sales receipts. She's been making a lot of money over the past six months, which is surprising, since it was winter and the lower Cape isn't exactly a booming metropolis in the colder months." Violet reached for a paper tag hanging off one of the paintings and showed Desiree the figure written on it.

She nearly choked. "Twenty-three hundred dollars?"

"She's always gotten a lot for her paintings, but she left behind so many. I've never known her to have this much stock. The clay pieces, too. Usually she made just enough to get by. She must have been planning this trip for a while."

"Wouldn't that be the icing on the cake? Is it so hard for people to tell the truth? Why would she do this to us?" Desiree ground her teeth together to keep her anger from tumbling out. "She plans a trip to rejuvenate her soul and leaves us here to figure out the life she's left behind? It's emotional blackmail, holding Grandma's house over our heads like this."

"It's *Lizza*." Violet walked to the far side of the cottage. "You grew up with a father who went to work every day from nine to five and was there on the weekends to take you to art lessons, dance, music—"

"I didn't take art lessons," she corrected her.

"What?" Violet's jaw dropped open. "You were incredibly talented, even as a little girl. Why did you stop?"

Desiree shrugged, not wanting to argue. She'd stopped drawing and painting in an effort to sever what few similarities she had to her mother. Instead, she focused on doing the exact opposite of what her mother might do at all times. The last thing she wanted was to become someone who could walk away from her child, and in her mind, any similarities could lead to that.

"Whatever the reason," Violet said angrily, "it was a mistake. I'd have given anything to have *half* your talent."

"What are you talking about? You used to make those gorgeous batik wall hangings, clothes, and pottery. I could never do any of that. I can barely sew." She sighed, reining in her angst and trying to come up with a plan. "What do you think? How do we figure out hours?"

Violet glanced at her, then back at the paintings. "You're really going to stay?"

"It would give us time to get to know each other." She couldn't deny that Rick had more than piqued her interest, too, but she wasn't about to tell Violet that. She didn't want her to think that was the only reason she was staying.

"We could split the hours. You take a day, I take a day, or morning and afternoon? But I'm not great at schedules. So…" Violet flashed a smile so genuine Desiree wanted to scoop it up and put it in her pocket for the times when they argued.

"I live by schedules," Desiree admitted.

"Then we're definitely going to drive each other crazy."

Desiree's heart raced at the prospect of staying for the summer and spending time with Rick, while getting to know Violet better. Both were as exciting as they were nerve-racking. "We might. Unless we both agree to try."

"If you're asking me to try to be more schedule-oriented, I can pretty much tell you I'll suck at it."

"Yeah, me too. I won't do well without a schedule." Her chance at a relationship with her sister was slipping through her fingers, and suddenly it felt like her *last* chance. Like if they couldn't be friends now, it would never happen, and that brought a wave of panic. "But what if we didn't drive each other crazy? I mean, my friend Emery is a wild woman and I adore her. We get along great."

"A *wild woman*." Violet nodded, as if she were mulling over the idea. "Emery, as in the girl who jumped out of a moving car? You think she and I are alike?"

"She was twelve, and in her defense, the car had been rolling to a stop and her favorite bag had fallen out the window, but yes, the one and only Emery. And I've never thought of you two being alike, but she's pretty wild, so maybe a little alike."

"I'm willing to give it a try," Violet relented. "I guess if we want to kill each other, we can always nix the idea and reevaluate."

Desiree let out a breath she hadn't realized she'd been holding. "Great!"

Violet pointed to the sign on a door in the back of the store. "'Your personal discovery awaits.' Interesting. Want to make bets on what's back here?"

"Nude paintings?"

She followed Violet into the back of the shop, and they both fell silent. A pink bar ran around the perimeter of the room about a foot from the ceiling, from which hung dozens of negligees, panties, bras, and other sexy paraphernalia. Beneath were tables with various adult *pleasure enhancers*. Desiree had never been inside a *pleasure* shop, much less seen so many things she couldn't imagine doing anything with. Fuzzy handcuffs and G-strings dangled from decorative iron trees like holiday ornaments.

"Whoa! Lizza owns a sex shop!" Violet picked up a giant purple *toy*. "This could cause some damage."

"Put that down!" Desiree whispered, her cheeks burning like the Sahara.

Violet turned it over, inspecting it while Desiree was secretly hoping to evaporate into thin air.

"*Ohmygosh.*" Her eyes shifted around the room. "I don't even know what half this stuff is, and you're away in third-world countries most of the time and *you* know?"

"Because I'm not a prude."

"That's a crappy thing to say. I'm not a prude. I've just never met anyone who I'd want to explore these kinds of things with. It takes trust and the right person."

"Babe," Vi said. "You are obviously an overthinker. Don't you ever just let your body decide what you'll do? Go with the moment?"

"Yes. I did that earlier, when I let Rick kiss me." She winced inwardly at her confession. She'd wanted to shock Violet, but it felt funny saying it aloud.

"He kissed you?" Violet picked up a plastic box, looking over the funky objects inside. "You didn't share that little piece of intel. How was it?"

A thrum of electricity darted through her. "You know that moment right before you kiss, when you can't think and your whole body is buzzing with anticipation?"

"I usually fly right through that sucker to the good stuff, but sure."

"My body's still buzzing." Desiree inhaled a lungful of cour-age, and her eyes moved over the table, taking it all in. "I would be too embarrassed to go into a store and buy these kinds of things."

"Why, if they're used for consensual, pleasurable sex? You're not buying slaves." Her sister picked up another box and read the side of it.

Desiree walked around the table, thinking about how lim-ited her sexual experiences had been. "Sex is private."

"Plenty of married couples use pleasure enhancers." Violet

put the box down and her gaze softened. "Please tell me you're not a sex-with-the-lights-off-only girl."

Desiree cringed. "Do candles count?"

"Okay, new plan. We're working together until you're so comfortable with these things, you can sell them to Rick's grandmother."

"That is *never* going to happen." She waved her hands, walking backward. "I'm not even sure I can sell this stuff to *you*."

"Give me the leash," Violet said, and Desiree gave it to her. "Put your hands out."

Desiree held out her hands. Violet turned them palms up and began piling on crotchless underwear, toys, and whatever else was unpackaged.

"What are you doing? Violet! Stop! Vi. Please. I'll drop them. I swear I will."

Violet laughed. "Perfect idea." She grabbed Desiree's arms and pulled them out to the side so the toys tumbled to the ground.

"No!"

Cosmos barked excitedly.

"Why did you do that?" Desiree stared at the toys at her feet.

"Okay, baby sister." She crossed her arms. "Pick them up."

"What? No. You made the mess."

Violet pushed a few more off the table, hoisted herself up, and sat on the now-empty spot. "I'll sit here until you do it. Pick the darn things up. Get used to holding them until you see them as nothing but pieces of rubber and plastic if you have to. Just do it. It's time to break you out of this Little Miss Innocent act and grow some hair on your chest."

Desiree laughed. "That's disgusting. Who wants hair on their chest?"

"It's just an expression. Trust me. You'll feel a lot better about your sexuality once you can own it." She slid off the table and picked up a man's G-string, then handed it to Desiree. "Hold it."

Desiree took it and looked away.

"Seriously? What are you afraid of? Is this how you're going to act with Rick? Look away?"

"No! But it's not like you'll be there egging me on just so you can tease me about it later." The room fell silent, and Desiree instantly regretted what she'd said. "I didn't mean that."

"I'm trying to help, not make fun of you." Violet started picking up the toys.

"I can do it."

They worked together restocking the table in uncomfortable silence. A while later, after they'd cleaned up and Cosmos had curled up by the door, Desiree promised herself she'd try harder not to snap or judge.

"I'm not a prude." She looked out the window, which was easier than looking at Violet while she bared this piece of herself. "With the right guy I'd consider these things. I think. *Maybe*. And I talk about sex with Emery, but it's harder with you. I don't really know you." She caught her reflection in the window and, over her shoulder, a reflection of the sister she longed to know.

More nervous than she could ever remember being, she faced Violet, and had a hard time reconciling her tentative expression with the headstrong woman she knew her to be. "But I want to. I want to be comfortable with all of this, and with us. With sharing parts of ourselves that we should have learned how to share years ago. But that doesn't mean it's going to be easy for me. I associate a lot of things with Lizza, like the ability to do things on a whim, and painting, and not returning messages, and it scares me. Or pisses me off. I'm never really sure which. I only know my skin crawls every time I do something she might do. I know that's horrible and unfair, because you grew up with her and she's your mother, too, but I can't help it. Even the idea of not having a schedule feels like it's like *her* to me, and—"

"I get it," Violet said. "I *totally* get it."

"You do?" Relief swept through her, and she wanted to keep the connection going, so she admitted, "And, embarrassingly, the guys I've been with have been less than *thrilling*. So when I hear other women talking about their escapades, I always feel a step behind. It's not that I'm a prude, but I'm also not the kind of girl who would just whip out one of those and be like, 'Hey, wanna play?' I want to be that free. I know you could do it. Emery could do it. But not me. I'm just not wired that way."

Violet smiled. "I get that, too. Certain guys make it harder to be that way. Some aren't very adventurous, or they suck in bed, and others suck you right into their bed and you never want to leave."

"Um..." Desiree wiggled her finger in the air. "I've never had that last kind of guy. I *want* to, but I can't really wear a sign that says 'I want a guy who's good in bed. Only experienced men need apply.'"

They both laughed, and the tension in the room came down a notch.

"How does a person *get* comfortable with all this?"

"Alcohol," Violet said emphatically. "Lots of it."

"Really? I'm a total lightweight. Two glasses of wine and I'll be doing things I shouldn't."

Violet headed for the door and Cosmos followed. "Three glasses it is."

"Wait. Now?"

"No time like the present. According to Lizza's sign, it seems like she didn't work every day. Today will be our orientation day. I'll grab some wine from the house, and we can close the doors so it's just us, drink until you're feeling *really* comfortable, and I'll show you what this stuff is."

"Sorry, Vi, but I am *not* going all girl-on-girl with you."

"Please, Des. *Really?* I'm totally into men, and their big…trouser snakes. I meant I'd *talk* you through it. Help you understand what all these things are for, so by the time we leave this cottage you don't feel two steps behind. No baby steps. We're going to jump in with both feet."

Feeling unusually sassy and excited at both the prospect of doing something like this with Violet *and* learning about all the naughtiness around her, she said, "What about you? You're perfectly willing to put me in an uncomfortable position, even if it'll help in the long run. Kind of one-sided, don't you think?"

"So, you want to know my Achilles' heel?"

"Yes! Do you have one?" Desiree couldn't imagine it.

"Oh yeah, do I ever. Maybe I'll tell you about it *after* I drink an ocean of wine and then some."

RICK PACED HIS living room with his phone pressed to his ear, listening to his partners, Craig and Michael, argue. He checked his watch for the tenth time in as many minutes. Rick had spent the past few months negotiating a six-million-dollar project to relocate two executives from the Austin area to DC.

They were on the cusp of finalizing the contract, and Craig had solidified a two-million-dollar project for next spring. Unfortunately, Michael had brought in only half a million dollars in the past nine months, and Craig was hammering him. He didn't blame Craig for losing it, but he also felt bad for Michael. His wife had left him for another man, turning his and their two little boys' lives upside down. But they'd been on the call for more than thirty minutes, and the closer it got to seven o'clock, the more his patience dwindled.

"Let's all take a step back," Rick said, interrupting. Normally he was the hothead, but he had a soft place in his heart for Michael, a childhood friend. He'd known Michael's ex-wife since childhood, too. Michael and his wife had moved to DC to join Rick and Craig's business. It was no secret that his ex-wife hated the area, and Rick wondered if she would have strayed had they remained in Hyannis.

"The bottom line is, we're partners. We're in this together. Michael, I know you're struggling with the divorce and keeping up with your kids, but Craig's right. You've got to get back in the game. And, Craig, if you or I were in his shoes, we'd expect to be cut some slack."

He headed outside and climbed into his truck. "I've got to get off the phone, but let's come up with a plan. Michael, sit down and figure out what new projects you can go after. Look at what's on the horizon, possible clients you can tap into. Referral sources you can put some energy into. Give us a timeline for expectations."

"It's been nine months," Craig pointed out.

Tell him something he didn't know. Nine painful months of watching his buddy fall down the rabbit hole. The man he admired like a brother had gone from being one of the most confident and successful salesmen he knew to barely holding himself together. But Rick wasn't about to give up on Michael, any more than he'd give up on Drake or Dean.

They made a plan to strategize next week. After he ended the call, Rick pulled out of his driveway and saw Drake walking toward the office. He rolled down his window and slowed to a crawl beside him. "Hey, bro. Thought you were going sailing?"

"We are. Serena had to run home to change." Drake glanced in the truck, which Rick had cleaned out earlier. "Have a date?"

There was no stopping his grin. "I'm taking Desiree out."

"The sweet *girl next door*?" Drake's brows drew down in a serious slant.

"The one and only. Oh, and by the way, she's literally staying next door in the old Summer House. Have fun tonight. I know I will."

A few minutes later Rick pulled into Desiree's driveway. Cosmos bolted out of a cottage, running toward the truck and barking up a storm. Rick pulled over and parked to avoid hitting him. He climbed from the truck and crouched, offering his hand.

"Hey, scruffy pool hopper."

Cosmos yapped and sprinted back to the cottage. The door was open and the lights were on, and Desiree's melodic laughter floated out from within. He pictured her eyes lighting up when she laughed, and couldn't resist following the pup inside the eclectic shop to see what had him so hyped up. Paintings and pottery and other types of art covered every surface.

"Wait, wait, wait!" Desiree's voice floated into the room, and he followed it to an open door in the back.

"This can't be right. Are you sure?" Desiree stood with her

back facing him, wearing the same sexy tank top and shorts she'd had on that morning, but now it was covered in a red lace and silk negligee. Violet stood in front of her, bent at the waist, her hands hidden from view by Desiree's body.

While Desiree's rear was as tempting and fine as he'd ever seen, it wasn't enough to distract him from the multitude of colorful lingerie dangling from strings around the room, and the plethora of adult-play items on the tables and shelves, or the mess of both strewn across the floor. In the corner of the room, a mannequin lay cockeyed, an empty wine bottle nestled in the crook of its arm. The girls had been busy.

"Hey there," he said with amusement.

Desiree spun around, eyes wide, mouth agape, wearing some sort of barely there negligee over her clothes, with leather laces up the center, and feathers where there should be fabric covering her breasts and at the juncture of her thighs.

"Rick," she said breathily, dragging her eyes down his chest and swallowing hard. "Geez, you're so flipping *hot*."

"Own it," Violet said, pointing up at the ceiling.

He arched a brow, having absolutely no idea what he'd walked in on, but... Sweet Desiree was definitely not as innocent as she appeared.

Desiree put a hand on her hip and thrust out her chest. Her hand slid off her hip, and she quickly put it back up again. Her eyes darkened as she sauntered over to him, full of wine-bravado—hips swaying seductively, eyes locked on his—and apparently completely oblivious to her outfit. Heck, the way she was moving, *he'd* almost forgotten about it. She rubbed her hands over his pecs and down toward his abs. "I have been *dying* to feel your muscles."

"Be my guest, sweetheart." He'd probably go straight to hell for not stopping her when she was clearly tipsy, but seeing his careful girl so uninhibited was a massive turn-on.

"Doesn't he look hot, Vi?"

"Scorching." Vi grabbed another wine bottle from a shelf and took a swig.

As her hands roamed over his chest, he felt guilty for enjoying every second of her feel-fest, and took her hands in his. "Sweetheart—"

"I really like when you call me that." She leaned forward, and feathers brushed over his clothes. Her eyes dropped to the space between them, and she gasped, stumbling backward and sending Cosmos into a barking frenzy as he jumped and tried to bite the feathers.

"Ohmygosh. It's not what it looks like!"

Cosmos ran circles around her, yapping.

"Yes, it is." Violet nodded. "It's *exactly* what it looks like."

Desiree tried to peel off the lingerie, but it got stuck on her shoulders. "I swear it's not. We were going to work, and then we talked, and then—" She tore the bottle from Violet's hands and thrust it at Rick, looking guilty and crazy cute. "*This* happened, and..." Her eyes dropped to the lingerie. "Oh no! Then *that* happened. Just shoot me. Shoot. *Pow. Bam.*"

He reached for the bottle and set it on the table. "There will be no shooting. But, sweetheart, you look really cute." He glanced at Violet, who was having way too much fun at her sister's expense.

Desiree's cheeks flamed. "Ohmygosh. I should never drink. We weren't...It's not..." She started yanking at the straps. "It's stuck. I can't"—*tug, tug*—"get it"—*tug, tug*—"off."

Violet doubled over laughing. "I like you when you drink!"

"You're a horrible influence." Desiree glared at her, still

struggling to get the leather laces untied and swaying unsteadily.

"True," Violet said with an emphatic nod.

Rick framed Desiree's face as he'd done earlier, gazing into her pleading eyes until she stopped struggling and focused on him. Like the dawn of a new day, the tension drained from her face. All the jokes and innuendos that were on the tip of his tongue slipped away, and his insides turned to mush. What was she doing to him?

"I've got it," he assured her, and carefully untied the contraption, peeled it carefully from her clothing, and set it on the table, aware of Violet watching his every move. Without giving Desiree time to give in to the embarrassment playing over her features, he gathered her against him and said, "You're incredibly sexy when you're tipsy."

That earned a sweet smile, but she quickly buried her face in his chest. "I'm so embarrassed."

He was captivated by how quickly she went from being completely unguarded to genuinely vulnerable. "Why? Because you and your sister had a little fun in your *toy* shop?"

"That's what I'm talkin' about," Violet chimed in, and bent down to pick up the pup. "Come on, Trouble. Let's give these guys some privacy." She blew Desiree a kiss and motioned with two fingers pointing from her eyes to Rick's, mouthing, *I'm watching you.*

He chuckled, but he liked Violet's protective nature.

"It's not *our* shop. It's our mother's." Desiree winced. "That sounds *so* bad." She lifted her eyes to the ceiling and laughed. "Welcome to my crazy summer life."

"I think I'm going to like your crazy summer life."

Chapter Five

DESIREE SURVEYED THE messy shop and the wine stains on her tank top. Reality sobered her up, but she was still light-headed. Unfortunately, she wasn't so drunk that she didn't realize how badly she'd made a fool of herself. She could hardly believe Rick was still looking at her like she was the most beautiful, interesting person he'd ever seen. Either she was totally misreading him, he was nuts, or this was by far the luckiest night of her life.

She was caught between wanting more of this free, light feeling, and being terrified by how quickly it felt like that freedom—not the alcohol—could become an addiction. She began straightening up to distract herself, and fell back on her safety net, defining who she had always been.

"I'm really not like this," she assured Rick. She knelt to pick up the items on the floor, and realized Vi was right. Whether it was from the wine, the fact that she'd already stepped into Mortification Land and there was no further damage to be done, or because she and Vi had used the colorful pleasure rods as swords in a Battle of Shlongs, she no longer felt funny touching them. She realized Violet hadn't told her what her Achilles' heel was. She'd have to remember to ask her the next time…*we drink together?*

Rick crouched beside her and gathered a number of toys in his arms. He could hold a *lot* of them, and not once did his focus stray from Desiree. "*This?* As in someone who likes to cut loose every now and again?"

She shifted her eyes away and pushed to her feet, setting the toys on the table. "No, as in someone who wears slutty lingerie and drinks before a date. I haven't showered, my shirt is stained…I'm sorry, Rick."

He unloaded his armful on the table and took her hand, drawing her against him again. He felt safe and solid, and when his eyes turned serious, she didn't know what to expect.

"You just accelerated the first half of our date. Now I can forget the wine and we can get straight to the taking advantage of you part."

He paused long enough for alarm bells to go off in her head. And then a slow smile crept across his face, turning those bells into dirty little chimes.

How the heck did he do that with just a look?

"I'm kidding," he said. "If I remember correctly, I gave you my number when you were drenched like a kitten caught in a storm. A sexy-as-sin kitten, but still. Desiree, I don't care if your shirt is stained, if you've had a few drinks, if we stay here and take a walk on the beach, or if we go out to a fancy dinner. I just want to spend time with you."

She breathed a sigh of relief. She was used to being wined and dined by men who would never say anything like *sexy-as-sin kitten*, and they definitely would have issues with her being tipsy and sloppy on their first date. Everything about Rick was refreshing and tempting.

"If you're worried about what I think of all of this," he said with a serious tone. "Don't. It's life. It's fun. Besides, I've been known to sneak into my brother's house and fill his drawers with ladies' lingerie before his dates."

"Really?" She loved how he made her laugh.

"Heck, yes."

"I can't believe you're really not turned off by my wine drinking and sloppy clothes and all this...*stuff.*"

"Not even a little. But if it'll make you feel better, go shower and change and take care of whatever else you might be worrying about, and I'll pick up in here. Unless you're using this as an excuse to blow me off?" A devilish grin lifted his lips. "In which case, I'll have to turn on the charm and show you what you'd be missing out on with that very bad decision."

"You can be even more charming than barely knowing me and being willing to change your plans and clean up my inappropriate toy mess?"

"Only if you're lucky."

She wanted to be lucky. *Very* lucky. No part of her wanted to leave him, not even for a minute. "I'd take you up on that very generous offer, but you'd probably clean the place out, and then I'd have to bring Cosmos over to swim in your pool morning, noon, and night as payback."

"That would make me the lucky one." Rick patted her butt, and she clamped her mouth shut to keep a squeak from slipping out. "Go do whatever it is you need to do, and I'll start loading up my truck."

How about you load me up?

Holy moly.

Rick made her feel bold and sassy. He was opening a door to who she used to be. Who she'd *forgotten* she was. She'd suppressed the sassier side of herself when she'd graduated from college. Sassiness had no place around three- and four-year-olds. But apparently Little Miss Sass was done being held back and was trying to rush to the head of the class.

"No, thanks," she said. "I think I'd rather stay right here with you."

"Don't trust me alone in the store with her?" He grabbed the mannequin and set the empty wine bottle on the table. "She's pretty sexy, and she doesn't complain when I curse or get mad when I leave the toilet seat up."

"She sounds like the perfect girlfriend." Picking up a box with MR. MASSIVE printed on the side, Desiree said, "But maybe she'd like to meet a *new*, battery-operated boyfriend."

"Someone's selling women a load of bull. I'd say that's Mr. Tiny."

She rolled her eyes and laughed. "Such a man."

"I'm all man, baby." He grabbed a whip from the floor and tapped her butt with it. "What exactly *was* going on in here?"

She gasped and grabbed hold of the whip. Their eyes connected, sending heat coursing down her body. How was she supposed to form a response when he was looking at her like she was *dinner*? And why wasn't she running away?

Because dinner would be amazing with you. Dinner, dessert, tomorrow's breakfast. The whip dropped from her fingertips. The sinful look in his eyes made her wonder if he could read her thoughts.

"Um…" He'd asked her a question. *What were we doing? Right.* "It started out as a sisterly bonding thing," she managed. "And somehow turned into one ridiculous joke after another."

"And this is your mother's shop?" He picked up a pair of pink fuzzy handcuffs, dangling them from his index finger. "Not that I'm into cuffs, but it looks like Mama knows how to party."

She took the cuffs from him and set them on the shelf, glad he wasn't into handcuffs. *Am I glad? Yes! Of course I'm glad. I think. Hm…* She tried to focus on her mother, which was surprisingly safer than where her mind was heading. "My mother is an anomaly. I don't really know or understand her."

"That must be difficult." He stopped straightening up to give her his full attention.

She'd never shared her feelings about her mother with anyone other than Emery, and she wasn't quite ready to share them now. Especially since she didn't trust what might come out of her mouth at the moment. Apparently wine was the key to loosening up *and* the key to saying things she shouldn't. She kind of liked the combination, but her thoughts about her mother weren't cute or funny.

"It is what it is," she said, hoping she sounded casual. "How about your parents? Are you close to them?"

A look of longing washed over him, and just as quickly it disappeared. "My mother lives in Hyannis, where I grew up. She's great. Strong. Doesn't take guff from anyone. She loves the outdoors, and spoils Mira's son, Hagen. And my father…" His tone turned mournful. "He was a great guy. Unfortunately, he died when I was a teenager."

That sobered her up completely, her heart breaking for him. They had more in common that she'd imagined. Her mother might be alive, but Desiree could barely remember a time when she'd felt like Lizza was more than a ghost. "I'm sorry. That must have been really hard."

He nodded. "It was a long time ago." His jaw tightened, and she sensed he didn't want to talk about it.

They finished cleaning up, and as they left the cottage,

Desiree found herself thinking about her mother and Violet again. She might not have a chance with her mother, but maybe something good could come out of this summer after all. A sometimes-cantankerous relationship with her sister would be better than no relationship at all.

She locked the door behind them, shivering against the brisk night air.

"Cold?" He wrapped his arms around her, his broad body warding off the evening chill. "I have a sweatshirt in the truck."

Maybe *two* good things could come out of this summer.

"And exactly how would that be better than being in your arms?" slipped out. Clearly she was going to have to get used to her inner sass coming out if she planned on spending any time with Rick. Which she did. *Hopefully a lot of time.*

His lips quirked up, and *oh* how she loved the haughty grin. "They're not mutually exclusive."

Their eyes held for a long, hot moment. It was all she could do to say, "Okay."

He kept her tucked against him as they crossed the driveway. She'd never dated a man who was possessive, and she wouldn't have imagined that she'd like it, but she was becoming very attached to the feel of Rick's hands on her. There was something addictive about him. He grabbed a sweatshirt from his truck and helped her put it on. It hung to the edge of her shorts, and that, too, felt warm and wonderful, like she was wearing a piece of him.

He rolled up the sleeves and brushed his fingers tenderly over her cheek. He did that a lot, touching her face, her hair, her hands, her arms, and she found herself wanting more.

"Boy, do I like seeing you in my sweatshirt."

"Not exactly the sexiest outfit for a first date."

"You couldn't be more wrong. You look beautiful, and now I can pretend you have nothing on underneath." He winked, and put an arm around her. "Are you hungry?"

She was too busy thinking about *him* imagining *her* with nothing under the sweatshirt to think about food.

His gaze moved to her mouth, lingering long enough for her mouth to go dry with anticipation, before drifting lower, hovering around her breasts, and then sliding down the length of her legs. His jaw clenched, his grip on her became stronger, and his eyes? *Ravenous.*

"Food," he practically growled.

She couldn't help but laugh as he helped her into the truck.

As he pulled out of the driveway, he reached across the seat for her hand, touching her for what felt like the hundredth time in two days. A little thrill raced through her as his big, warm palm swallowed hers. It was such a small thing, but it felt significant, and their hands fit together perfectly.

"Have you been to the Night Affair yet in Truro?" he asked.

"I haven't been anywhere. I just got into town yesterday."

He squeezed her hand, his eyes darting back to the road. "Good. I haven't had a chance to check it out yet, either."

He drove through Wellfleet to Truro, which was only a few miles away. Rick parked on a side street, and as they headed for the event, the air buzzed with the din of the crowd, the beat of the music, and the heat pulsing between them.

"This reminds me of the festivals back home, in Oak Falls, Virginia," she said, taking in the colorful lights twinkling against the dark sky and people milling around tented booths. A band played on a grassy lawn, where people danced and ate at picnic tables.

"You're from Virginia? I live in DC."

"I thought you lived here, at the resort."

"I do for now. We're renovating a recreation center. I'm going back to DC next month, after the work is done. I bought the resort as an investment with my brother, Drake, and our friend Dean. They'll run it when I go back home in a few weeks."

She mentally calculated how far they lived from each other.

"How long are you in town?"

"I don't know exactly." How could she not know what her plans were? That wasn't like her at all, but then again, the last twenty-four hours had been anything but normal. "Violet and I are watching my mother's business for the summer, and I have to be back at school in mid-August. I guess I'm here for five or six weeks. Unless my mother comes back sooner."

They blended into the crowd and Rick draped his arm over her shoulder, pulling her closer. "Are you a teacher?"

"Mm-hm. Preschool."

"A naughty preschool teacher." He smiled down at her. "I bet all the single dads find reasons for extra parent-teacher conferences."

"Hardly, and I'm not exactly naughty." Although seeing the glimmer of heat in his eyes made her want to be.

He leaned down and spoke with his mouth right beside her ear. "You were pretty naughty tonight."

His gravelly, seductive voice made her insides whirl. "I have a feeling I'll never live that down."

They made their way to the food tent and ate chicken on a stick as they walked around looking at books and crafts and handmade clothing. Rick was easy to talk to, and Desiree felt happier than she had in a long time. After they finished eating, they stopped by the dessert display.

"Please tell me you're not one of those girls who survive without sweets." He flashed that killer smile, making her stomach flutter.

"Nope. I like everything. My best friend, Emery, teaches yoga and Pilates. I take her classes several times a week, and when I take the night classes, we almost always go out for dessert afterward." They were just like the women Emery made fun of.

"Sounds like a great friend."

"I love her like a sister. I can't imagine what I'd do without her." If Emery were there now, she'd be rooting for Desiree to cut loose and jump Rick's bones. Her hormones were doing enough pushing; she didn't need Emery's pressure.

He took her by the shoulders and turned her away from the booth. "Are you allergic to anything?"

"No. Why? What are you up to?"

"Live dangerously, Desiree," he taunted. "Don't turn around."

She heard him talking quietly to the vendor but couldn't make out what he was saying. Anticipation bubbled up inside her. "Rick? Despite what you saw tonight, I'm not very good at living dangerously."

She felt the heat of him behind her.

"One more second, beautiful."

Every time he called her *beautiful* or *sweetheart*, she melted a little inside. His seductive voice and those smoldering eyes, coupled with a few well-placed *sweethearts*, made her mind wander down a dirty path. She felt herself smiling and wondered if he knew he could use those endearments to his advantage.

He draped an arm over her shoulder, holding a bag and a

drink in one hand and startling her from her thoughts.

"Dessert."

Why, oh why, was she thinking he would make a much better dessert than whatever was in that bag? It's like he'd blurred the well-defined boundaries she usually lived within. "Wonderful. What is it?"

"If I told you, it would ruin the fun." He guided her to the next booth, where they were selling incense and scented candles.

"Oh, I love candles," she said, bending to smell them. "I'm kind of a candleaholic. My apartment is full of them."

"Now we're getting somewhere. I'm going to learn all your secrets, Desiree, and then you're in trouble. What's your favorite scent?"

Her mind was reeling with the worst kind of cheesy answers, all of which revolved around him, and she tried—*oh, how she tried*—to keep them from coming out, but there must have been something in the air, because out popped, "You could just bottle yourself up, add a wick, and I'd be very happy."

The sinfulness staring back at her set her body aflame. Oh great. Now she was thinking about his *wick*. Lighting it, touching it, tasting it. Holy cow. What was going on? A little wine, a little Violet, and a day in a sex toy shop, and suddenly she couldn't stop thinking about sex. With *him*.

"That can be arranged." His deep voice snapped her back to the moment.

"Summer," fell hard and fast from her lips. "Anything *summery*," she added, hoping to distract him from her earlier answer. But he was watching her, and she knew he was waiting for that sexy girl who was clawing around inside her and turning up her sassiness about a hundred notches to find her way out.

She focused on the salesgirl behind the table, who was

pointing out candles with summery scents, but her mind was still wrestling with thoughts of Rick's *wick*, and his eyes, and the heat of his hand on her waist.

"…Summer Night, and Summer Romance," the salesgirl said. "We also have Coconut Delight and Sandy Harbor."

Rick gazed into Desiree's eyes with as much heat as hope, and she felt herself disappearing into them.

"What do you think, Desiree? Are you up for a summer romance?"

Summer romance? She wasn't a summer-romance girl. She was a first-date-dinner-and-a-movie girl with a polite good-night kiss. A three-week-rule girl. If she wanted a guy after three weeks of dating, she'd consider sleeping with him. But right this second, she was a holy-moly-please-light-my-fire girl.

No.

Just say no.

I'm going to say no.

She swallowed hard, stood up straighter, the way she did when she faced her students' parents, reminding herself she took pride in being a responsible person. *I can do this.*

She gazed up at Rick, who had yet to take his eyes off her, and her inner sexy girl gagged that good-girl chick, and "Absolutely," came roaring out.

RICK STRADDLED THE bench of a picnic table near the band where they'd chosen to eat dessert and guided Desiree into the same position, straddling the bench and facing him. He reached behind her, put his hand on her butt, and hauled her forward, until her knees pushed between his legs and the bench.

"Much better."

"Not very ladylike," she said with a tease in her eyes.

He bit back the dirty, though honest remark that sat on the tip of his tongue. *You could sit naked on my lap and you'd still look ladylike.* What had gotten into him? He wasn't a scumbag, and he didn't say things like that to women. But Desiree was awakening primal desires he'd buried beneath seventy-plus hours of work each week for years on end.

Reminding himself to slow down, he said, "I want to see your face."

He lit one of the candles they'd bought with the complimentary matches the salesgirl had thrown in as the band began playing a fast-paced song.

"I wouldn't have pegged you as a romantic," Desiree said.

"What would you have pegged me as?"

"I don't know. You're not like the guys I know."

"Are they mostly teachers and single dads?" He tossed out a line, hoping she'd bite. He was dying to know if she dated often and what her life back in Virginia was like. He was all for blowing the competition out of the water.

"No, definitely not. I would never date one of my students' fathers. I don't date much, and according to Emery, the guys I usually go out with are a little boring. She calls them 'nice.' But you're a nice guy, and you're not at all boring."

"Hey, nothing wrong with nice," Rick said.

"No, she's right. Nice guys *can* be a little boring." She whispered the word *boring*.

He looked around. "Are they here? The boring guys? Why are you whispering?"

She smiled, and he wanted to see that smile all day long.

"Because it feels rude to say it out loud."

"That's the preschool teacher in you speaking. People say Drake is a nice guy, and he's not at all boring. Then again, he's also persistent and opinionated, but not like me. I'll get in people's faces and speak my mind. It's a bad habit of mine, learned it from my father."

"Like Violet," she said.

He nodded. "Probably very similar. I like her, by the way. She watches out for you."

She squared her shoulders. "I don't need watching over."

"Everyone needs someone to watch out for them." Thinking of how different his life had been since he returned to the Cape and how great it was spending time with his family and friends, he added, "Life gets lonely without close friends."

"I have close friends, but I can take care of myself." Her brow wrinkled, and she took a sip of the iced tea he'd bought with their dessert. "Who watches out for you?"

"Drake. Dean. I don't know, friends and family."

A wistful look washed over her face, and he remembered her comment about her mother. He wondered if she had any family in Virginia. "You didn't seem to want to talk about your mother, so I won't push even though I'm curious. But can I ask about the rest of your family? Do you have any other siblings? Is your father in the picture?"

"I have no other siblings, and my father's definitely in the picture. He's an investment banker, and he was transferred to Connecticut last year, but we're still close."

He was glad to hear that. She was so cagey about her mother, he wondered what was really going on, and it made him want to protect her from whatever it was.

"And we've already established that Violet watches out for you."

"She's a whole other story. My family is complicated, Rick. I don't want to bore you with the details."

"I can handle complicated, and I'm sure I won't find it boring."

She looked down, fidgeting with her hands.

"I'll tell you what. Let's eat dessert, and when, and if, you ever want to talk about it, I'd love to listen." He pulled a container from the bag. "Close your eyes."

She did, and folded her hands in her lap, which was about the cutest thing he'd ever seen. It was easy to picture her patiently leading a class of preschoolers, teaching them letters and games and how to make friends, keeping her naughty side locked up tight. She was kind and careful and perfectly self-aware, especially when she was thinking naughty thoughts and became flustered and turned on. He loved that so much, he wanted to push all her buttons.

"I can feel you looking at me," she said sweetly.

"I'm undressing you with my eyes."

Her eyes remained closed, but her mouth curved up. He didn't know what had inspired him to play this game. He'd never done it before. But she seemed to be coming out of her shell more and more, and he wanted to keep peeling away those layers until he saw the very heart of who she was, not who she wanted everyone else in the world to believe she was.

"I'm going to put something in your mouth," he said, thinking a slew of dirty thoughts. "And you tell me what it is."

"You didn't tell me this was a game of trust. It's a good thing we're not playing naked." Her cheeks pinked up, and her fingers curled tight.

She had no idea what she was doing to him when she said dirty things in that sweet voice. "I'll add naked desserts to our list of things we should do together. Open up that pretty mouth of yours, beautiful."

He set a piece of dessert on her tongue, and a blissful look came over her.

"Mm—" Eyes closed, she licked her lips, swallowed, and licked her lips again.

Holy. Cow. That sound, her mouth…

"Oh my gosh. That is delicious. What is it? Chocolate, strawberry, *something*?" She licked her lips again, eyes still closed.

Every stroke of her tongue brought him closer to taking the kisses he was dying for.

"I know what it is," she said excitedly. "It's on the tip of my tongue."

He was about to offer to lick it off the tip of her tongue when her eyes flew open.

"Cheesecake! Right?" Before he could confirm it, she pressed her hands to his thighs and said, "Let me do you!"

She was so sexy, looking at him with those big green eyes, her hands squeezing his thighs. He wanted to pull her onto his lap and kiss her breathless. But she was so excited, he also wanted to keep this going.

"Anytime, sweetheart."

"You are so bad. See? The guys I know would never say that. Or call me 'sexy as a kitten,' or look at me like you are *right now*." Her voice trailed off to a whisper, and she fidgeted with the edge of the sweatshirt. "I like the way you look at me."

"That's a good thing, because I like looking at you, and I plan on doing it all summer long." He was trying his hardest to take things slow, but he was *this close* to kissing her, and once he did, he wasn't going to stop.

Her smile twitched, and her gaze flicked up to his. "So, you meant it when you asked about a summer romance?"

"Yes, I meant it. But don't worry; you're not locked in to anything. One date. Two. *Forty.* This will be whatever you'd like it to be." He couldn't remember the last time he'd wanted to look past a first date, but he found himself hoping for *forty.*

"What do *you* want it to be?" A sea of emotions swam in her eyes—hope, trepidation, *lust.*

He wanted to take her in his arms and experience every one of those emotions firsthand. To give her reasons to smile, to discover what was going on with her mother and what made her the careful woman she was. He didn't know what was going on inside him, but whatever this surge of desire and protectiveness was, he didn't want to fight it. But he sensed that she'd been hurt, and though he couldn't pinpoint where or how, he'd do everything within his power to keep her from getting hurt again. And that meant starting with not being too aggressive or scaring her off.

"I'd like it to be a daily occurrence." He probably should have said he'd like to see her again tomorrow, and they'd take it one day at a time, but he was only capable of so much restraint. And at that very second, as music played and couples danced, the air between Rick and Desiree beat with a rhythm all their own, and his resolve to go slow frayed even more.

"I'd like that," she said. "Very much."

Their eyes remained locked for so long, he felt himself leaning in at the same moment she waved her hand nervously and said, "Close your eyes and open your mouth."

It took him a second to remember they'd been playing a game. He did as she asked, and a sweet, chocolaty treat touched his tongue. When he closed his mouth, he felt her fingers slip out. *Forget the chocolate. I want those fingers back.*

He opened his eyes and caught her watching him intently, sucking the chocolate off her index finger. Her eyes widened, and her finger fell from her lips with a *pop.* For a beat, everything stilled. Her eyes bored into him with the same storm of emotions as earlier, and his resolve shattered. Their mouths collided, and he threaded his fingers into her silky hair, taking the kiss deeper. She grabbed his shirt, keeping him close, and man, how he loved that. She tasted so sweet, kissed him so hungrily, he didn't want to stop, and when she made the sexiest sounds he'd ever heard, he knew he wasn't going to. Not yet. Not when kissing her was so much better than his fantasies.

His arm circled her waist, holding her as close as they could be in that position. He wanted to lift her onto his lap, to feel her legs around his waist, her sweet curves pressed against him, but they were out in public, and no matter how much she'd opened up, he knew she was pushing her boundaries. And he wanted to push them, over and over again.

They kissed through the remainder of the song, and into the next, and by the time they came up for air, they were both breathless and she was flushed. He wasn't typically a passionate kisser. He liked to rush things along and get to the good stuff. But as he waited for the disclaimer Desiree seemed compelled to state every time she tiptoed out of her comfort zone, he realized he *was* a passionate kisser. He'd just been kissing the wrong women.

He was surprised when her disclaimer didn't come.

She touched her lips, as if they were still tingling, as his were, and he couldn't resist kissing her again, softer this time, longer, deeper. Oh yeah, he'd been kissing the wrong women, all right. He did not want to rush through Desiree's kisses. He wanted to pile them on, to batten down beneath them for the winter and ride them into spring.

"I wanted to dance with you," he said as they came up for air. He needed her to know he hadn't planned on ravishing her, but he was unable to stop.

"Kiss me now," she said breathlessly. "Dance another time."

She didn't need to ask twice.

Rick's senses surged and skidded as they made out like they needed each other to breathe. Everything blurred together, the sensual sounds slipping from her lungs, the feel of her knees pressing against his inner thighs, her hot little hands on his arms. None of it was enough, and he fought against his own desire to take her back to the truck, pull off on the first dark street they came to, and make love to her. But that wasn't *slow*. *This* wasn't slow, and it wasn't enough, either. He needed to feel her against him.

He tore his mouth away. "Dance with me."

Rising to his feet, he practically lifted her to hers and swept her into his arms. Their eyes met for only a split second before their mouths came together in a kiss hot enough to join metals. Their bodies took over, swaying to their own sensual beat. Her hands claimed his back, her hips pressed against him, making his body throb with desire. His hands moved down her back, to the dip at the base of her spine, holding her tight. She moaned into the kiss, and her nails dug into his back through his shirt. They kissed and danced, lost in a world all their own, their emotions pouring out when they broke away for a few short seconds at a time.

"Love kissing you." His hands slid south, holding her butt, and earning another heady moan.

"Don't stop. Kissing *or* touching," she pleaded.

As if he could.

Rick didn't know how much time had passed as they devoured each other, dancing beneath the stars, but eventually he realized that they were the only ones dancing; there was no music. The sparkling lights had gone out, leaving only the light of the candle. He smiled against her lips, and her eyes opened, sucking him right into another lustful kiss. She melted against him with the force of an ocean, constant and demanding.

"I don't want to stop," she said breathlessly.

He brushed his lips over hers. "We don't ever have to."

Sometime later—half an hour, an hour, he wasn't sure—they made their way to the truck, stopping every few steps to devour each other. She snuggled up to him on the way back to her place, kissing at the stoplights, the sexual tension in the truck an inescapable entity all its own. When he parked in front of her house, he didn't want the night to end, and at the same time, he didn't want to take it so far that she had a chance to regret a minute they'd spent together.

He took her face in his hands and gazed into her eyes, intending to tell her as much, but no words came. Their mouths joined like metal to magnet, in an urgent, exploratory kiss. She quivered against him, sending a surge of heat through his veins. Her hands moved over his chest, his arms, his *thighs*. She was right there with him. He leaned into her, and she went willingly onto her back, never breaking their connection. His mouth moved over hers with reckless abandon, and when her hips rocked up, he nearly lost it. He shifted her up toward the passenger door, wishing they were anyplace other than the cramped cab of his truck. He pushed his hands beneath her, lifting her hips so he could grind against them, and sealed his mouth over her neck, earning more sinful, breathy noises.

"You feel so good," she said. "Don't stop."

He wanted to strip her bare and make her lose her mind, but they were in his *truck*.

"Don't stop," she pleaded.

He had a cottage, she had a house, and they were making out like horny teenagers in her driveway. This was not how he'd imagined they'd end up, but he was powerless to resist her.

"Let me touch you and take you over the edge, baby," rushed out before he thought to stop it.

Her eyes opened, and he feared he'd blown it.

"Sorry, sweetheart. I got carried away." He pushed up on his palms, and she wrapped her hand around his neck, tugging him back down.

"*We* are getting carried away," she said with a shy smile. "I don't usually..."

"We don't have to." He touched his lips to hers, wishing he had used the head on his shoulders instead of letting the one between his legs lead.

She guided his hand to her thigh. "I *want* to."

Her breathy plea obliterated his control.

A long while later, he gathered her against him in the tight space, and they shifted onto their sides. Her cheeks were flushed, her eyes hazy. Pleasuring Desiree was unlike anything he'd ever experienced. It didn't matter that they hadn't made love. Sending her soaring brought him immense pleasure, and more than that, it had unearthed something inside him that made him want to hold her, protect her, and make her *his*.

"There's my beautiful girl."

She pressed her forehead to his chest. "I don't usually..."

"Shh. I don't either." He tipped her chin up and gazed into her eyes. "All that matters is this, right here. You and me and this powerful thing happening between us."

Chapter Six

DESIREE AWOKE EARLY the next morning with the need for structure, which wasn't surprising given that things had been in such turmoil since she'd arrived. Except last night, which hadn't been tumultuous in the same sense that the rest of her life was. It had been surprising, exciting, and wonderful. She'd never gotten completely lost in a man like that before, much less in a *truck*. But she couldn't have pried herself away from Rick if she'd wanted to. She'd *craved* him. And feeling his body against hers had made her want him all the more deeply. Even after their rampant make-out session, they'd had a hard time separating. They'd shared so many *one last kiss*es that she thought Violet might find them lip-locked on the porch in the morning. She touched the tiny spot beside her lip where his whiskers had left a little burn, and a shiver of heat skittered through her. The man knew how to kiss, and touch, and say all the right things. He'd left her body humming for hours, which was probably why she'd woken up with her head spinning and the need to get her arms around her new summer plans.

She picked up her phone, her pulse quickening as she reread the text Rick had sent shortly after he'd left last night. *Sweet dreams, beautiful. I miss you already.* She'd had so many conflicting thoughts—Were they moving too fast? Was she getting caught up in him because of the craziness in the rest of her life?—and his text had soothed her worries. He seemed to know just what she needed.

Boy, does he ever.

He'd been open and honest about what he'd wanted, and that had made her want him even more.

She had never had an orgasm with a man before. Not once, and certainly not with nothing more than kisses and his hand. But their molten kisses alone had brought her right up to the verge of release, never mind what he'd done with his hand.

She chewed on those thoughts throughout the morning as she walked around the house making a to-do list, starting with her outdated bedroom and bathroom. She'd taken one of the two bedrooms on the third floor. She liked the privacy and the gorgeous bay views out the nearly floor-to-ceiling windows, but also, it had been her grandmother's bedroom, and it provided a sense of stability she desperately needed. But if she was going to be there for the summer, she needed to get bedding from this century. She spotted Violet on the beach with Cosmos, and she warmed all over. *My new family.*

She carried that thought with her as she continued on her list-making journey. Crossing the hall, she passed the narrow door that provided access to the stairs leading up to the widow's walk. She used to sit up there for hours as a little girl, dreaming of all the ways her mother might suddenly show up for a lengthy visit, instead of the quick forty-eight hours at the end of her vacation. She debated going up now, but she wasn't ready for the emotions she knew would trample over her when she did. Instead, she pushed open the heavy wooden door to the other bedroom, swallowing hard at the sight of her mother's art studio in progress. The ceiling and walls had been stripped down to the ancient framework and rafters. Unmatched wooden tables were littered with painting supplies, some of which were open, the paint dried up. Masking tape secured sketches of women to the studs, and the windowsill was home to a host of paintbrushes, pencils, paints, magazines, and jars of dingy water with paintbrushes sticking out like lost bones. Half-finished paintings sat on easels and rested against studs.

She took a few steps into the room, inhaling the scents of her mother's chaos and unearthing memories she didn't realize she still held on to. She didn't have many memories from when Lizza and her father were married, and she was never sure what was real and what she'd fabricated out of desire or resentment. But as she stood in the midst of her mother's studio, flashes of the past rushed in. She remembered standing in her mother's studio in her childhood home, trying to get her mother's attention. Talking hadn't worked. Singing hadn't worked. She'd nearly yelled, and still she hadn't broken through her mother's trance. Her hands sweated as she remembered knocking a jar of paint off a table and the horrified expression on her mother's face. Her chest constricted from the memories. She spun on her heels and stormed out, closing the door behind her. She leaned against it, palms to her chest, waiting for her heart to stop racing before she headed downstairs.

She'd forgotten how high the ceilings were and how each room felt twice as big as rooms in more recently built homes. She was glad her mother was remodeling. But as she moved from room to room, she wondered where the expensive renovations had taken place. The dark hardwood floors were still worn and scuffed, and there were cracks she remembered from her childhood in the drywall. Even the kitchen, though spacious, with a big center island, hadn't been updated beyond a new refrigerator.

She was working at the kitchen table when the door to the patio opened and Cosmos's nails clicked across the floor. He went paws-up on her leg, and she lifted him into her lap, wet paws and all. He licked her chin, his eyes sparkling, like she was the best surprise ever.

"Morning," she said to Violet, who had on the same black bikini top she'd worn yesterday and another pair of cutoffs. She looked relaxed and ready to hang out on the beach, but Desiree hoped she'd help her out with the items on her list.

"What are you working on?" Violet peered over her shoulder.

"I made a list of things we need to do to get the shop going. I didn't see a sign out by the road, so I thought maybe we could make one so people know we're open. Unless you saw one stored away somewhere? I didn't check the closets. I guess I'll do that first." She made a note to check the closets. "I also made a plan for working at the shop." She knew Violet had a hard time with schedules, so she didn't call it that. She pushed the notebook across the table. "I alternated mornings and afternoons, so neither of us is stuck there all day."

Violet smirked. "A *schedule*? Seriously?"

"It's a *plan*, not a schedule." Ignoring the deadpan look her sister was giving her, she pushed a little harder. "Why not? I'd like to know when I need to work and when I can go to the beach, or out with Rick, or—"

"Sorry, Des, but I really do suck at schedules." Violet pushed the notebook away. "Although I'm glad you're hooking up with Rick. That should loosen you up."

Why had she thought this was going to be the easy part of

getting organized? A schedule was rudimentary. It wasn't like she was asking Violet to *make* the schedule.

"I'm not *that* uptight. But I do like to know my plans. Otherwise, how will we know who's running the shop and when?"

"We live in the same house," Violet pointed out. "I'm pretty sure we'll figure it out."

"I'm sorry, Vi. I thought I could try to do this without a schedule, but I can't even *begin* without some sort of plan. It won't work for me. I'm just not wired that way. I like knowing where I have to be and when I have to be there so I can plan my week."

"Plan your week? No wonder you're so uptight. And just call it what it is. A *schedule*."

Desiree fought the urge to roll her eyes. "Look. I'm not asking for much. Just give me an inch and at least consider it? If you don't like what I've laid out, we can change it. It was just a starting point."

Violet sighed. "I'll look it over, but I'm telling you, schedules are not my thing. It's not like I don't want to stick to them. I'm just not good at it."

"I appreciate you trying," Desiree said, hoping for the best. "At some point we need to go through Lizza's things and figure out how much the mortgage is. I was so shocked at her leaving, I forgot to ask."

Violet reached on top of the refrigerator and tossed an envelope onto the table. "I found this in the den."

Desiree took the envelope. "I looked around the whole house and I can't find any renovations except in her studio. And that's a mess. The walls and ceiling have been ripped out, but it looks like she was using it that way. I can't figure out where she's spent enough for a mortgage of any substance. It makes me wonder if there's any debt to be paid. It would be just like her to lie about that, too."

Violet pointed to the envelope.

Desiree withdrew and quickly scanned the contents from the envelope. "Is this some kind of joke? How could she get a fifteen-year mortgage for *three hundred thousand* dollars? She doesn't have a pot to pee in. When she said there was a mortgage for renovations, I was thinking, fifty, maybe sixty thousand."

Violet waved her hand around the room. "The house is worth millions. Bay-front property on Cape Cod. Think about it."

"But *why* would the bank give it to her? She doesn't even have a real job." She set Cosmos on the floor and paced the kitchen.

"She probably sold them on the idea of reopening the inn, and everything on the Cape is hugely expensive. Renovations that cost fifty thousand in Virginia are probably twice that here. The question is, where's the money? She said she's been renovating, but obviously that's about as true as the reasons she brought us here."

"The next mortgage payment is due in *three* weeks. Why would she do this? Before Grandma's funeral, I hadn't seen her for years. *Years*, Vi." She paced. "Wasn't it enough that she ruined my childhood? Does she really need to mess up the rest of my life, too?"

"Careful, Des. You're going to pop a vein or something." Violet pushed herself up and sat on the counter, her bare feet dangling, like it was just another summer's day.

"How can you be so infuriatingly calm?" She was too angry to even begin to figure out how they'd come up with the money for the next mortgage payment. She had savings, but that was her hard-earned money to be used in case of emergencies. She didn't earn much, and it had taken her a long time to save it up.

"Because while you're whining about how she ruined your childhood and you're not used to her antics, *this* is what I grew up with. This is normal for me." Violet pushed from the counter.

"What does that mean?" She glared at her sister. "And I'm not whining. I'm just pointing out a fact."

"Trust me, you were a lot better off in Virginia with your father than traveling the world with her. You have no idea what it was like moving every six months, never having friends long enough to build relationships. Never knowing what country I'd be in next." She shoved her feet into a pair of black leather boots by the kitchen door, grabbed her keys from the counter, and stormed outside.

"Wait!" Desiree chased after her and grabbed her arm.

Violet spun around, her eyes throwing daggers. "It's not your problem."

"It *is* my problem. I never thought about what you were going through. I thought you loved living with her, that you were just like her. Free-spirited and perfectly happy traveling around the world."

Violet turned away, jaw clenched tight.

"Please don't drive off. You're my sister, and we're in this together. We may not know each other very well yet, but we've got all summer." The tension around Violet's mouth eased. Not a lot, and if she weren't looking for it, she might have missed it. But it was enough to make her want to try harder.

"I'll take away the schedule," Desiree offered, hoping it would help.

Violet smiled, and an incredulous laugh fell from her lips. "You didn't even want to stay for the summer in the first place."

"I know, but maybe this is our chance to finally become the sisters we were never able to be when we were growing up."

"We're so different." Violet looked over Desiree's yellow tank dress and strappy sandals.

"But we came out of the same womb," Desiree gently reminded her, making them both smile. "You rushed up here when you thought I was in trouble. That *has* to mean something."

"Yeah, that I didn't want to lose the only person I have in the entire world besides *her*. I always thought that one day we'd, I don't know, be able to hang out together. Find a way not to fight when we saw each other. And then I thought you were *dying* and we'd never have the chance. And if she's the only person I have in this entire world, then I'm truly fu...*screwed*."

"I've wanted that, too," Desiree admitted.

An untrusting expression washed over Violet's face. "You don't have to say that to make me feel better. I'm sure when you're at home I'm the last person you think about."

It didn't surprise Desiree that Violet didn't believe her. They had nothing to base trust on. A couple of stressful weeks over the summers when they were younger hardly built a solid foundation. But they were on the cusp of a new turn in their relationship, and it was shrouded in possibilities. Her thoughts unexpectedly turned to her date with Rick. Apparently, this was her summer for stretching her boundaries in all directions. She inhaled a jagged breath, wondering how she'd survive so many emotions and changes at once.

"I do think about you. Maybe not in a *missing you* kind of way anymore, because we don't have that type of relationship, but I've always wished we did. Or could," Desiree reiterated. "Come on. Please, Vi? Let's both agree to give this a chance. How hard can it be to sell paintings and sexy stuff?"

Violet laughed. "*Fine.* Just turn those sad puppy eyes away from me." She knocked Desiree with her shoulder. "She really messed us up, didn't she?"

"I don't know. You're a world traveler and I'm a preschool teacher. We're not doing so bad." As she said it, she realized it was true, and she needed to stop thinking about how her mother had ruined her childhood. She hadn't ruined it as much as she'd broken her heart. "I'm sorry I didn't realize you were unhappy when we were younger. I wouldn't have stopped coming here to spend time with you."

"Des?" Violet asked as they walked toward the house.

"Hm?"

She held the screen door open for Desiree to walk through. "Stop being so good. It's really annoying."

"WHY ARE DATES so nerve-racking?" Desiree held up two dresses and turned toward her laptop, showing Emery her choices. It was nearly seven o'clock, and Rick would be there soon to pick her up.

"Don't you have anything sexier to wear? And you're nervous because you made out like horndogs last night and you know you're on the brink of jumping his bones." Emery made kissing noises.

"I am not going to jump his bones on the second date." Desiree's insides heated at the idea of jumping Rick's bones.

"If I were you, I'd shed my clothes so flipping fast," Emery pushed. "You really need to get new curtains. Those flowery things behind you are total mood killers."

Desiree looked at the curtains, thinking about Rick in her bed. "Can you please stop talking about making out and *moods*? You're making me even more nervous." She tried to focus on choosing an outfit. She hadn't thought she'd be dating, and almost everything she'd brought was either too casual or too proper. "I don't know where he's taking me, so I was trying to err on the conservative side."

Violet popped her head into Desiree's room. "Hey. I picked up the flyers. Did you get the signs done? And who weeded the patio? Does Lizza have a secret gardener? And if she does, is he hot? Tatted-up with a big co—"

"Violet!" Desiree pointed to the laptop.

"Sorry. Hey, Emery." Violet came into the room wearing the same outfit as earlier, with a black hoodie over her bikini top.

After their talk this morning, she and Violet had worked together creating flyers advertising *Devi's Discoveries - Art and Personal Explorations*, and sent them to a local printer. Desiree hadn't been able to bring herself to go back into her mother's studio, so while Violet was out putting up flyers, Desiree weeded the brick courtyard by the cottages. It made the place look a thousand times more welcoming.

"Hey, Violet." Emery waved. "Since I'm not there to drag her butt out to the store, can you take Desiree out to get curtains? And please tell me you have something she can wear tonight on her date with Rick?" The two had never met other than a few brief hellos on FaceTime, but it was amazing how easily a friendship could develop that way.

At least for them.

On some level, it bothered her that Emery and Violet could communicate so easily. But on another, she was glad for it. She and Vi had never even thought of keeping in touch that way when they were younger. Then again, Vi hadn't owned a computer until her late teens, when the space between them had widened like a canyon.

"Tomorrow night, Des," Violet said. "You and I are going to Hyannis to get bedding and towels. I cannot sleep on pink sheets one more night." Hands on hips, she ran an assessing eye over Desiree. "Didn't you say he took you out with a stain on your shirt last night? Why bother primping?"

"Because he's seen me drenched and stained. Don't you think he deserves to see me cleaned up?"

"I think he's already hooked," Violet said. "But let me see what you have."

"Des, I have to run. I've got a class tonight," Emery said. "Good luck, and let me know how the bone jumping goes."

"Bone jumping?" Violet's eyes lit up.

"*Thanks*, Em. I appreciate that."

"Love you, too!" Emery ended the call, and Desiree closed her laptop.

"How about this?" Violet held up a coral minidress with a halter top, which Desiree had bought with Emery last summer when they'd gone to Ocean City for the weekend. The straps tied behind her neck.

"It's pretty casual." She slipped off her bra and into the dress, feeling mildly self-conscious about undressing in front of Violet.

"First, those lace panties are fricking hot. Good choice. And unless he's taking you to the Wicked Oyster, you can wear that dress. Besides, with that tan you're rocking, you look incredible.

Throw on some hoop earrings and maybe a few bracelets, and he'll be jumping your bones by dessert."

She did a mental happy dance knowing Violet approved of her panties, and quickly reminded herself that after last night's make-out session, she should get ahold of her raging hormones and slow things down. "I don't want him to jump my bones by dessert." She started to take off the dress, and Violet grabbed her hand, stopping her.

"Desiree, you look *pretty*, not slutty. Don't you realize how hot you are? You could wear baggy pants and a sweatshirt and he'd still want to jump your bones."

Secretly pleased with Violet's praise, she glanced at Rick's sweatshirt hanging over a chair in the corner of the room. She'd tried to give it back to him last night. *Keep it. I like seeing you in my things.*

"Okay. I'll wear it, if you're sure it's okay."

Her sister held up a pair of dangling gold earrings. "It's better than okay, and these are perfect. You don't need hoops or bangles. You look amazing just as you are."

A knock at the door sent Desiree's heart racing, and Cosmos sprinting down the stairs. "That's him."

"Whoa, babe. Chill. I'd give anything to feel whatever it is that's making you blush." She grabbed a sweater from Desiree's closet and handed it to her. "It'll be cold later."

Desiree stared at it for a second, warmed by her thoughtfulness. She put on the earrings as they descended the stairs. "And I'd give anything for your sense of calm. Any tips?"

"Jump his bones before he can jump yours." Violet winked and pulled open the door.

Holy mother of hotness.

Desiree's breath whooshed out of her at the sight of Rick

wearing a pair of dark shorts, flip-flops, and a white button-down rolled up to his elbows, exposing his muscular forearms. He looked beyond handsome, but it was the rakish look he was giving her that practically melted her panties off.

RICK'S GAZE DRIFTED right past Violet to Desiree, stunning in a bright, summery dress that showed off her gorgeous legs. Would it be rude to plow past Violet and take Desiree in his arms? He'd noticed last night when they were kissing on the porch that his whiskers had left a little scratch beside her mouth. It was almost gone now, but he was glad he'd taken extra care to shave right before their date.

"If you two stare like that any longer, you're going to burn holes through each other." Violet pulled Rick inside by his wrist and leaned closer to Desiree. "I think you need to wear shoes." She picked up Cosmos and headed upstairs.

Desiree looked down at her bare feet. "Oops."

"Shoes are overrated." Rick wrapped his arms around her waist and leaned down to kiss her cheek, wanting a much more intimate kiss. But after last night he didn't trust himself to stop at just one. "Hi, beautiful. I thought about you all day."

"I thought about you, too," she said.

Man, he liked knowing that. "I thought we'd hit the Pearl for dinner, and then Drake and some of our friends are having a bonfire on the beach." The Pearl was one of the nicer restaurants in Wellfleet, with a second-story deck that offered beautiful views of the harbor. "It should be fun if you're up to it."

"Sounds perfect. I've never been to a beach bonfire." She

glanced at her feet again. "Just give me a second to grab my sandals."

He watched her hurry up the stairs, unable to remember the last time he'd wanted to introduce a woman to his friends and family. He'd much rather be alone with Desiree, but his nephew had specifically asked him to come, and he'd do just about anything for that little guy.

A short while later they were seated at a table overlooking the marina. Rick reached for Desiree's hand, lacing their fingers together. "Should we risk a glass of wine tonight?"

"One, yes. Three, no," she said with a sweet smile. "The last thing you need is a sloppy drunk on your hands."

"I think you're mistaken. There's no scenario in which I wouldn't want my hands on you."

Her cheeks flushed, and he leaned in closer. "How can I miss you this much after one date?" He pressed his lips to hers, wishing he could kiss her forever, but the waitress arrived.

They ordered dinner, and a few minutes later she brought their wine. After she left, he moved to the seat beside Desiree, wanting to be closer.

"Did Violet tell you Cosmos went for a swim again this morning?"

"What? No." Her brow wrinkled. "I'm so sorry."

"It's okay. I'm going to have to get him a puppy pool. I was hoping to see you when I brought him back, but Violet was sitting on the porch and she said you were still asleep." He lowered his voice and said, "I think Cosmos wanted me to sneak up anyway."

She pressed her lips together, as if she were holding back a naughty thought.

Let it out, baby. Let it out.

Her eyes darted away, and she took a sip of her wine. "We'll take care of it. I promise. I wonder if he dug under the fence and escaped."

"Let's take a look together tomorrow and see what we can figure out." He squeezed her hand. "You're absolutely irresistible when you're flustered."

"Well, you're not getting a very good impression of me with my inebriated state last night, my mother's misbehaving dog, and the toy shop." She whispered *toy shop.* "Not to mention how fast we…" She blushed a red streak. "Last night."

He couldn't resist sliding one hand to the nape of her neck, drawing her closer, and brushing his lips over hers. "I think you've made an excellent impression, especially when you get flustered."

Her lips parted and a puff of air escaped. "I'll probably get flustered a *lot* tonight."

He lowered his lips to hers, turning her playful smile into a series of eager kisses. He desperately wanted to deepen the kiss, but he knew she'd be embarrassed. As much as he loved seeing her cheeks pink up, battling with the hunger in her eyes, he forced himself to come up for air.

"I'm sorry," he said. "I'll try to behave."

She touched his hand and said, "Don't behave too much, or I might have to put you in a time out."

She was going to be the death of him. Could a man die from sweetness overload?

"Don't worry, sweetheart. I don't think I'm capable of being *too* behaved with you. Unless, of course, you have a naughty corner. I'd do just about anything to land there."

Her eyes bloomed wide. She downed half her wine and whispered, "*I don't have a naughty corner!*"

He laughed and gave her a chaste kiss, then forced himself to sit back and put enough space between them to keep him from taking *that* any further. *For now.*

He took a drink to distract himself from her tongue running nervously across her lower lip, and when that didn't work, he went for conversation. "What do you think would have been different if we'd met under different circumstances?"

"You mean besides *everything*?"

"I hope you're kidding, because I really like who you are," he said more seriously.

"Thank you. But a lot would be different. I'm floundering a little being here this summer."

"Because you're watching your mother's business and you're not into the items she carries?"

She sat up a little taller, her expression serious. "That and the whole reason we're here. My mother is the kind of person who lives her life on a whim, without any regard for who she hurts along the way."

"And you've been hurt by her whimsical lifestyle?"

She nodded, and it made him ache and angry at once. Holding her hand, he put his other arm around her, wishing he could take away whatever pain her mother had caused.

"Violet is my half sister," she explained. "We have different fathers. She's two and a half years older than me, and we grew up together until I was five, when our parents—our mother and my father, Violet's stepfather—divorced. Lizza, our mother, took Violet and moved overseas to teach."

He ground his teeth together at the thought of Desiree as a trusting little girl having her world ripped out from under her. No wonder Violet was so protective of her. She was trying to keep anyone else from hurting her baby sister.

"They moved from one country to another while Lizza taught on six-month contracts, sometimes shorter or longer, but you get the idea. I lived with my father in Virginia, and saw them once or twice a year for a few days at a time when we were young. Violet and I spent some time together here at the Cape, but by the time we were teenagers, it was just a few disconnected and uncomfortable days each year." Her gaze lowered to their joined hands. "I've never talked about this before, except with Emery."

"I'm sorry, and thank you for trusting me enough to share it." In an effort to lighten her mood, he said, "Is this the same Emery who says you date 'nice' guys?"

"The one and only. You listened to everything I said last night, didn't you?"

Imagining all she'd gone through, the truth came easily. "How could anyone be with you and not listen to every word you say? What you've gone through is what's made you the incredible woman you are. I want to hear everything you're willing to share."

"It actually feels good to tell you. It's hard to have all of this in my head *and* try to relax. I really like you, and I want to relax." She looked down at their joined hands and smiled. "Just promise me that if you run for the hills, you'll drop me off first."

"Yeah, because *that's* likely to happen." He laughed, and her smile reached her eyes. "I'm not going to judge you by your mother's actions, if that's what you're worried about. And I'm not going anywhere without you by my side."

"You make my heart go a mile a minute." She took another sip of liquid courage. "I've never felt like this before."

He leaned in closer. "I might use that to my advantage later, but unless you want me to do so now, I'd suggest we move to safer ground, because that look in your eyes makes it seriously *hard* for me to concentrate."

He forced himself to put distance between them *again*. "Tell me what it was like when you did see them."

She swallowed hard, her brows knitting. "As you can imagine, those visits were stressful and disjointed. There was no time to get reacclimated to one another before they were leaving again. During the summers, Violet and I would come here to stay with my grandmother, but they weren't joyful reunions. We didn't really know each other, and as we got older, it became even more awkward, and we spent less and less time together. And then I went to college, and our visits became even more sporadic."

Regardless of how good she said it had felt to tell him, he saw pain in her eyes. He rubbed his thumb over the back of her hand, hoping to soothe it. "I'm sorry you went through that. It must have been heartbreaking."

"It was. And frustrating." A small smile lifted her lips. "I told you it was complicated."

She was revealing so much of herself, he felt even more protective of her. "And I told you, I can handle complicated."

That brought a bolder smile, and a sigh of relief. "That's good. Because it gets even more so."

He couldn't imagine that she'd been through more than what she'd already described.

"Before last year at my grandmother's funeral, it had been a few years since I'd seen either Lizza or Vi. And then out of the blue, a few days ago I received an email from Lizza saying she needed me to come to the Cape to prolong her life."

Holy crap.

"I felt about how you look right now. Like *what the heck*, right?"

"Something like that," he mumbled.

"When I got here, I found out she wasn't sick. She was *bored* looking after the house, which isn't surprising considering she never stays in one place very long."

"Wow, Desiree. I'm sorry, but who would do that to her daughter? I'm having a really hard time liking your mother right now."

She laughed, and it caught him by surprise. "You and me both. Anyway, the long and short of it is that she'd also sent an email to Violet saying *I* needed her here to help prolong *my* life. I had only just arrived, and Lizza was all packed up and ready to leave. Right before she climbed into a cab she told us she'd taken out a mortgage on the house, and unless we wanted to lose our grandmother's estate, we needed to stay and run her business to pay the mortgage. Now she's off at an ashram for the summer."

She told him about the lack of renovations being done and their plans for marketing with flyers and signs. She'd clearly accepted that this was her lot for the summer, and she was facing it head-on.

"No wonder you feel off-kilter. You're a strong, loyal woman, Desiree. I think most people would have turned around and gone back home, leaving Lizza to clean up her own mess."

She took another sip of wine. "Don't give me too much credit. I wanted to leave, but I couldn't strap Violet with all of this. It's so crazy, it doesn't even feel real."

Thinking of when they'd lost his father, he said, "I know all about things being so far out there they don't seem real." He pushed those memories away, as he'd been doing his whole life, and focused on the brave woman baring her soul before him.

"Maybe it's a blessing in disguise." *Because it brought us together.* He tried to lighten the mood and earn one of her beautiful smiles. "Think of it this way. You're learning a new trade, living in a beachfront house *without* the headache of renovations, and you have time to get to know your sister. I'd say that's a heck of a good summer."

Her smile reached all the way up to her eyes, and then all that brightness smoldered. "You left out the best part of all."

He put an arm around her, drawing her closer. "That you're dating a guy who's getting more into you by the second?"

"Yes. *That.*" She lowered her voice and said, "You should probably seal that thought with a kiss."

"If I don't, can we visit the naughty corner?" He slanted his mouth over hers, swallowing her sounds of surprise and turning them into something *much* sweeter.

Chapter Seven

WHEN THEY ARRIVED back at the resort for the bonfire, Desiree and Rick left their shoes in the truck and crossed the dunes to find the others. The sand was cold beneath Desiree's bare feet, but she was warm snuggled up against Rick's side. She had worried that her confession would make him think twice about getting any more involved with her, but as they walked along the shore, serenaded by the bay lapping at the sand, she knew it had brought them even closer. They'd talked and laughed over dinner, and she'd shared so much of herself that she felt like Rick knew her better than most people who had known her for years. But when the flames of the bonfire came into view, her nerves sprang to life, pushing all that goodness to the side.

"You okay?" he asked.

"Just a little nervous."

He stopped walking and wrapped his arms around her with a wide grin. "I promise you will like them, and they will adore you."

"Why won't I *adore* them?"

He laughed and touched his lips to her hers. "You are forever the teacher, aren't you? I'll have to be more careful with semantics. You will *adore* them." His eyes darkened, and that playful grin turned serious. "Just don't adore them too much. I don't share well."

"Is my big, confident guy jealous?" She flattened her palms on his chest, going up on her toes, anxious for another kiss. "What happens when you get jealous?"

"I up my game," he practically growled, before taking her in a toe-curling kiss that had her winding her arms around his neck to keep him from breaking their connection.

She needn't have worried. He kissed her until her knees weakened, and she sank down on her heels, holding on to him in an effort to remain standing. When their lips finally parted, he went back for more, leaving her mouth tingling and her body electrified.

"I…" She swallowed hard to try to force her fuzzy mind into gear.

A wicked grin spread across his face, and he kissed her again. "You know I can't resist you when you get flustered."

His voice was gravelly and low, and she imagined him saying it to her in a dark bedroom, where she was sure to be flustered with an experienced guy like Rick. That thought sent her mind scrambling again, and he must have seen it, because he lowered his mouth to hers, kissing her deep and slow, until she was sure she'd turn to liquid and wash away with the tide.

She came away breathless and put her finger over his mouth to give herself time to find her legs again. He smiled and puckered up, pressed a kiss to her finger, and then he sucked it into his mouth, swirling his tongue around the tip.

"Rick." She pulled her finger from his mouth and stole a glance up the beach, toward the sounds of laughter and guitar music. She fought her needy self, which begged her to drag him up to the dunes and continue making out, but she couldn't leave his family wondering where they were.

"My delicious Desiree, you push all of my buttons." He wrapped his hand around her wrist and kissed her palm. "I warned you about being flustered," he said in a playful voice, as if he hadn't just sent her world spinning. "Come on. Let's go get jealous and flustered."

A little boy sprinted down the beach toward them, his mop of brown hair blowing in the wind as he plowed into Rick's legs. "Uncle Rick!"

"Hagen, my man." Rick hoisted him into his arms and kissed his cheek.

"We're roasting marshmallows," Hagen said, his bright blue eyes dancing with excitement. "And me and Dad made *In-va-rar-y* sand castle."

"That's great." Rick put his hand on the small of Desiree's back and said, "Des, this is my brilliant nephew, Hagen. Buddy, this is my girlfriend, Desiree."

It had been so long since she'd been called a girlfriend, she was momentarily stunned. Rick winked, as if to say, *Go with it.* She *was* going with it, all right. And she wasn't freaking out inside or feeling like she wanted to hold back. Seeing her big, brawny, pushy man with sweet Hagen helped bolster her decision.

Hagen's eyes turned serious. "Hi."

"Hi. I'm surprised you know about the Inveraray Castle. It's a beautiful one."

"I know about lots of castles. Mom says castles are handsome, and their grounds are beautiful." He wiggled out of Rick's arms. "Hurry up and get there before Uncle Drake eats all the marshmallows." He took off running toward the group.

"Slow down around the fire," Rick called after him, melting Desiree's heart a little more. "Hagen and Matt, my sister Mira's husband, have been studying castles. They're planning a family trip to see a few of them over the winter. Last summer they visited libraries down the East Coast."

"He's adorable," she said. "How old is he? Six or seven?"

"He's seven. Hagen's a cool kid. He loves—*adores*—books and facts. Probably like your children will one day." He put his mouth beside her ear as they approached the bonfire and said, "I bet my sweet, naughty teacher wants three kids and a white picket fence."

She'd dreamed of marrying a man who was as loving and stable as her father, and of being the type of mother she always wished she'd had. He'd pegged her so perfectly, she wondered what else he saw in her.

A tall, dark-haired man pushed to his feet, flashing a friendly smile. "There's the man of the hour. Hi. You must be Desiree. I'm Drake, Rick's older brother." He gave her a quick hug. "I'm glad you made it."

"It's nice to meet you." She glanced at Rick, sighing inwardly as he blew her a kiss.

A pretty brunette wearing shorts and a sweatshirt hugged her next. "I'm Mira—their sister and Hagen's mom. My son thinks you're very pretty."

"Oh," Desiree said, surprised. "Well, thank you, Hagen. He's adorable. I can't wait to see the castle he's built."

Mira reached for another dark-haired man's hand. The way he was looking at Mira told her he was Matt.

"He and Matt built it," Mira said.

Matt embraced Desiree. "Nice to meet you. We'll show you the castle after you get put through the paces with this crew."

A perky brunette wearing cropped jeans and a purple hoodie pushed between them. "Hi. I'm Serena. I work for the guys at the resort."

"And we grew up together," Mira chimed in.

"And she and Drake had a fling," said a muscular guy who was sitting on a blanket playing the guitar.

Serena waved her hands. "No fling. We just work together."

Drake glared at the guy. "No, we did not have a fling. Come on, Dean." He took the guitar from Dean and gave him a nudge toward Rick and Desiree. "This is Dean, our business partner—and a troublemaker."

"How's it going?" Dean gave her a friendly hug.

Rick reclaimed her with an arm around her waist and said, "Welcome to *my* crazy summer."

She liked the playfulness of his friends and family. Everyone settled on blankets and chairs around the bonfire. Matt and Hagen roasted marshmallows, and Drake and Dean gave each other a hard time.

Serena handed her a stick and a bag of marshmallows. "We have chocolate and graham crackers, too."

"Sounds delicious." She took the stick, and Rick grabbed the bag of marshmallows.

"I've got it," he said as he slid a marshmallow onto the stick, licking the sweetness off his fingers with a lascivious look in his eyes. *Oh boy. May I have another, please?*

Dean picked up his guitar, playing again.

"Rick tells us you're staying at the old Summer House Inn," Drake said.

"Yes. It was my grandmother's house. My sister and I are running my mother's art gallery for the summer."

"Mira, we should check it out," Serena said. "Is it open all the time?"

She told them how they were just starting to figure out the hours and get the word out about the gallery, and decided *not* to mention the sex toy shop.

"Why don't we come by one afternoon when we can both slip away. Maybe while we're there we can help you brainstorm ideas to get the word out," Mira suggested. "I just set up a co-op, and Serena is a wiz at marketing."

"That sounds perfect," Desiree said, already feeling a kinship with the easygoing girls.

Hours passed in a carefree night of music, marshmallows, and playful banter. Rick kept a hand on Desiree's leg, or his arm around her, the whole time. Hagen showed Desiree the castle he and Matt had built and explained the history of the structure in seven-year-old terms, blowing her away. It was a magical feeling, being swept into the inner circle of such warm, close-knit friends. She wished she and Violet could get along this easily. *Maybe one day…*

Rick nudged Desiree's shoulder, holding a roasted marshmallow between his fingers. "Can I interest you in a little warm, creamy goodness?"

With the seductive tone of his voice, and the way he was visually devouring her, he might as well have been naked and offering her something far more sexual. Her eyes darted nervously around the group, worrying someone else might have had the same interpretation. Matt pulled Mira to her feet and began dancing. Drake and Dean were now both playing guitars. Drake's eyes were locked on Serena, who was taking a selfie with Hagen, and Desiree wondered if there was something between Drake and Serena after all.

She turned back to Rick, relieved she was the only one with

the dirty mind.

Rick's eyes darkened as she opened her mouth and bit into the marshmallow. She put her hand up to block her mouth as she chewed. He moved it away and sealed his lips over hers, slathering the sweet, sticky treat over her tongue. It melted into their half laugh, half kiss, and she dissolved into him. He drew back just far enough so she could see the heat in his eyes as he sucked the stickiness off his fingers, igniting flames beneath her skin. *I want to do that. I want to suck your fingers, lick marshmallow off your entire body. Lick and suck, and—*

"You've got that flustered look again," he said in a heady voice.

Anticipation climbed up her limbs, but she caught sight of Hagen in her peripheral vision, and as Rick moved in for another hot kiss, she put her palm to his chest. "Rain check. Hagen might see us."

Rick made a guttural sound. It was so sexy, she nearly ate her words and kissed him. He rose to his feet, bringing her up beside him, and headed away from the group.

She hurried to keep up. "Where are we going?"

"Dancing."

Remembering last night's dance, she couldn't stop grinning. A good distance from the group, he gathered her close and began moving seductively. She could feel his arousal. His mouth came down over hers as his hands moved up and down her back in a dizzying pattern. He took the kiss deeper, cupping her butt and making her whimper with need. With the bay breeze at her back, and her hot man pressed against her, her body begged for more. He gazed into her eyes, looking at her like he was wrestling with his emotions.

"Sorry, beautiful. I have been wanting to do that all night.

Seeing you with my family did something to me." He tightened his hold on her. He'd been doing that all night, too, as if he were afraid the air slipping between them might steal her away. "I hope you weren't overwhelmed by everyone."

"Not at all. You're lucky. If I had a family like that, I don't think I'd ever move away."

RICK TOUCHED HIS forehead to Desiree's, thinking about what she'd said. He was lucky. *Real* lucky. He had a great family and friends who were as close as blood. Thinking of the reasons he'd left the Cape all those years ago, he said, "Sometimes the hardest place to be is where everyone knows you best."

Confusion rose in her eyes, and he drew her against him, hoping to put that conversation aside for a while. As they danced in the moonlight, he thought of all Desiree had revealed to him, admiring her ability to keep such a positive outlook when her life had been turned upside down by the very woman who should have been watching out for her.

Just like last night, Rick lost track of time and space and anything but the woman in his arms. He didn't know when his sister and her family had left, or how long ago Drake and Dean had stopped playing their guitars. All he knew was that as they broke away from a particularly hot kiss, he *needed* to be alone with Desiree.

"What do you say we get out of here?"

She glanced at the bonfire. "Sure, but we should say good-bye."

He didn't want to share her any more than he already had, but he respected her too much to deny her the chance for a proper goodbye. They headed back to the group and said they were taking off. As Serena hugged Desiree, promising to come by the shop soon, Rick picked up Drake's guitar.

"Mind if I borrow this?" he asked his brother.

"No. Go ahead," Drake said. "You okay?"

Drake knew him so well. He only played when he thought of his father, and right then, thoughts of his father were following him like a shadow.

"Do you play?" Desiree asked.

"A little." He draped his arm over her shoulder.

"Oh, please," Serena said. "These three were in a band together as teenagers. He's really good."

"Okay, we're out of here." Rick dragged her away before anyone could share stories of him disappearing into music after he'd lost his father.

"Why didn't you play with the guys tonight?"

"And miss holding you? No, thank you." He kissed Desiree's cheek as they headed down the beach toward her place. "I'll bring your sandals by tomorrow."

"Good. That means I'll see you again."

He smiled down at her. "Did you have any doubt?"

"Well, you did call me your girlfriend, so I guess I shouldn't, but..."

"But nothing, sweetheart. A daily occurrence, remember?" He stopped walking and dropped to one knee, resting the guitar over his other and holding tightly to her hand. "Desiree, will you go out with me tomorrow, and the next day, and every day thereafter, until you either get sick of me or leave the Cape?"

She covered her mouth, but nothing could hide her radiant smile. "Yes, you silly man."

"'Silly' doesn't sound very manly," he said as he rose to his feet.

She cuddled against him as they walked along the shore. "On the right man, 'silly' is as hot as 'strong.'"

"Really? Huh. I'll have to amp up my silliness."

Desiree laughed. "You're wonderful just as you are. Full of surprises. Oh, shoot. Tomorrow night I'm going out with Violet. I'm sorry. I totally forgot."

"Ditching me already?"

"Hardly, but I think our sheets are from the Colonial days. We really need to get new ones."

"Have fun. I'll hang out with Dean and Drake, and we'll get together Friday night. That is, if you're free."

"I'm definitely free," she said, lacing her fingers with his.

When they reached Desiree's house, they sat in the sand and Rick played his guitar, singing songs that made Desiree smile. He wanted to play all night long, just to see the joy in her eyes.

Deep into the night, when Desiree looked a little sleepy, he played "I Wanna Be That Song," by Brett Eldredge, and sang it to her. And there, with the moon glistening off the water and his girl sighing dreamily beside him, he knew he was falling hard. He wanted to *be* the song that got her high and made her dance and made her fall. He wanted to *be* the melody that made time stand still for her, filled her up, and kept her young. He wanted her to believe she was right where she should be. By *his* side.

She sighed, and those penetrating green eyes of hers washed over him with so much emotion, he felt like she saw right through him.

"There's something incredibly sexy about the way you wear your emotions on your sleeve," he said. "What are you thinking right now?"

"A lot of things. I was thinking about how nice it was to see you joking around with everyone, and wondering if Violet and I could ever be as close as you and Drake. And I was thinking about Mira and Hagen, and how incredible it must be for her to have found someone who loves her and her son *so* much." She glanced up at him with soulful eyes. "But mostly, I was thinking that this has been the most romantic night of my life, and I don't want it to end."

"Then we won't let it."

Chapter Eight

"I HAVEN'T BEEN up here in years." Desiree looked over her shoulder with a pensive yet excited look in her eyes as she and Rick ascended the stairs toward the widow's walk. She'd loaded him up with pillows and blankets from a closet on the second floor. When they reached the top of the stairs, she stepped into the small cupola and inhaled deeply. "I was afraid to come up here alone, and I can't guarantee that it's not rotted out by now."

"Why were you afraid? The house seems stable despite a few cosmetic things that need attention. I haven't looked closely, but from what I saw outside, there wasn't anything that made me think it was in disrepair."

"It wasn't that so much as memories. This is where I'd come to be alone. But now that I'm thinking about it, it really could be rotted out."

He smiled. He glanced out the door, searching the darkness with his contractor's eye for broken railings or missing balusters. He reached up and flicked the light switch by the door, and dozens of tiny orange lights sparked to life, illuminating a newly renovated, freshly painted widow's walk. Beautiful ornate balusters supported wide railings. An unusually deep bench, the size of a queen bed, was built into the perimeter, topped with thick colorful cushions.

Desiree latched on to his arm. "Rick," she said in a shaky voice. "*Lizza.* She must have done this. The orange lights. That's my favorite color. When I got here, she was wearing a long orange dress. I thought it was a coincidence." Tears welled in her eyes.

"She must have done this for *you*, Des," he said, his chest full and happy for her. "You said you were the only one who came up here, right?"

"I was. My grandmother told me that my mother used to come up here. That was the reason I first started. To see if I could, I don't know, get a sense of her."

He knew all about reaching for someone who wasn't there. He'd spent a lifetime holding on to a ghost. "And did you? Get a sense of her?"

She shook her head, her eyes clearer now. Shifting the blankets and pillows into one arm, he grabbed the door handle, looking to her for approval. She nodded, and he pushed the door open. Cool air swept over them. Desiree crossed her arms against the chill, and he set the guitar and blankets on the cushions.

"I forgot how much colder it was up here." She stepped outside and ran her hand along the railings as he closed the door behind them. "It's so beautiful, but *why* would she do this? Nothing else in the house has been renovated." She waved at the bench. "When I was growing up, there was no bench or anything. I'd just throw pillows and blankets on the deck and plop right down."

She was talking so fast, he knew she was nervous. He set the pillows up against the railing, watching her as she gazed out over the water. The breeze carried her hair away from her face, and she looked even more radiant than usual, despite the part of her that must be coming undone.

He wrapped his arms around her from behind. "She put a lot of thought into this, Des."

She turned in his arms, hope and confusion battling in her eyes.

"Sweetheart, I know what it's like to be reaching for a ghost that always slips through your fingers. What I don't know, but it seems like you have a chance to find out, is what it's like to catch one. Don't let your questions hold you back from feeling all the joy of knowing you're on her mind a lot more often than you thought."

Her expression turned serious. "It's just…Why wouldn't she tell me she did this, or leave a note, or *something*?"

"Because maybe she has just as much fear over what it means as you do. Or maybe she's not the kind of person who leaves notes. I think the important thing is that she's clearly making some kind of an effort."

"She's so crazy. Look how she got me here." Her forehead wrinkled in contemplation.

"Do you still want to hang out up here?"

"Yes. It's just a lot to take in."

A few minutes later they settled against the pillows with their feet stretched out in front of them. He covered their legs with a blanket, and when he put an arm around her, she rested her head on his shoulder.

"It seems like a lifetime ago when I'd sit up here dreaming of my mother surprising me by showing up on a boat, or parachuting onto the beach for a long visit instead of the quick day or two at the end of my summer vacation. Crazy little-girl dreams."

"Not so crazy, and dreaming is good. After we lost my father, I swore I heard him everywhere. Walking around the house, his voice in the wind, and I'd dream about what I would say to him if he were there. Sometimes I still do."

"Big-boy dreams," she said, and tipped her face up toward his. "What was your father like?"

"That depends who you ask." Love and longing twined together inside him, bringing his truth to life. "To me he was bigger than life. He was aggressive, never let anyone or anything stand in his way. I thought he was indestructible. The strongest, smartest man alive."

"Like you," she said. "You come across that way."

He scoffed. "I'm glad you think so, babe, but he was so much more of a man than me. But like I said, if you ask Mira, she'll say he was too strict, and Drake thinks he was overzealous, although they both adored him."

She smiled. "Good word."

He leaned down and kissed her. "My girl likes me to use the right words."

"Do you want to talk about him?"

"No." He kissed her again, but instead of deepening the kiss, he held back. He realized he wanted to share this part of himself with her after all. When their lips parted, he said, "Yes. I'd like to tell you about my father if you're sure you want to hear it."

"I do. When we were dancing earlier, you said 'Sometimes the hardest place to be is where everyone knows you best.' That's always been my safest place, with my friends and my father. Last night you said Drake and Dean and your friends were the ones who watched out for you. Aren't they the same people who know you best?"

He shifted his eyes away, struggling against a wave of emotion.

She took his chin between her fingers and turned his face toward her. "Do you want to let me in?"

"You're *in*, Des. You're in so deep I can't stop thinking about you." He clenched his teeth, and she pressed her lips to the tight muscles in his jaw.

"*Geez*, everything you do…" He turned on his side so he could look into her eyes. "My father would have liked you. You're smart and sweet, and strong, and you don't put on airs. He used to say, 'Never trust a person who puts on airs, and for Pete's sake, don't marry one.'" He laughed, remembering the way his father's eyes would turn serious when he'd say that last part. "He was a custom homebuilder, and all I ever wanted was to grow up to be just like him. We used to talk about making Savage Custom Homes into Savage and *Son*."

"I love that," she said. "You followed in his footsteps. I bet he's smiling down on you every day, so proud of the man you've become."

He swallowed against the ache that had festered inside him for more than a decade and a half. "I'd like to think so. He also taught us other things. How to play the guitar, how to Jet Ski, parasail, surf. You name it, he taught us."

"A music-loving adrenaline junkie?" she asked.

"I don't know if it was that as much as he loved life, and he never wanted us to be afraid of anything or let anything hold us back. Although, cliff diving, now, that was a pure adrenaline rush. Maybe he was a bit of an adrenaline junkie."

"You cliff dive? I'd be afraid to *look* over a cliff."

He pulled her closer and kissed her smiling lips. "I'm going to teach you to do all of those things."

"In your dreams, big boy."

"Trust me, baby, you're in my dreams. Although I think you'd be more accurate to call them *fantasies*."

She blushed, but her eyes went dark as a forest, and his body ignited. He groaned, and she trapped her lower lip between her teeth.

"If you keep looking at me like that, I'm going to stop talking and devour you."

"Okay," came out in a rush.

As his mouth came down over hers, she pushed at his chest, laughing. "No. Wait. I want to hear the story."

"And I want to kiss you," he said more harshly than he meant to.

"If you kiss me like you usually do, until my brain cells fry and my body turns to butter, I'll never hear the rest."

"Baby, you're killing me. Now I'm thinking of my hands all over you." He kissed the corner of her mouth. "And your hands on me." Her eyes closed, and he kissed each lid. "And my mouth *everywhere*."

Her eyes flew open.

"Too much?" He'd pushed too far.

She shook her head, nodded, and then she shook her head again.

My mixed-messages girl. "Sorry, babe. I'll tame my eagerness."

"No," came out fast and loud, and she clamped her mouth shut, eyes wide. When she spoke again, her voice was husky. "I mean, I like your naughty side, but I want to hear about your father. Hold on. Let me put on my teacher face so you can tell me without wanting to kiss me. Then we can…see about those kisses."

She held her hand in front of her face, a sexy giggle slipping out, and he breathed deeply, trying to rein in his desires. It was a continuous losing battle. She lowered her hand, eyes serious, her face a mask of patience and calm as she stared at his chin. She lifted her gaze, and the second their eyes met, the space between them electrified.

"Talk *fast*, Rick," she said breathlessly.

"Can't. It's not a fast subject."

She trapped that plump lower lip again. He was holding on to his control by a thread.

"There's this thing I do with my really eager students." She ran her finger down the center of his chest, driving him out of his mind. "I let them run around and get all their energy out so they can concentrate."

Oh, heck yes.

She fluttered her long lashes and said, "Maybe we should…"

Their mouths collided in urgent, hungry kisses. He took them deeper, and she eased back on the cushion, moaning loudly. How had he resisted her for this long? Her soft curves molded to his body like nothing he'd ever felt. Pure feminine perfection. She threaded her fingers into his hair and held on tight, bowing up beneath him and rocking against his arousal. His head told him not to make too much of it, but his hands were on a mission, traveling down her hips and taking hold. He loved everything about her body, the way her hips filled his hands, her softness pressed against his hard frame. He needed more of the woman who was making him feel and think and wish for something besides the next big business deal. He slid one hand to the base of her skull, and she tipped her head back, giving him better access to the rest of her.

He didn't want to miss an inch, and took his time kissing her chin and the column of her neck up and down and around toward her nape, inciting the most lascivious noises from her sexy mouth. When he kissed a path along her breastbone, she arched, offering more. He wished he could tear the dress right off her. But she was the best thing that had come into his life for so long, he didn't want to misread her.

"Rick," she pleaded, holding his gaze as she tugged at the little bow behind her neck. The fabric drifted over her magnificent breasts, and she pushed it down, leaving no room for misinterpretation.

She closed her eyes, and it was too much. He needed her right there with him, to *see* her desire in those gorgeous green eyes. "Look at me, sweetheart."

Her eyes fluttered open, so needful he could drown in them.

"Desiree," was all he could manage. His heart swelled as if he'd been given the greatest gift of all. Her trust.

DESIREE WANTED RICK like she'd never wanted anything in her life. He was real, and passionate, and so very attentive and careful while still being insanely rugged, all of which made her want to *take* and be *taken*. His mouth claimed hers, spread heat like wildfire through her core, her limbs, to the very tips of her toes.

He gazed lovingly into her eyes, sending her heart into a tailspin.

"I love kissing you, sweetheart."

He captured her mouth in a demanding kiss, and she wanted his demands. No man had ever elicited this type of overwhelming response. Not even close. He took her lower lip between his teeth, tugging gently, and she held her breath, *wanting*, and a little nervous.

Okay, a *lot* nervous as his eyes found hers again. The hunger in his gaze, while visually seeking permission, unraveled her, unleashing some kind of inner beast, and she gave in to the lust coursing through her.

After driving her to the brink of madness, his kisses turned soft, like tiny treasures he pressed to her lips, her cheeks, her chin, as she lay relaxed and sated in his arms. They still hadn't made love, and he didn't push, didn't make her feel guilty. In his arms, she felt special and wanted.

Without a word, he righted and tied her halter, smoothed her dress over her thighs, and pulled a blanket around them as she snuggled in closer. Energy deliciously depleted, maybe now she could focus on talking.

Chapter Nine

"YOU ARE AN excellent teacher," Rick said, reveling in the feel of Desiree, warm and safe against him. "You knew just what we needed."

She tipped her face up. "Well, that was like recess for me. I'm completely relaxed and ready to talk, but it was more like snack time for you, and probably left you all revved up. I understand if you'd rather not talk."

He pressed his lips to hers, glad she wasn't embarrassed after how she'd given herself over to him. "I thought you weren't a naughty teacher."

"You bring out the naughty in me. But I kind of left you hanging."

"Don't worry about me, beautiful. Pleasuring you is enough for now. I enjoyed every second of it."

"You're very generous," she teased, and moved beside him, lying on her back and gazing up at the stars.

She'd gone through so much emotional turmoil since she'd arrived at the Cape, her resilience astounded him. He laced their fingers together, wanting to do more for her, to be the man to make her dreams come true.

"What's the one thing you'd like to do while you're here

this summer?" he asked.

"Other than spend time with you?" She met his gaze, and he touched his lips to hers.

"That's the best answer you could have given."

"It was honest," she said softly. "There are things I want to do, like get to know Violet better and figure out what our mother did with all of the money she borrowed."

"I know you have a lot on your plate, but what do you want to do that isn't driven by your circumstances?" he asked. "Is there anything you've always wished you could have done? For you, not to repair your relationships with them."

"I've always wanted to go out on a sailboat. It seems like the most romantic thing in the world, drifting at sea in the moonlight."

The sense of desperation that accompanied memories of the night of his father's death clutched at him.

She touched his cheek. "What is it? Did I say the wrong thing?"

"No." He leaned into her touch, trying to smile but knowing by the concern in her eyes that he failed. Images of his father flashed in his mind. *Buck up, big guy. Nothing in life is worth that look.* He missed him so much he ached, and he wanted to share the man who meant everything to him with Desiree.

"Being on the open sea can feel like the ultimate freedom. Driven by the wind, with the sounds of the boat slicing through the water, and the flutter of the sails. It's as much of an emotional rush as it is a physical one. My family used to go sailing a lot."

"Sounds like there's a 'but' coming."

He turned on his side again, and she turned with him, gazing into his eyes. She had a calming effect on him that was as strong as her ability to heat him up. He put his arm over her and pulled her closer. Her gaze was warm and her touch comforting, easing the knot in his gut.

"There is," he admitted. "A big one."

"Your father?"

He nodded, his throat thick with emotions. "My father used to say that a few days at sea could make or break a family, and it turned out, he was right. We lost him the summer after I turned fourteen. My family was sailing off the coast of North Carolina on our way back home. We'd been on the water for a couple of weeks by then. It was evening, and the sky up ahead was a little gray, but we'd sailed through storms before, and it didn't look like it was going to be much more than rain."

He paused, his pulse speeding up with the memory. He ground his teeth together, steeling himself, and forced his words out as fast as he could. "The trickery of Mother Nature is that one minute you're looking at a clear sky, and the next it's tar black, with violent gusts of wind. That evening the winds hit hard and fast, sixty-five, seventy miles per hour. We managed to get the jib down, but the mainsail only halfway before the storm was upon us. I can still taste the brackish water, still feel my body sliding across the deck as the boat lurched, heeling into the storm. It all happened fast. My father was hollering for us to hold on. My mother had grown up on boats. Her father was a fisherman. She was hunkered down with Mira in the cabin, and I remember seeing Drake on the other side of the boat. He turned as a swell tipped the boat sideways and water crashed over the deck. He lost his grip. It took only an instant, and he was sliding toward the edge. I dove for him." He blinked against damp eyes, unashamed of his emotions.

"I caught his arm, and just as he found his footing, the boat lurched again in the choppy water, and I lost mine. We grappled on the deck to keep from being thrown into the water. I turned just as the boom smacked my father in the head, sending him overboard. With the torrential rain and erratic movement of the boat, we couldn't see ten feet in front of us, and when you're staring into a black angry sea...It swallowed him so fast. We threw a life vest, but..."

He paused, fighting against the images slamming into him. "Everything kind of blurs together after that. The wind was howling, and we were dodging the boom, shining the flashlight into the water. Drake told me that I fought so hard to go after him, it took all his strength to hold me back. The whole thing lasted ten, maybe fifteen minutes, and cleared as quickly as it hit. But he was gone."

Tears streaked Desiree's cheeks, pulling more from him. She threw her arms around his neck.

"I'm sorry, sweetheart. I didn't mean to make you cry."

"Me?" She pulled back and looked deeply into his eyes. "I can't imagine how you must feel. I'm so sorry."

"Me too, babe." *More than anyone could ever know.* He wiped the tears from her eyes.

"But you're not afraid of the water? I don't think I'd ever go in again."

"I'm not afraid of the water, as you know from the night we met. I powerboat, water-ski, parasail, paddleboard. You name it, I do it. My father wouldn't have wanted us to let his death stop us from doing the things he'd taught us. But sailing?" He shook his head. "I can't bring myself to do it. Too many memories. My father used to say the sea was his mistress. He'd wax poetic about the sounds and the way he felt when we were coasting along. Those kinds of memories are hard to deal with, but they don't come up often. Before we bought the resort, I was working seventy, eighty hours a week in DC, too busy to think about anything but the next deal. I hadn't been back to the Cape for any extended period of time, just a few days here and there. It was easier to keep the memories at bay that way. But being with Drake dredges them up. He still goes out on the sailboat. We keep it down at the marina."

"So, he's moved past it?" she asked. "At least you had each other to talk about it and help each other through."

Not exactly. "Believe it or not, Drake and I haven't really talked about it much. It was hard enough getting through every day afterward, and it was easier to bury ourselves in our daily lives. I think Drake's dealt with it pretty well, though. He had to. He's only left the Cape for a few months at a time to open his music stores, but his life is here."

"And you?" she asked carefully.

Leave it to his brave girl to ask the hard questions and get under his skin. For once in his life, he didn't want to avoid the issue. Had Drake or anyone else asked the same question, he might have scoffed and said he'd dealt with it. But after all Desiree had been through, he wanted to be honest with her.

"I've dealt with losing my father. I was pretty angry for a while, and I was a troublemaker. I was the kid who skirted every line. My mother would tell me to be home by ten o'clock and I'd come home at ten oh two. I was *that* kid. Growing up and moving to DC helped put some distance between that night and my emotions."

"I can totally see you as a rascally teenager, even if you hadn't lost your father. You seem to have that way about you." She touched his hand. "But what did you mean when you said that being around the people who knew you best was the hardest place to be? You don't think anyone blames you or Drake, do you?"

"No. The sea is a prickly beast. My father had drilled that into our heads. But I see my father in my family, around my mom's house, and that's tough sometimes. Drake looks a lot like him. And when I see Mira, I remember my father used to push her out of her comfort zone. He never wanted her to feel like she couldn't do something, so he showed her that she could. I still remember when he first took us water-skiing. Mira didn't go parasailing, or anything like that, but she put on a brave face and got up on water skis. You know, in that way, you remind me of her. You face what's in front of you. That's weird comparing you to my sister, but…" He shrugged.

"As long as you're not secretly into incest." The tease played in her eyes, and he was thankful, because he didn't want to get swept any deeper into the painful memories or a downer of a conversation.

He tickled her ribs, and she squealed.

"What happened to that sweet, careful girl I was dating?"

"You freed her from her confines with wild kisses and…*more*. Finish your story. And your mom? How did she deal with it?"

"My mom was a pillar of strength. She had three grieving kids, and she plowed through life taking care of us. She had her ups and downs, but she was focused on making sure *we* healed. She wasn't going to let us use our loss as a crutch, and she stepped into my father's shoes and got us all right back out in the water. She was right there doing water sports with us, and it was just what we needed."

Her eyes moved over the bright orange lights splashing against fresh white paint, and she smiled. "It's funny how someone can do one thing, and it can change deep-seated emotions. In my case, *years* of emotions. I still have uncomfortable feelings toward my mother, but this"—she tapped the bench they were lying on—"it softened me toward her. I didn't think she understood me or knew who I was, but I think, like your mother knew what you all needed, maybe mine knows more about me than I thought."

"I hope so, sweetheart. I truly hope so." She yawned, and he asked, "Do you want me to take off so you can get some sleep?"

"No. I want a slumber party, like we planned."

He smiled, feeling tremendously lighter than he had earlier. "A slumber party? Does that mean I get to do a panty raid?"

"That would require panties." She slid down on her back and pulled him down over her. "Kiss me, Rick. Let's replace all our sad thoughts with happy ones."

Chapter Ten

DESIREE DRIFTED IN and out of sleep, lulled by the even cadence of Rick's breathing as he slept with his arm and leg draped over her, as if he were afraid she'd disappear in the night.

Thud!

Her eyes fluttered open, quickly closing again to shut out the bright morning sun. Rick tightened his hold on her, and she snuggled back in.

Thud!

She started, blinking more fully awake, and tried to identify the noise she'd heard. Rick nuzzled against her neck, making her want to disappear into last night again, baring their secrets, kissing and touching, and experiencing one epic orgasm after another. If he could bring her such pleasure with his hands and mouth, what would it be like when they finally made love?

"You okay, sweetheart?"

"I thought I heard something." The crisp morning air whisked over her cheeks, and Cosmos yapped inside the house. "Maybe Violet isn't here. I should probably—"

"We were told to take down these walls."

She and Rick bolted upright at the sound of deep male voices followed by more barking.

"Are you expecting someone?" he asked.

"No!" She scrambled to her feet, searching for her underwear as Rick stretched.

He peered over the railing. "I think your mother's contractors have arrived. Those are Cape Renovators trucks. They do excellent work."

"I wonder what work she's scheduled." She tossed one blanket into the air after another. "Do you have my underwear?"

He wrapped his arms around her. "No, but I'm pretty sure they won't know you don't have any on. But now that I remember..." He slid a hand beneath her dress and squeezed her bottom.

"I can't go down there without them!" She twisted out of his arms, and he hauled her back, grinning as she tried to wriggle free. "Rick! Don't you hear Cosmos going crazy? I need to get inside."

"Violet had to let them in, right?" He brushed her hair from in front of her eyes and tucked it behind her ear as she peered around him, scanning the floor for her underwear. "This is our first morning together, and we only get to experience this very special moment *once* in our entire lives. I know you're frazzled, and I hear Cosmos, and the guys, but I'm pretty sure nothing bad will happen in the next sixty seconds while I say good morning to my beautiful girl."

Her eyes met his, and her frantic heart took notice, slowing her down enough to realize how romantic he was being. She inhaled deeply, blowing it out slowly and smiling. "Hi."

"There's my girl. Good morning, sweetheart." He pressed his lips to hers. "It was nice being close to you last night."

"*Very* nice." She wound her arms around his waist, glad she'd taken a break to soak in his goodness but still thinking about the people in the house. "But…"

"No worries. Let's find those missing panties, and then we'll go down." He made quick work of shaking out and folding up the blankets. When he shook the last one, her panties flew up in the air. She snagged them and put them on. Three minutes later they were standing face to face with three burly men—and one very amused Violet—on the third floor of the house.

"Well, well, well," Violet said, sidling up to Desiree. "I thought you stayed out last night." She leaned in close and whispered, "What kind of *frickery* was going on upstairs?"

"Violet!" Desiree felt her cheeks flame. She scooped Cosmos up, trying to settle him, and herself, down. She shot a look at Rick, who was stifling a grin and shaking his head.

Stepping away from Violet, Desiree turned her attention to the oldest of the three men, hoping they hadn't heard her sister's comment. "Hi. I'm Desiree Cleary, Violet's sister, and this is my boyfriend, Rick Savage." It felt good to call Rick her boyfriend. *Really good.* "You're here to do the renovations?"

"That's right. Rob Wicked and sons at your service." He took off his baseball cap, revealing a shock of black hair, flecked with silver. A friendly smile stretched across his face. "These are my boys, Zeke and Zander."

One of his sons flashed a cocky smile and thrust out his hand. "Zeke Wicked. Nice to meet you."

He had the same thick black hair as his father and bright blue eyes like his brother, who was busy lusting over Violet in her bikini top and shorts. Maybe Desiree should take her clothes shopping.

"Hi. I'm Zander." With a rake of his hand, he pushed his longish brown hair away from his face and winked at Violet.

Zeke elbowed him, and Zander grinned.

Violet narrowed her eyes as if she were putting him through some sort of mental test. His smile never faltered. He obviously wasn't afraid of failing.

This should be fun. "I guess you guys have already started in the studio?"

"The studio?" Rob put his hat back on. "You mean the room with all the painting supplies? No, ma'am. We have strict orders not to step foot in that room until the two of you give us directions on what you'd like done."

Desiree looked curiously at Violet.

"Don't look at me," Violet said. "I have no idea what she's asked them to do."

"I can give you the rundown. Starting on this floor, we're taking down these walls." Rob pointed to the walls that separated the hall from the bedrooms. "On the second floor, we're combining the two front bedrooms into one, and on the first floor, we're removing the wall between the dining room and the kitchen and—"

"What?" Desiree looked at Violet again. "No."

"You can't do that," Violet said. "This house has been this way forever. It's practically historic. You can't change the structure."

"Can we put this process on hold?" Desiree asked. "We thought you were here to fix drywall and, I don't know. The kitchen and bathrooms, maybe? And I guess you already renovated the widow's walk, which is gorgeous, by the way."

"They did?" Violet asked.

"Yes, and it's beautiful," Desiree said as Violet plowed past her and headed upstairs to the widow's walk.

"Zander and I finished that up last week," Zeke said with a proud smile.

"Rob," Rick intervened. "Desiree and Violet have just been thrown into managing this project, and the house has sentimental value to them. Would you mind if they take a look at the contract and design plans before you get started?"

Desiree was relieved that he'd stepped in. Her mind was running in too many directions to speak rationally.

Violet came down from the widow's walk raving about how awesome it was, took one look at Desiree, and said, "Don't worry. We're not going to let anything else happen."

Zeke and Zander left, and Rob stayed to review the plans. After going over the proposed renovations, it became clear that the house would no longer even feel like Summer House Inn. This was another piece of her family that her mother could take away. Maybe Lizza hadn't finished the widow's walk for Desiree after all. Maybe it was all just part of the general renovations, to bring Summer House Inn back to life so she could sell it.

"I don't understand any of this," Desiree finally said. "Rob, can we cancel the contract?"

Rob shook his head. "I'm sorry, Desiree, but we've already had the structural drawings done, and there's a no-cancellation clause in the contract. The good news is that Ms. Vancroft did say that if you two wanted changes, we had her permission to work with you, within the confines of the monetary contract. But the bad news is that our architect is backed up for five weeks. So, I'm afraid if you decide to make changes to the plans, we may need to wait to get started closer to the end of the summer."

Panic gripped her. "Vi, if they start when Lizza's here, she'll make *all* of these changes."

"I know you have to get back to teach," Violet said. "But I'll stay, and I won't let her destroy the house."

Rick took Desiree's hand. "Sweetheart, I'm a licensed architect. I can do the drawings for you and Violet and have them done quickly."

She wanted to leap into his arms, but she didn't want to be an imposition. "You're finishing your own renovations at the resort. Are you sure you have time? And what will it cost?"

"I wouldn't have offered if I wasn't sure."

"It doesn't matter what it will cost," Violet said. "I'll sell everything I own. Except my bike. No way. Or maybe you'll take a few nights on the widow's walk with Des as payment?"

"Violet!" Desiree covered her face.

Violet splayed her hands. "I'm just thinking of creative financing."

"Nobody needs *creative financing*, and you're not selling anything," Rick assured them. "I'll make the time, and we'll get this all worked out."

RICK CROUCHED BESIDE the bookshelves he was building in the new recreation center later that afternoon and eyeballed the level. *Perfect.* He pushed to his feet as Drake came down the hall.

"The old place doesn't look too shabby, does it? You have to admit, we make a great team," Drake said.

"We've done quite a job. Once we get furniture, stock it with games and books, it'll be a great gathering place. The patio and fire pit will really make it, though. Put on a holiday event, advertise it during the weeks before and during the Oyster Festival to get the word out. If we advertise it well enough, we should be pulling in solid bookings by year three." Winters were harsh on the Cape, and tourism was almost nonexistent then, but they'd winterized the cottages with the hopes of making their mark as a Cape winter destination. "And if not, we've lost nothing by ridding ourselves of the restaurant overhead and headaches."

"I agree. Like I said, we make a great team." Drake gave him *the look.* The one that said, *You know you want to stay.*

Rick didn't respond. Drake had been on him to move back for good ever since he arrived last year. When they'd first bought the resort, Rick had agreed to stick around until it was fully renovated, which should have been this past March. But they'd made a last-minute decision to turn the restaurant into a recreation center, and he'd agreed to stay and handle the renovations. He had a feeling the late decision had been driven by Drake's wanting him to stick around. If Drake knew how hard Rick was falling for Desiree, he'd try to use that to get him to stay, too.

"Guess things went well last night?" Drake was relentless. "You missed our run this morning."

Rick moved to the other side and began securing a shelf to the wall. "Yeah, we had a good time. Thanks for lending me your guitar."

"No worries. You need all the help you can get to turn a girl on." Drake smirked.

"You realize I have tools in my hand, right?"

Drake laughed. "It's been a long time since you've had a girlfriend. Everyone really liked her." He grabbed a shelf and set it in the bookcase they'd installed earlier.

"I had no doubt they would."

"Bring her sailing Friday night with Pete and Jenna? Pete's father is watching Bea and we're going out around ten." Pete and Jenna were Matt's brother and sister-in-law, and Bea was their almost-four-year-old little girl. "Mira's waiting to hear back from Mom to see if she can babysit Hagen so they can go, too. It'll be fun. Dean and Serena are going."

"Sorry. I'm taking Desiree out. I was hoping you could help me get a few things set up on the dunes." He'd been thinking about it all morning, as they'd walked around her house and made a list of the things she and Violet wanted to change. Renovating the kitchens and bathrooms and replacing some of the windows were the biggest aspects of the project; the rest was cosmetic—drywall, paint, replace a few fixtures. They even wanted the hardwood to remain scuffed to retain the home's character. Depending on the fixtures and appliances they chose, the renovations should come out to be less than the initial budget. He'd have a talk with Rob on their behalf when it was time, and ensure they received whatever money remained. They'd also checked the fence off of the kitchen, where Violet had let Cosmos out yesterday morning. But they hadn't found any missing pickets, holes, or cracks the pup could fit through. Cosmos, it seemed, was as elusive as Desiree's mother.

"The dunes?" Drake laughed. "Not exactly your usual date."

"There's nothing *usual* about Desiree, and I don't have a 'usual' date."

"Sailing is more romantic than the dunes. Come on. Change your plans?" Drake stroked his jaw. With two or three-days' scruff, he looked even more like their father. "Why are you looking at me like that?"

Rick crossed his arms, meeting Drake's serious gaze. "Like what? Like you're pressuring me to do something I don't want to?" The familiar stare-down ensued. How many years would it take for Drake to back off? *How long will it take before I can stop seeing Dad when I look at him?*

Mimicking his brother's stance, Drake planted his legs like tree trunks and crossed his arms. "You haven't gone sailing with us once since you got back."

"I've been a little busy." He motioned toward the stairs. "I'm heading up to"—*escape your pressure*—"check out the tiles in the bathroom and make sure they set properly." They'd renovated the second floor into an apartment.

"I'll go with you." Drake followed him up. "Mira and Serena said you looked at Desiree like you were totally into her."

"Yeah? Like you look at Serena?" He crossed the living room and went down the hall to the master bathroom. Eyeing the tiles, he wished Drake would back off.

"You have to get past this."

"No idea what *this* is." Rick moved through the spacious bathroom, checking the shower tiles, the caulk lines, anything to keep from looking at Drake.

"Rick. You haven't gone sailing since Dad died."

"What are you, my therapist?" He pushed past Drake and headed down the hall, into the other bathroom. "It's not like I have time, or live on the water when I'm in DC. I'm lucky if I get home before eight or nine most nights."

"Look at me," Drake demanded in the commanding eldest-brother voice he'd adopted in the years after their father died.

Rick spun around, sure his eyes were casting daggers. "What?"

"Why do you think you're fighting moving back here with your family, where you belong?"

"I have a business to run. I don't have time to mess around on the water like you do." Rick held his brother's stare.

"You did that, Rick. You make yourself work all the time."

No kidding. Think I want to talk about it? "Why is it perfectly acceptable that you own music stores off the Cape and travel for them, but my business being out of state is an issue?"

"Because I didn't stop doing one of the things I loved most when Dad died."

Something inside Rick snapped. He closed the gap between them, and years of rage and hurt came flying out. "You're right. I haven't gone sailing. Big deal. Is that the measure of a life well lived? If I've freaking sailed or not? I can't help it. It sucks, but every time I think about going on that boat, on any freaking sailboat, I remember how much he loved it, and it *kills* me."

"Rick…" The concern and love in Drake's eyes warred with the ghost swimming between them, and there was nothing his brother could do to slay it.

Only Rick could do that. "I don't have time for this." He needed to get Desiree's drawings done.

He pushed past Drake, descending the stairs at a fast clip, and stormed down to his cottage. Memories of that awful night lurked like villains as he worked on the drawings late into the night.

Still wired from the conversation several hours later, he rolled up the completed designs, hopped in his truck, and drove down to the marina, determined to do something, though he didn't exactly know what. He noticed Desiree's sandals on the floor of the truck, and his chest constricted.

It was after midnight. The restaurants and shops were closed. A few stray cars were parked by the pier. A couple stood by the boathouse kissing, and Rick's mind sped straight to Desiree. She'd texted earlier. *Hope you're having fun with the guys. Miss you!* She'd made his night and distracted him from his argument with Drake for a little while. But even thoughts of his brave, beautiful girl couldn't quiet the ghosts as he crossed the parking lot, shoulders rounded, hands pushed deep in his pockets, eyes locked on the pavement, and *I can do this* running through his mind like a mantra.

That awful night came rushing back in an angry flash of the boom carrying his father overboard, and Rick froze. With his heart in his throat, he turned back toward the truck, determined to outrun the memories.

You chicken fool.

He grimaced, uttered a curse, and headed for the marina again. His pulse raced so fast he thought he might pass out. Sweat beaded his forehead despite the cool air as he forced his legs to carry him forward. He was vaguely aware of the couple he'd seen kissing driving away, leaving him alone in his tortured state. More memories crashed over him—Drake holding him back, their voices disappearing in the rain as the angry sea swallowed their father.

He paced, pushed both hands into his hair and clutched his head in a futile attempt to stop the memories from flooding in. He took three long strides toward the truck and stopped.

His mind reeled back in time again as he stood there shaking, unable to move forward. He'd stood here before. First a number of years ago and then again a few months ago. He'd stood in this same place, staring down the ghosts of his past. He hadn't been able to face them then. Why did he think he could do it now?

Life takes you where you need to be, when you need to be there.

He started as the memory hit him. He'd almost forgotten the woman who had said that to him. She had been sitting on the dock drawing the night he'd come out a few months ago. They'd talked for a long time about what it was like to miss the people they loved. And he'd made a comment about not knowing why he'd thought he could deal with it. It was her response about timing and life that brought Drake's voice back to him now.

Why do you think you're fighting moving back here with your family, where you belong?

Why, after all this time, was Drake pushing him so hard? *Why am I pushing myself?* He knew those answers. They were easy compared to the turmoil of uncertainty consuming him. For the first time in years he'd spent long stretches of time with his family and friends, instead of hiding behind mounds of work miles away. He'd laughed more over the last several months than he had in a decade. He'd gotten a chance to *live* again, and he'd met someone who touched him in a way that made him want to slow down. Only slowing down on the Cape meant dealing with his demons, and he wasn't sure who he'd be when, or if, he came out the other side.

He spun around one more time, staring down at the boats tethered to their moorings. They were imprisoned, just as he was shackled to his past. He shifted his eyes to the other side of the marina, thinking of Desiree. Wasn't his confession enough for one twenty-four-hour period? *Confessions*, he reminded himself. Being honest with Drake would surely cause his touchy-feely brother to want to talk about it ad nauseam. He wasn't any better prepared for that than he was for what he'd set out to do tonight.

Grinding his teeth together, he stalked over to the pier, staring out at the jetty where he'd first seen Desiree, and tried to catch his breath. He filled his mind with her. Her smile, her touch, her blushing, beautiful face. And when his breathing calmed, and his heart was so full of her it no longer ached, he climbed in his truck and took the long way back to the resort.

He pulled over on the side of the road, picked a handful of tiger lilies, and scoured his truck for paper, but couldn't find any. He stopped at the resort office to write a note for Desiree, and rolled it up as he had the drawings. He eyed the decorative bottles on the windowsill, smiling as an idea came to him.

When he finally collapsed for the night, visions of Desiree followed him into his dreams.

Chapter Eleven

DESIREE HUMMED TO the music streaming from her phone as she cooked breakfast Friday morning. She'd risen with the sun, or rather, with Cosmos, who had claimed the foot of her bed as his own last night. She didn't mind. She'd missed Rick, and she'd woken up excited to see him. And, she realized, to face the day. Yesterday she and Violet had broken new ground when they'd realized they were on the same page with regard to the renovations. Who knew two sisters who grew up on opposite sides of the world could agree on something so big so easily? They were in complete agreement with leaving the structure of the house intact, but as they'd found out last night while they were shopping, their decorating tastes were still miles apart. Desiree preferred bright colors like coral and white, while Violet went for purple and black. They'd have to deal with that at some point and come to a compromise for the kitchen and bath renovations, but for now Desiree was holding tight to their budding kinship.

Her heart skipped a beat as she glanced at the note Rick had left on the front porch, tucked inside a bottle and tied with twine. She'd nearly tripped over Cosmos when they'd found it on their way outside this morning. He'd also left an array of gorgeous tiger lilies, the renovation drawings, and the sandals she'd left in the truck. She'd taken a picture of the beautiful way he'd laid it all out and sent it to Emery with the message, *Hot Jet Ski guy is the most romantic man I've ever met!* Emery had replied, *If he has a brother who is single, I'll be there tonight!* which had sparked a phone call that had lasted almost an hour.

It had taken Desiree a solid twenty minutes to get the note out of the bottle, and she'd been beaming ever since. She read it for the umpteenth time.

> *Good morning, beautiful,*
>
> *I'm going to bed wishing you were in my arms, but I hope you had fun with Violet. Take a look at the kitchen and bathroom plans and let me know if you want revisions. Can't wait to see you tonight. Wear something that can get wet and dirty, and bring extra clothes.*
>
> *Now you're thinking naughty thoughts.*
> *I bet you're blushing, too.*
> *Love that.*
> *So, so much.*
>
> *Xo, R.*

She'd texted him earlier, and promised he'd be *generously* compensated. Desiree wanted to blame Violet's influence on that racy comment, but this was all *her*, and it felt good to own it. Although her sister *had* taken great pleasure in teasing her last night about their "rooftop romp." So much so that by the end of the evening, Desiree was not only no longer embarrassed by it, but she was also tossing teases into the pot. They'd definitely bonded last night. They might not be besties, but they were making progress. Violet had even agreed to help her organize their mother's studio, which Desiree was thankful for. She wasn't looking forward to facing it alone.

She tossed a piece of cooked egg to Cosmos, who was curled up on his bed by the door to the patio, tuckered out from their earlier walk. They'd wound through the quiet back roads, bringing memories of when Desiree and her grandmother had taken walks together in the early mornings. She'd always been an early riser, and this morning, after their walk, she'd gone down to the Wellfleet Market and picked up groceries. She'd chatted with a few women at the market, and noticed a sign for a yoga class taking place on the beach. Emery would love that. Life there was small-town quiet, just like back home. But nothing compared to the sights and sounds of Cape Cod Bay. *Or the sights and sounds of Rick*, she thought as she dished her eggs onto a plate, added a few blackberries and a garnish of twisted orange slices.

"What is that scrumptious smell?" Violet stretched as she ambled into the kitchen. She leaned over Desiree's shoulder, smelling of mint toothpaste. "Have enough for me?"

Desiree snagged a piece of toast from the toaster, set it on the plate and handed it to Violet. "Brie and blackberry omelet. Enjoy."

"Someone's been busy this morning." Violet carried her plate to the table as Desiree served herself. "Did you pick the flowers? They're a nice touch."

"Rick left them on the porch, along with the drawings for the kitchen and baths." She'd used the glass bottle as a vase. The pretty flowers brightened up the whole kitchen.

"Wow, he's really going for boyfriend of the year, isn't he?"

"He's definitely a thoughtful guy." *And an amazing kisser, listener, toucher…*

Violet took a bite of the omelet and her eyes widened. "Mm. Des, this is incredible. What other hidden talents do you have besides picking up hot guys and cooking?"

She handed Violet a cup of coffee and sat down to eat. "I'm hardly talented at picking up hot guys. Rick was a fluke." The best fluke *ever*, but still a fluke. She'd never actually tried to pick up a man, but she *was* a talented cook. "My father taught me to cook. We used to watch the Food Network and choose recipes to try, and on weekends, I'd make fancy breakfasts for us. Now the only person I get to make fancy breakfasts for is Emery. She takes full advantage, showing up at my house at the crack of dawn every few weeks and claiming she's emaciated because her fridge is empty."

"The more I hear about her, the more I like her. You should invite her up."

"Maybe." As much as she loved Emery, her first thought was that if she was entertaining her friend, she'd have less time alone with Rick. Selfish? Yes, but just this once, she wanted to be.

They reviewed the plans and called Rick to let him know they were perfect. He said he'd get them to Rob, and after making Desiree blush about her compensatory comment, they ended the call, and she and Violet ventured up to the studio.

"I don't see why you're always blushing." Violet stood in the middle of the studio, surveying the mess. "Sex is rejuvenating. It's like the fountain of youth. And not just sex, but all that comes with it." She laugh-snorted. "See how I did that? All that *comes* with it? The weight of a man's hard body pressing down on you, the look in their eyes when they're just about to lose it. Nothing in this world can bring couples closer together than an act of pure, raw passion."

"Trust," Desiree said without thinking.

"Well, duh. Even if you're just having sex and there are no emotions involved, you have to trust the guy. But when there are emotions? Passion can take a couple from zero to love in a heartbeat." Violet shrugged. "So, you shouldn't be embarrassed because you've slept with the guy."

"I told you last night that we haven't done that." Desiree crossed the room, no longer thinking about the uncomfortable feelings her mother's studio evoked. Her hammering heart had nothing to do with *that*, and everything to do with the desires she'd been trying to tamp down since she'd spent the night with Rick. She didn't want to tamp them down anymore, and Violet's diatribe all but opened the gates. Desiree wanted to run them down and let her inner sexy girl come charging out.

"I don't see what's wrong with this," Violet said, snapping Desiree out of her fantasy. "Why does she need drywall or organization to work? She's an artist. This feels fantastic to me. Inspiring, without any confines to stagnate her thought process. I say we leave it as is."

She went to the corner of the room and disappeared through a doorframe Desiree hadn't noticed the first time she'd gone in. "I guess you didn't check this closet when you were looking for signs. Come help me. That big wooden thing in the back is a sidewalk sign. See the hinges at the top? It folds out, and you can paint the store name on the sides." She frantically tore open a big cardboard box.

"What is all this stuff?"

Violet's jaw dropped open. "Pottery supplies, all brand-new! Clays and glazes, stains, tools." She pointed to the equipment in the back of the closet. "That's a kiln, and behind it? Those are pottery wheels. One's motorized. And that shiny one has a kick wheel. I get off on kick wheels."

They dragged the sign, machines, and supplies into the room, and Violet began emptying the box.

"Aren't you worried about using her stuff?"

Violet scoffed. "She tricked us into coming here. As far as I'm concerned, it's all fair game."

"I thought we were organizing?"

"That was before we found all of this!" Violet held up two boxes of clay. "I haven't done pottery in *two* years. I miss it like you'd miss schedules if you had to go without. But we need signs, so get busy painting them. It's not like anyone's going to come to the gallery until we get the signs up and hand out the flyers. Knowing Lizza, she probably painted on the beach and sold her paintings to people who walked by. I promise we'll get on schedule tomorrow."

She inspected the potter's wheel with such a joyous expression, Desiree didn't want to take that away from her. "You do realize you just promised me you'd get on a schedule, right?"

Violet waved her hand dismissively. "I'd give you an orgasm if you'll let me do this for a while."

"Ew."

Violet laughed. "You definitely need to hang out with me more. You're too literal. Either that, or you need to get laid."

Desiree rolled her eyes. "Why are you so crude?" She looked over her mother's paints and brushes.

"Why are you so uptight?"

Desiree let her comment go as she gazed out the window, trying to figure out what to paint on the sign and wondering if she *could* still paint. After a while she carried an easel over by the window and secured a canvas to it. She was annoyed, because she wasn't uptight, but then again, she knew Violet was probably annoyed with her for taking issue with her cursing like a sailor. *On the other hand, we're in the same room and about to embark on something for a common goal.* The teacher in her thought that was well worth a little annoyance.

"Aren't you going to use the wooden sign?" Violet asked as she made room on a table for her supplies.

"I don't even know if I can paint anymore, Vi. It's been years, and I have *one* chance to get the sign right. I figured I'd practice." She gazed out the window, taking in the long dune grass blowing in the breeze and the ridge where the dune crested and the world seemed to fall away. A little boy with a blue floppy hat was playing at the edge of the water. He put his toes in and dashed across the sand. Her mind reeled back to her first few summer vacations there with Violet and their grandmother. Desiree had wanted Violet's attention so badly, she'd made a total pest of herself, following her sister everywhere, begging her to play, or talk, or swim.

She glanced across the room at Violet, remembering what she'd said about growing up traveling with Lizza and never having friends for long enough to build relationships. Maybe Violet was right, and she should count herself lucky for growing up with the stability and comfort of one house, one community, and friends like Emery, whom she'd known forever. The thing was, she hated knowing that her sister had been lonely. It made her wish for those times with Violet even more.

As she selected and lined up the paints, her thoughts turned to Rick. He was rustling up so many parts of her that she'd either buried or forgotten, or simply hadn't realized she possessed. It was definitely possible to build relationships in short periods of time. The heart had a way of embracing certain people for a million mysterious reasons. She glanced at her smart-mouthed, tattooed sister and found herself hoping Violet would find someone, if only for a few days, or a week, or a *summer*, who would help her experience the parts of herself she was hiding, too.

DESIREE STARTED WHEN Violet tapped her shoulder, causing her paintbrush to slip to the edge of the canvas.

"Vi," Desiree complained, and tried to blend in the smear with the rest of the rippling water.

"That's me," Violet said in a small voice. "I remember that striped dress. Grandma made it, and I *hated* it."

Desiree blinked several times, feeling as if she were coming out of a fog. "I was just painting the water…" She studied the painting. Bold strokes and fine lines in dozens of shades of blues, grays, purples, and pinks brought the bay to life. Long blades of dune grass sprang up between rough wooden boards, on which she'd painted Violet from behind, as a little girl. Her knees were pulled up to her chest, her thin arms wrapped around them. She'd painted from memory, without any cognitive thought.

"That's the deck at the edge of the dunes." Violet touched Desiree's arm, as if she needed something to stabilize her.

"You used to sit out there, brooding. I'd watch you sometimes."

"Des, this is amazing. Look at what you've created. My hair looks like it's blowing in the wind. And that ugly striped dress looks like it's moving, too. You even cinched the waist with that stupid, girly bow. You could sell this."

"No," she said too harshly. "I mean. It isn't *that* good." *And it's you. I want to keep it.* She dropped the paintbrush in the bottle of water and stared down at her hands, unable to believe she'd been so transfixed. She turned away from the painting, unsure of how she felt about this connection to her mother.

"Des, you *have to* paint. You haven't moved from this spot since morning, and it's"—she pulled out her phone—"five thirty."

"What? Oh no. Can you please, please, *please* clean up? Rick's going to be here in a few minutes, and I need to shower and change."

"IT WAS LIKE I was in this trance while I was painting," Desiree said, as she and Rick walked down the beach toward the resort. "It kind of freaks me out. I've spent my whole life trying *not* to be her." She'd shown him the painting she'd made, and her artistic talent had blown him away.

He adjusted the backpack with their extra clothes on his shoulder and drew her against him, knowing exactly what she needed. Because after last night, it was what he needed, too. He gazed into her eyes, and as he'd hoped, her troubled look eased. Heat and a sense of something bigger whirled around them, between them, inside *him*, unstoppable and explosive. Her hair swept over her cheek, and he gathered her long locks in one hand, holding it away from her face, earning the sweet smile he'd dreamed of last night.

"I know you're bothered by your newfound talent, but someday you might feel differently. You might be glad you have something in common with your mother. You never know how things will change. It doesn't mean that you'll turn into her or treat other people, or yourself, differently. It's just one of those things that you might one day be thankful for."

He realized he was asking her to accept something that was probably as hard for her as his father's death was for him. But what he'd said was true. Feelings about people and events could change on a dime. No one knew that better than Rick. Until the night he'd told Desiree about the reasons he no longer sailed, he hadn't wanted to, or been able to, share it with anyone. And now he wanted to conquer it.

She breathed deeply. "It's just so hard. Accepting that I'm like her scares me, but I guess you could be right."

"I could be wrong, too," he said honestly. "But being with you has helped me to see that I need to deal with the parts of my father's death that still haunt me. I *want* to do that more than I ever have, and that's because of you. I'm not trying to push your mother on you. I know how much she's hurt you. I'm just saying, maybe you should leave that door open until you've had time to think about it. Painting seems to have brought you and Violet closer together. It might be worth thinking about instead of closing that door completely."

"Maybe you're right."

She went up on her toes and touched her lips to his, and when she pressed her hands to his neck, he took the kiss deeper. She made one of those sexy noises he loved, and desire flooded him. When she melted against him, rubbing her soft body all over his, and pushed her hands into his hair, heat shot through him.

He reluctantly tore his mouth away and looked down at his erection. Drake would have a field day with that. "Not exactly family friendly."

"Oh my." Her cheeks flamed, but her smile turned wicked.

He took a step away, trying to calm down while she stood there beaming, looking hot and sexy and so darn lovable he could barely stand it.

She sauntered up to him with an extra-confident sway of her hips and said, "Put your feet in the water. It's *cold*."

"Nothing will help if you keep acting like that." He swept her into his arms and carried her into waist-deep water. She clung to him, but she didn't scream or complain. She lowered her lips to his, kissing him deeply.

"Better?" She touched her finger to his lower lip, and he sucked it into his mouth. Her eyes darkened, and she slid a second finger between his lips. "You're definitely going to the naughty corner."

"That's not exactly a threat."

"It was meant as a promise." A glimmer of mischief rose in her eyes, and they kissed again, long and deep, which did nothing to lessen his arousal. He wished to heaven he hadn't arranged a surprise for Desiree. He'd carry her right up to his cottage and love her until night fell, and then he'd love her all the way until morning.

When he finally carried her back to the beach, she asked, "Where are we going that I needed to bring extra clothes?"

"It's a surprise."

Her eyes widened with excitement. "Another sexy slumber party?"

"How can you be so cute *and* the hottest woman I've ever known? I want to have a slumber party with you every night. In my bed. Your bed. The widow's walk. The beach. My truck. Wherever you'd like, as long as we're together. But I don't think much slumbering will be going on."

She pressed her lips together, but her smile bloomed anyway. "I want that, too."

Chapter Twelve

"THERE YOU ARE!" Serena's voice broke through their reverie. She was jogging toward them, her open hoodie swinging over a green bikini. Drake stood by the Jet Skis a few feet away, staring at Serena's butt.

Rick had been so focused on Desiree, he hadn't realized they'd reached the resort.

"I was worried that you'd changed your mind. We're so excited for you! I can't believe this will be your first time on a Jet Ski." Serena hugged a very shocked Desiree, who was looking at Rick like she'd swallowed a frog.

"What exactly are we doing tonight?" Desiree asked.

Serena covered her mouth. "Oh, no. He hasn't told you?"

"Not yet," Rick said, giving her a thanks-a-lot look.

"Sorry," Serena said. "I'll just…" She pointed to the Jet Skis. "Give you two a moment alone."

Desiree's eyes slammed into him with a mix of excitement and shock.

"Ohmygosh. Jet Skis?" She grabbed his hand. "I've never been on one. I can't drive one of those."

"You don't have to," he assured her. "You'll ride with me. All you'll have to do is hang on. You said it was tempting the night we met, and I thought it would be fun. Drake and Serena are taking one out, too, but there'll be no racing, no horsing around. It's just a quick Jet Ski ride to get us to your surprise. But we have to go now, because it's illegal to ride after sunset."

"Way to give a girl time to decide." She squeezed his hand. "What if I fall off?"

"You won't. They have a very wide base, and I won't make any sharp turns or erratic movements." He gathered her close and felt her heart beating frantically against his. "I promise I won't do anything dangerous. You'll wear a life vest, and if you're uncomfortable, we'll stop."

"And you think I'll like it?" Her brows knitted.

"I do, babe, or I wouldn't have planned it. I know you're cautious, and I promise I'll always be careful with you. But you like to have fun, Des, and I don't want you to miss out on a thing."

She glanced at the Jet Skis again, nibbled on her lower lip, and drew in a deep breath. "I guess this can't be any more difficult than juggling a classroom of feisty preschoolers." With a wide smile, she said, "It looks like today is my day for scary, unexpected adventures. Let's do it."

He picked her up and spun her around. "You're going to love this. I promise."

"Well, I love *this* part of it! I'm going to have to agree to do things more often."

His mind went straight to the gutter, and his expression must have given him away, because she flushed so hard he had to kiss her again.

Ten minutes later, with the backpack stowed in the storage compartment, life vests securely in place, and having given Desiree a quick lesson in Jet Ski safety, they were ready to ride.

Drake and Serena shared a Jet Ski, and Drake gave Rick a thumbs-up.

"No wild stunts!" Desiree said.

"Only in the bedroom, sweetheart."

Rick started out slow, with Drake and Serena trailing them. He had to hand it to Drake. He hadn't given Rick a hard time about storming out last night, or pushed him any further about not going sailing with them later tonight. Drake was also doing him a huge favor by driving Rick's Jet Ski back to the resort later. He definitely owed his brother big-time.

"Faster!" Desiree yelled.

That's my girl. He kicked up the speed. The wind stung his cheeks, and Desiree clung to him as they flew through the water.

When they arrived at the private stretch of beach owned by Dean's brother, Jett, where the rest of Desiree's surprise waited, she *whoop*ed! She'd loved the ride, and hopefully she'd like the rest of the surprise just as much. Tonight they had the property all to themselves.

Drake and Serena pulled up beside them and cut the engine.

"Hey, man, I appreciate your help tonight," Rick said as he and Drake stepped off the Jet Skis.

"That's what family's for." He pulled Rick into a quick embrace and said, for his ears only, "I'm here for you. Whatever you need, whenever you need it."

"That was amazing!" Desiree said as Rick helped her to her feet. "*So* fun! I can't believe I ever called you *reckless*!"

"She knows you already." Drake laughed, and Serena smacked his arm.

"Hey!" Drake hoisted Serena over his shoulder and carried her into deeper water.

"Don't you dare!" Serena hollered. "I'll kick your butt, Drake Savage!"

Rick helped Desiree remove her life vest, rid himself of his, and tossed the backpack on the beach. "When did my girl call me reckless?"

Her cheeks flushed, and she blinked up at him with big, innocent eyes.

He'd had her wrapped around him for the last forty-five minutes, listening to her melodic laugh and wishing he had a GoPro so he could have seen her elation unfold. And now she was looking at him with that sexy, vulnerable look? The one that drove him out of his mind?

That devastatingly delicious lip sprang free, and she said, "The first time I saw you racing around on the Jet Ski."

As Drake and Serena sped away, Rick hauled Desiree against him. *Alone at last.* He gazed into her honest eyes, his heart tumbling. "Babe, the only thing reckless about me is how fast I'm falling for you."

DESIREE AND RICK held hands as they strolled along the beach, and as the sun began setting, they made their way up a sandy path toward the top of the dunes. Lush bushes with vibrant purple and white flowers appeared between patches of dune grass, as if seeds had rained down from above and taken hold haphazardly. When they reached the crest of the dunes, it was like walking into a dream. In a sandy clearing by the edge of the dunes was a thick orange blanket, several big, colorful throw pillows, and an enormous picnic basket. Rick lit two torches that sat a few inches off the sand, bringing the whole romantic setup into clearer view. Rose petals were spread along the blanket, trailing from where they stood. And at their feet, Rick had drawn two hearts intersecting in the sand, with their initials in them. Her heart felt like it might beat right out of her chest.

"Rick…"

He was watching her with so much emotion in his eyes, she felt her knees weaken. He took her hand and guided her around the message in the sand and away from their little love nest, to where he'd tied pretty blankets up between two low trees, creating a barrier. "Dean's brother owns this property and the beach below, so we have it all to ourselves."

He crouched by them, lighting another lantern, and dropped the backpack behind the blankets.

"Even though we're alone and there's no chance of anyone seeing us, I assumed you might want a dressing room," he said as he came to her side and pointed beyond the hanging blankets. "And just over the ridge, by my truck, is a bathroom. I'm sorry I can't take you sailing to drift beneath the moonlight." *At least not yet.* "And taking you out on a powerboat wouldn't even come close to giving you the romantic night you dream of."

She stepped closer, her chest full. "Sailing is off my list. I know how hard that would be for you, and I don't want you to feel pressure because of my silly childhood dream."

"Your dreams aren't silly at any age."

"Rick, all dreams don't have to be realized. Especially not at the cost of making you uncomfortable." This incredible man was making her heart work overtime. "This is so much more than I could ever hope for. On top of everything else, you made me a *dressing room.* And I love it even more because it came from here." She touched the left side of his chest.

Framing her face with his hands, he brushed his lips over hers, and her entire being flooded with awareness. He didn't kiss her, didn't say a word, just stood so close her body tingled with anticipation. He touched her cheek so tenderly, she didn't want to move, or breathe, for fear of missing a second of it. As the minutes passed, her senses spun. She smelled his raw, manly scent, felt his chest brushing against hers, his hips rocking in a slow sensual motion bringing rise to a desperate pulse inside her. One hand moved to her back, his fingers pressing into her. His lips swept over her cheek, then along her lips again, and up beside her ear. He didn't speak, but she heard his thoughts, felt his desire. They stayed like that until darkness fell around them. And just when the tension had her strung so tight she was sure she'd snap, he lowered his mouth to hers, unleashing an explosion of sensations.

Lust surged through her veins like an awakened river. She grabbed at his back, his arms, his head, needing to be closer. His tongue plundered her mouth just as it had in the widow's walk. Her body electrified with the memory, and a needy noise escaped into his mouth. His hand cruised up the back of her tank top, crushing her to him. She loved how big he was, how strong. He was shirtless, and she wanted to feel his skin on her, over her, around her. They stumbled and kissed to the blanket, stripping their clothes off as they went, and destroying his sandy message.

"I brought dinner, but I'm starved for *dessert*."

"Greedy."

They both stilled as she ogled him, salivating for a taste of the man who was breaking through all her barriers, setting her free from the confines of her own mind. She didn't have to look at his face to know he was aware of her every breath, probably waiting for her to pull back on the reins, but tonight, for him, she was cutting herself loose.

AFTER THEY CAME down from the clouds, they lay beneath a blanket, their naked bodies entangled like twisted vines. They kissed and talked and held each other in comfortable silence for long stretches of time, listening to the distant sound of the bay and the dune grass rustling in the breeze.

Rick pressed a kiss to Desiree's forehead. "Are you cold? Hungry?"

"I'm not moving from my new favorite spot," she said sweetly. "You're like a personal heater, and I don't care if I starve."

He laughed, but he felt the same way. "Good. Me either. Tell me something about you that I don't know. What's it like to be surrounded by little people all day?"

She smiled, the way she had each time she'd talked about teaching. "It can be the most wonderful, fulfilling job in the world, or the most trying. Usually, it's a little of both. Pre-schoolers are curious and eager to learn, which makes each of their discoveries really exciting. Probably one of my favorite things is when they think they can't do something and then prove themselves wrong. Nothing beats the pride in their eyes."

As her love of her work poured out, he realized how much enthusiasm he'd lost for his own.

"No two days are the same, and no two children are the same," she said. "What works for one might send another into tears. It's a balancing act."

"Did you always want to be a teacher?"

She snuggled closer, and her voice went soft. "I always knew I wanted to work with children and be a positive influence in their lives. When I was in high school, my father suggested I volunteer at a summer program for three- and four-year-olds to see if I liked it, and that was it. I knew what I wanted." She gazed into his eyes, her fingers moving slowly over his skin. "It's funny how sometimes you just *know* something is too right to be wrong."

"Like us."

"Like us," she whispered. "That's something else we have in common. You always knew you wanted to be a builder, like your father. Did you ever entertain the idea of being something else?"

"Not once. When I set my mind on something, I'm not easily deterred."

"Really? I couldn't tell. It's not like you were persistent when we first met."

"And you were sweet and sexy and curious, but *careful* not to let me know how badly you wanted to get in my pants."

She gasped. "I did *not* want to get in your pants!"

"Until tonight," he teased.

She flushed, and he touched his forehead to hers. "Desiree, you are the sweetest, most passionate creature on this earth, and I hope you blush like that until we're old and gray."

"*We're…?*" she said breathlessly.

"Slip of the tongue."

He came down over her and laced their hands together, holding them beside her head. "We're too right to be wrong."

He took her in a series of slow, intoxicating kisses. In seconds, he was drunk on *her*, lost in the way she moved sensually beneath him, breathing harder, then hardly breathing at all. He kissed her jaw, ran his tongue along the shell of her ear, and his emotions came pouring out in one heated whisper after another.

"I can't wait to make love to you." He brushed his lips over hers.

"Yes," came out in a rush of hot air.

As their bodies came together, he held Desiree close, never wanting to let her go, and spoke heatedly into her ear. "Feel that, sweetheart?"

"Mm," she said with the softness of a sated lover. "Amazing."

"*Real*, baby. We're as real as it gets."

Chapter Thirteen

SATURDAY MORNING, AFTER waking up entangled with her boyfriend, Desiree and Rick had made love...*twice*. First, wild and passionate, and later, slow and soul-fillingly amazing. She'd never considered herself a spiritual person. How could she when the mere word reminded her of Lizza's taking off to follow her "calling," and leaving Desiree behind. But making love with Rick was more than a physical and emotional experience; it *was* spiritual. A coming together of mind, body, and soul. After that blissful wake-up, she'd taken Rick's advice, and instead of closing the door to painting, she'd left it open and painted several signs for the shop.

Several busy days, and sinful nights, passed with taking long walks, making sweet *and* passionate love into the wee hours of the morning, and sharing more of their secrets, hopes, and dreams. Before Desiree knew it, Wednesday arrived with sunshine and an influx of customers at Devi's Discoveries. The road signs Desiree had made were working wonders. *Thank you, Rick.* She'd been putting them up along Route 6, and Violet had passed out flyers in the area. The flyers had worked so well, this morning Violet drove to the neighboring towns to hand out more.

"I'd like to buy these." A stout woman with curly silver hair set two items from the personal exploration shop on the counter. "And how much is this?" She held up a pottery mug with a fishtail handle.

Desiree had been nervous about leaving the door to the personal exploration shop open, but Violet had threatened to stand outside the cottage telling customers, *Be sure to check out the enormous vibrators in the back room*, if she didn't. Boy, was she glad her in-your-face sister had insisted. Between the gallery and the shop, they'd been clearing a grand each day, and on Monday they'd earned nearly three thousand dollars, having sold one of their mother's paintings. Today they'd already made almost a thousand dollars, most of which had come from the sale of *personal discovery* items.

"It's thirteen dollars," Desiree answered. "It's one of a kind."

"Are you the artist?" the woman asked excitedly.

"No." *My mother is.* An odd sense of pride came with that thought, and Desiree had to work hard to move past it. "Lizza Vancroft is the artist."

The woman clutched the mug to her chest with a hopeful smile. "Is she here?"

"No, I'm sorry. She's away for the summer." As an afterthought, she added, "Rejuvenating her creativity." She rang up the purchase, thinking about Lizza. The shop was truly packed from top to bottom, and in the studio, just as her mother had said, there were enough pieces to carry the shop for at least a few months. Maybe Lizza really had depleted her creativity while she was there. It still didn't excuse her for making it seem as though she was *dying*, but that was Lizza.

The shop remained busy throughout the afternoon, and every customer wanted to chat about something—the weather,

the artwork, the property. She'd met two people who remembered when the Summer House Inn had been a go-to summer-
vacation spot. One gentleman said his family had stayed there
when he was a little boy, and he remembered the kind woman
who had run it. It warmed her to hear him speak of her
grandmother. They'd begun renovations earlier in the week, and
it was amazing how a fresh coat of paint could breathe new life
into tired-looking rooms.

When things slowed down she texted Violet, who was supposed to have returned from putting up flyers hours ago. *I've
been swamped all day. Great job with the flyers, but where are you?*
Desiree had been picking away at weeding the gardens along the
driveway while Violet manned the shop, but today she had
hoped to surprise Rick with lunch. Thanks to Violet, that idea
had gone out the window.

She headed outside to the easel she'd set up by the front
door and worked on a painting of the gardens she'd begun
yesterday in between customers. Pulling from memories, she
brought to life wild grasses, burgeoning hydrangeas, daffodils,
azaleas, tiger lilies, and her favorite, orange trumpet creepers.

A stream of yappy barks broke her focus. Cosmos darted
between the bushes at the far side of the property, heading for
her at record speed. She'd put him in the fenced yard outside
the kitchen while she was working and wondered how he'd
gotten out again. She stepped away from the painting as Mira,
Serena, and Rick burst through the bushes. Her heart skipped at
the sight of her big, handsome man tearing across the lawn in a
pair of shorts and a tight white T-shirt. Their eyes locked, and
pure lust stared back at her.

"Grab him!" Serena yelled.

Desiree scooped up Cosmos, who was dripping wet, wishing

she could grab her man instead. "What have you done now?" Cosmos wriggled in her arms, covering her face with puppy kisses. She couldn't stop grinning as the others caught up.

Rick skidded to a stop beside her. "Hey, babe. The scoundrel got in the pool again." He kissed her lips, the only spot Cosmos hadn't touched.

"He climbed the fence!" Serena petted Cosmos. "Such a smart boy."

Rick glared at her.

"You have to admit, he's a smart dog," Mira said to her brother. "Look at this, Des."

She held out her phone, showing Desiree a video of Cosmos standing on his hind legs, stretching as tall as his little body could possibly reach, and hooking his paws over the top of the fence. He jumped three times before hauling himself up and over. He darted into the pool, sending the swimmers into a frenzy of screeches and laughter.

"Oh my gosh! I put him in the fenced-in area this morning. I never imagined he could climb out. I'm so sorry." Desiree lifted Cosmos up and looked into his twinkling dark eyes. "You have been a very creatively naughty puppy."

He yapped, his tongue lolling out of his smiling mouth.

"I've never seen a dog do that," Serena said. She and Mira were wearing shorts and tank tops, looking like they'd just come from the beach, though Desiree knew Serena worked most days running the front desk.

"I'm going to have Dean install flower boxes on the outside perimeter of the pool fence, and I was thinking he should do it on the inside of your fence, too. Is that okay? It should keep the troublemaker from climbing over." Rick grabbed the pooch's face and pressed a kiss to his snout. "Grr."

Desiree laughed. "That's fine, and I'd really appreciate it. He could get hurt running across the parking lot, and I'm pretty attached to him. But can you blame him for wanting to go swimming? I mean, it *is* summertime." *Wow, I sound like Violet.*

"You're right," Rick said. "I'll buy him a kiddie pool for your fenced-in area, too." He winked. "The rest of the materials for the patio were delivered earlier. I've got to get back before Drake screws things up. We're going to try to finish it up tonight, so I'll be a little late." He leaned in close and whispered, "You look even sexier in that little pink number than you did this morning. I can't wait to tear it off of you later. *With my teeth.*"

"You better hope he brushes them first," Mira said under her breath.

"I can't believe you heard that." Desiree glared at Rick.

He shrugged. "Sorry. I thought I was being discreet." He leaned in with a mischievous look in his eyes and said, "But I do love when my girl gets flustered."

Desiree swatted him playfully, earning a hearty laugh, but inside she was swooning over their racy relationship. "You're a *beast*. Go do your work."

He gave her a chaste kiss, and she watched him walk away.

"You realize that's my brother's backside you're ogling," Mira teased.

"Oh gosh, sorry." She carried Cosmos into the gallery and grabbed his leash from beside the door, hooking it to his collar. "Come on in and look around."

"I'm glad you and Rick found each other," Mira said as she looked around the shop. "I've never seen him this happy. Maybe you can get him to realize he needs to be *here*, and not in DC."

Desiree's stomach lurched, thinking about how short a time they had left together. He said he was there for another month when they'd met, and it had been almost two weeks. A couple more weeks would never be enough. She'd known exactly what she was getting into with Rick. A *summer* romance. But she hadn't realized she could lose her heart so quickly.

"But I'm leaving, too," she said wistfully.

"Well, that's easy to fix. We'll just have to start convincing you to stay." Serena peered into the back room. "*What* is *this?* Desiree! You didn't tell us you had a porn shop."

"What?" Mira followed her into the back room.

If they'd have come in a week ago, Desiree might have shriveled up with embarrassment, but now she'd handled, talked about, and sold everything for inappropriate fun. Embarrassment had no place in this salesgirl's life. *Except when it comes to Rick's whispered promises.* As much as she loved his dirty talk, when they weren't in the heat of the moment, she still blushed a red streak.

"It's my mother's 'personal exploration shop,' *not* mine. I'm just the salesgirl. I swear, if my teacher friends saw me now, they'd think I was a whole different person. Back home I spend my days talking to little people and keeping my thoughts and language as pure as I can." She picked up a bottle of lubricant. "Then I come here, thinking my mother is dying, and learn all about *this* and adult toys. I sold five of these today. *Five.* I didn't think people really used it that much."

"Just think of how much wider your vocabulary is now." Serena picked up a bottle of lube. "Now, boys and girls, this is called a *lubricant.* Can you say *lubricant?* Oh, what's it for, you ask? Well, after being around sticky fingers all day, Miss Cleary likes to get a different type of sticky—"

"Geez!" Desiree snatched the bottle out of Serena's hand. "You sound like my friend Emery."

"You have a dirty-minded best friend, too?" Mira eyed her bestie. "Serena has worn off on me, so watch out. Emery might wear off on you."

She didn't need to know it was *Rick*, not Emery, who had unlocked her inner sexy girl.

Mira held up a pair of edible underwear. "I'll be back later for these."

"Why stop there?" Serena held up a whip. "Turn it up a notch. You can't get this stuff anywhere around here. I think the closest place is P-town. We were going to brainstorm about marketing. Do you have time now? You could corner the market on this stuff *so* easily."

"I've been so busy since we set out the signs and flyers, I think we'll be okay. At least for now." Desiree heard voices in the gallery and went to investigate.

Cosmos barked at a young couple who was looking around with confused expressions. Desiree picked up Cosmos. "Hi. Can I help you find something?"

The couple shared a secret smile, and the guy handed her a flyer. "We got this at the Earth House. Is this the right place?" The Earth House was an eclectic record and clothing shop a few miles away.

Desiree quickly scanned the flyer. *Best sex shop around!* It went on to list a few of their products, and the address. Swallowing her shock at the changes her sister had made to the flyers, she said, "It sure is," and waved toward the open door, catching sight of Mira and Serena inspecting a box.

Violet's motorcycle roared into the driveway, and Desiree carried Cosmos outside. Violet climbed off her bike and took off her helmet, carrying it under one arm as she sauntered across the driveway.

"Have a fun afternoon?" Desiree set Cosmos on the ground.

Violet bent to pet Cosmos. "Actually, yes. It's been a long time since I've wanted to get to know a place. I hit some of the shops in Brewster, and went down to Breakwater Beach."

Desiree swallowed her complaint about Violet blowing off their schedule. Violet was a wanderer, like their mother. For her to want to get to know the area said something, and it felt like progress.

Serena and Mira came outside giggling.

"Do you get to test the products?" Serena asked.

"No!" *Can I? Do I want to? Oh my gosh. I think I might!*

Violet smirked. "That right there is the look of someone who wants to break the rules."

"Oh, I love breaking rules," Serena said.

Desiree introduced the three of them, then popped inside to check on the customers. When she came back out, Mira had a troubled look in her eyes.

"I'm a mother," Mira said. "Breaking rules isn't really my thing."

Violet scoffed. "Are you kidding? Naughty mommies are the bomb." She eyed Serena. "I think it's time we dare these girls into finding their inner badass."

"We're going to get along *so* well." Serena rubbed her palms together. "We could dare them to get arrested."

Mira and Desiree said, "No," in unison.

"No arrests," Violet said, and Desiree breathed a sigh of relief. "Something simple but different for them. Crotchless underwear."

"Yes! Crotchless!" Serena squealed. "At Rick's goodbye party in two weeks. That's the perfect send-off for two lovers. But you have to come, Violet."

Desiree felt like she'd been body-slammed. *Rick's goodbye party.* How could they already be planning to say goodbye when she felt like they'd just found each other? She crossed her arms against the longing taking hold and forced herself to focus on the thought of wearing crotchless panties around Rick and how thrilling it would be. *For both of us.* She imagined letting it "slip" that she was wearing them and Rick being unable to control himself. A thrum of excitement rushed through her, pushing the longing to the side. Oh yeah, she would wear those panties for him.

"Think I'd miss seeing my sister squirming like a schoolmarm in those sexed-up panties?" Violet shook her head. "No way."

Feigning her best annoyed expression to cover her new-found riskiness, Desiree said, "You *know* Rick has spent the night all week." She lifted her chin and said, "I am perfectly capable of owning my inner bad girl *without* a dare."

"You can't even say bad*ass*," Violet pointed out.

"I don't have to be trash-mouthed to be a bad…*girl.*"

"I can say 'badass,' but I can't go crotchless at a bonfire," Mira said. "My son, Hagen, will be with me."

"Is he looking up your shorts?" Violet asked.

"Well, no, but still…" Mira's voice trailed off.

"Mira!" Serena waggled her brows. "Think of the payoff afterward. I want to do it, and I don't even have a man!"

Desiree was imagining all the ways she could taunt Rick. He'd lose his flipping mind! But she wasn't going to *bet* on their sex life. Instead, she decided to turn it around on Violet. "I don't need a dare."

Violet's eyes widened in surprise.

"I'm going to do it anyway, but I'm not telling *you* when," Desiree added. "That's private. But…since I'm going to do it anyway, you have to stick to a schedule for a week. Seven solid days of showing up on time to a fair and equitable work schedule."

Violet rolled her eyes.

"What's the matter?" Desiree taunted. "Not bad*ass* enough to handle it?"

RICK PUSHED TO his feet, wiped the sweat from his brow, and gazed down at the beach, where Matt and Hagen were busy creating another elaborate sandcastle. Matt had been a professor at Princeton before getting a major publishing contract and falling in love with Mira. He'd chosen to write full-time and remain at the Cape, rather than going back to teaching. Every time Rick saw how happy their family was, he thought about how much his father had missed out on. But today he turned those thoughts on himself. He'd spent more than an hour on the phone with his partners earlier. The battle between them had become so contentious, Rick found himself wondering why he was fighting so hard to go back. He'd invested well, and had more than enough money to live on. But he'd built his business from the ground up, and walking away would mean leaving a piece of himself behind. A big piece. The successful, prove-he-could-do-it-for-his-father piece.

"What do you think?" Drake called out to him.

It took a moment for Rick to realize Drake was talking about the patio they'd been working on for the past two days.

His eyes swept over the earth-toned stones covering the width of the recreation building and spilling out in a wavy pattern toward the beach with a built-in fire pit on the far right. He imagined playing his guitar and sitting by the fire with Desiree on a cold winter night. Maybe they could swing up for the holidays together.

"We did a heck of a job," he answered.

"Dad would have loved this." Drake pointed to the fire pit. "Can't you see him sitting over there with one arm around Mom, telling some story about his days as a fighter pilot?"

Rick laughed, remembering his father's penchant for embellishing. "The man could lie like a rug."

Drake motioned in the direction of Matt and Hagen. "I'm glad Hagen's got Matt. Mira's a wonderful mother, but there's a difference between a father and mother, and their relationship with sons."

"Single parents bring up kids all the time. Look at us."

"We were teenagers when we lost Dad. That's different. Do you think Mom would have laughed at us burping the alphabet? Or thought it was 'epic' when we rode our dirt bikes into that mucky marsh? Remember? She made us hose off outside and yelled at Dad for taking us to a diner when we were so dirty."

Rick smiled with the memory. "Man, we were lucky to have him."

"Yeah. They say women are the ones with the ticking clock, but how can you be around Hagen and not think about it?" Drake wiped his hands on his shorts and pushed the plate compactor to the edge of the patio. "Maybe it's easier for you, since you're not usually around him so much."

"Maybe that's why I never really thought about it until recently."

"Makes sense," Drake said. "Wait. You're thinking about it now?"

Rick shrugged. "Not in an I-want-kids-now way, but just in general."

"I think Desiree kick-started your heart again. About time, if you ask me."

"She wants to go sailing." The confession surprised him as much as it appeared to have surprised Drake. "I can't look at her without wanting to try to get on that boat."

"I'm sure she'll understand if you explain..."

"I did, and she does." He forced himself to ask the question he'd been carrying with him since he'd told Desiree about his father. "Why didn't we ever talk about that night?"

"I talked about it all the time," Drake said, meeting his gaze. "With Mom, with the grief counselor."

Blood pounded in Rick's ears as he opened a door he'd all but nailed shut. "I mean us, Drake. Why didn't *we* ever talk about it?"

"You didn't exactly want to talk back then." There was a hint of defensiveness in his brother's tone, and more than a hint in his eyes. "And you've clammed up ever since."

"Don't you find that messed up?" It came out as an accusation, and he hated himself for it, because it wasn't Drake's fault. "*We* were the ones on the deck. *We* were the ones who couldn't save him." His voice escalated, and he ground his teeth, regaining control, a silent war raging between him and his demons. "*Us*, Drake. Not the grief counselor. Not Mom or anyone else. We were in it together that night."

"We still are," Drake said evenly. "It's on *our* shoulders, and it always will be. We. Couldn't. Save. Him."

Pain gripped Rick so hard he couldn't move.

"Don't do this again, Rick," Drake seethed. "You've pulled away for seventeen years. I'm right here, and I'm ready to talk. Do you blame yourself? Is that what's kept you away? Because no one blames you."

Anger clawed up his torso, tightening like a noose around his neck. "No. And I don't blame you, either."

"Then what is it?" Drake pleaded.

"I don't know." Rick paced, hands fisted at his sides. "I *know* we couldn't save him. I thought I dealt with all of this. I can go *on* the water, *in* the water, *over* the water. But I get near a sailboat and I choke. Like I've never put it behind me."

The pain in Drake's eyes was palpable. "Because you didn't. Mira and I pushed through it when Mom made us. We went out on that frigging boat and cried, and cursed, and fought, until there was nothing left to be angry at. We let him go, Rick, but you refused. Don't you remember fighting with me when I tried to drag your ornery butt down to the boat a few weeks after the accident? You gave me a shiner." He laughed under his breath. "I had to tell everyone I beat some kid up just to save face from admitting my younger brother clocked me."

We fought? Rick didn't know if he should laugh or worry over having no memory of the incident. "I don't remember that."

"No?"

Rick shook his head.

"I knew a part of you had disappeared after we lost Dad, but I didn't realize *you'd* lost that part of yourself, too." Drake's voice turned thoughtful. "We were all in shock, but you buried your feelings so deep you were untouchable. As a teenager, you hid behind music, and sports, and never slowed down enough to think, much less feel. And as an adult...Bro, you *know* why you work eighty hours a week, hundreds of miles away from us. But since you've been back, there's been no place for you to hide."

"Tell me about it. I see him in everything. In you and Mira. Even Hagen," Rick admitted. "Sometimes it's too much."

"That's a shame. I see Dad everywhere, too. But I'm *glad* for it, because not a day goes by that I don't miss him. Getting a glimpse of him is a relief. A momentary gift."

"I want to feel that so bad, Drake. You have no idea. I think about that night all the time."

"I can only imagine," Drake said. "But how can you see the light if you don't get rid of the darkness? That night's still eating away at you. I think about that hellacious night, and I want to punch something, or take revenge on the sea. But—"

"There's no revenge for a prickly beast." Rick rubbed the knot at the base of his neck, breathing deeply and knowing his brother was right. He'd talked to the counselor, but he'd never done the one thing that mattered most. He'd lost his father that night at sea, but he'd never really let him go.

"I didn't plan on working eighty hours a week." He needed Drake to know the truth. "I wanted to make him proud, and I couldn't pull myself together here. Then things got away from me. Working became a way of life."

Drake raked a hand through his hair with a tortured expression. "I get it. But you're here now, and I'll do whatever it takes to get you back here for good."

Rick knew what he had to do. "Can you handle the patio?"

He took a step away and Drake grabbed his arm. "Forget the patio." He hauled him into an embrace. "Love you, bro."

TWENTY MINUTES LATER, Rick walked along the moorings as if he were walking the plank. The darkening sky mirrored his emotions as each heavy footstep brought him closer to the ghosts of his past. His heart beat violently against his ribs as he passed one, two, three boats, stopping at the fourth. His eyes remained trained on the wood beneath his feet, refusing to rise. Inhaling a lungful of brisk air, he forced his gaze upward. The dark cabin windows stared back at him like snake eyes.

They say the faces of those you've lost fade from memory. But even now, seventeen years later, Rick could picture his father's smiling eyes, his unruly dark hair bending at the wind's will, and his thick arms, defined by hard work and the relentless pursuit of living life to the fullest, as he reached over the edge of the boat.

Give me your hand, Ricky boy. I'll haul ya up.

Rick crossed his arms, a barrier between him and his father's ghost.

Afraid? What's the worst that can happen? You slip and fall in the water? Big deal. So, you swim, son. That's why you have limbs.

He smiled, despite his heartache. His father had always been infuriatingly positive. Getting on the boat should be a piece of cake, but tears burned his eyes, and the longing in his chest felt like a never-ending abyss he wouldn't be able to climb out of once he fell in.

Stepping on that boat meant...finally accepting his dad was gone?

He'd thought he'd done that the awful night they'd lost him. But if that wasn't the issue, what was? *If I knew the answer, I'd get on the frigging boat.*

Holding his breath, he reached for the bow with shaking

fists. Unfurling them was like bending iron. Closing his eyes, he touched his fingertips to the cool, sleek fiberglass, gritted his teeth, and pressed his palms flat.

See? Stable as the day is long.

His father's voice drew his eyes open, and his gaze swept over the cabin. Flashes of that awful night barreled into him, and he slammed his eyes shut again, willing himself to remain standing and accept the torture once and for all. He was done hiding, done running. His entire body battled him, from the bones in his feet trying to carry him away to the very tips of his fingers struggling to let go. But he stood strong as the howling winds and sheeting rain of seventeen years ago pummeled him anew. The erratic sounds of the choppy sea roared in his ears. The deluge of waves pounded over the deck, and the screeching of the boat's hardware sliced him open. The dense *whoosh* of the boom and the deadly *thud* sent him stumbling backward, as if he himself had been carried into the sea. He dropped to his knees, tears spilling down his cheeks. His shoulders slumped, and his head fell heavily into his hands, but he didn't run. He didn't fight the fear or the gut-wrenching agony as the memory of Drake holding him back from launching himself into the black water pinned him to the ground.

I'm getting on that stinkin' boat.

He forced his eyes open, and a hand shot down and grabbed his arm, hauling him to his feet. It took Rick a second to push out of the past and into the present, where Drake stood sure and steady before him.

"What are you doing here?" Rick's voice was thick with emotion.

"Whatever it takes."

Rick didn't hesitate, didn't give the past time to hold him

back from his future. With Drake by his side, he climbed onto the boat, determined to be the man his father had raised him to be, and the man Desiree deserved.

Chapter Fourteen

DESIREE LAY AWAKE watching the sun sneak through the new coral curtains, thinking about how much had changed since she'd arrived. How much *she'd* changed. With Violet in her life, her days were anything but structured. Her sister really did stink at keeping to a schedule, but Desiree was coming to accept that Violet wasn't being volitionally rebellious. It was just the way she was wired.

She rolled onto her side, careful not to wake Cosmos, who was lying on the foot of the bed, and ran her finger along Rick's strong, scruffy jaw. She'd never been the type of person to stay overnight with a boyfriend, because she had a busy schedule and liked to stick to it. During the summers, she usually tried to make it to Emery's early riser's yoga class a few days each week, and during the school year she liked to go over her lesson plans for each day before class. Getting off schedule at home would leave her feeling restless, but here, between the shop, getting to know Violet, caring for Cosmos, and her favorite thing of all, spending time with Rick, she barely had time to slow down and worry about anything. Or rather, worry about things like schedules. She had plenty of other worries, like had they chosen the right appliances and paint colors for the kitchen, and would the flower boxes keep Cosmos from escaping? Luckily, paying her mother's mortgage wasn't one of them. The sales from the shop were taking care of that. She'd even dropped the mortgage payment into the mail early.

She pressed a kiss to Rick's lips, acknowledging her biggest worry of all. How could she ever go back to being the person she had been, when he'd become such a big part of who she was now?

Cosmos creeped along the bed on Rick's other side and smothered his chin in kisses. Rick's lips curved up, and he tugged Desiree against him. Cosmos hopped off the bed with a whimper. The pup should be used to them by now. They could hardly keep their hands off each other, and still, every time they reached for each other in the morning, Cosmos whimpered. She wondered if her mother would notice or care if she took Cosmos back to Virginia with her.

The thought of leaving brought a pang of longing.

Rick rolled over, trapping her beneath him. "Morning, gorgeous."

He lowered his mouth to her neck and began killing her brain cells one kiss at a time. This was so much better than yoga and lesson plans.

"In a world with billions of people, how did I get lucky enough to find you?"

She struggled to hold on to her ability to speak as he kissed her neck, the crest of her shoulder, then worked his way up toward her ear. "You...*stalked* me."

His laughter vibrated through his mouth, and he kissed a path south.

"And I'd do it again," he said. "Tell me you'll still see me when we leave here."

She closed her eyes, going for humor instead of reality. "All the way to the front door, until you leave for your morning run."

He sank his teeth into her flesh.

"*Ouch!*" He hadn't bitten hard, but he'd surprised her.

He crawled up her body, pinning her beneath him again, his eyes dark and serious. "When you go back to Virginia, and I'm in DC."

"Oh," she said innocently. "I don't want to think about that right now."

"Aren't you the one who likes schedules and plans?"

"Mm-hm."

"Tell me you'll still be mine."

Her insides melted at the passion in his voice. "I want to see you, but can we not talk about it? It makes me sad to think about being apart. I know you work all the time when you're in DC, and you won't have much time for me, so I'd rather not talk about it right now."

Sadness replaced the determination in his gaze. "Sweetheart, I looked at a map and Oak Falls is just under two hours from DC. We'll make it work."

He'd looked at a map? He'd thought that far ahead?

He kissed her then, a long, languid kiss that turned her worries to dust. And then he loved her from the inside out, so completely there was no room for doubt.

An hour later, showered and dressed, Desiree and Rick took Cosmos for a walk. When they got back to the house, Zander and Zeke were upstairs painting the hallway on the second floor. Desiree had been enjoying making elaborate breakfasts for Rick and Violet, and the last few mornings, she'd made enough for Zeke and Zander, too. Rob was in and out, but he'd made it over for eggs Benedict two days ago.

She pulled out the ingredients for Belgian waffles with blueberries and cream, while Rick did his best to distract her. He was dressed for his run, which meant he was gloriously naked, save for a pair of shorts and running shoes. He wrapped his arms around her from behind, nibbling on her neck and rubbing his body against her.

"Drake will kill you if you're late again." She leaned her head to the side, allowing him better access to devour her.

"Like I care?" He turned her in his arms and brushed her hair from her shoulder, placing several openmouthed kisses there.

She hooked her finger into the waist of his shorts. "All it takes is a few kisses and I'm hot and bothered again. I think you've turned me into a nymphomaniac."

"That makes two of us." He buried his hand in her hair, his eyes smoldering. "I've never felt like this before, and I can't get enough of you. After my run, I'm coming back with Dean to install the flower boxes around your fence. And after that…" He lowered his mouth to hers, kissing her until her legs turned to jelly. "Maybe we can sneak away alone for a little bit?"

"Good morning, sex maniacs."

Desiree started, pushing away from Rick as Violet snickered, but Rick tightened his grasp. He never let anything come between them, and it was just one of the things she adored about him.

"Geez, Vi. Think you could give us some warning?"

Violet snagged a blueberry from the counter and popped it into her mouth. "Gee, Des. I don't know. Think you can give me some warning before the nightly headboard banging begins?"

"Geez," Rick uttered.

"Aw, look how cute Mr. Massive is when he blushes." Violet grabbed another handful of blueberries.

"Violet!" *Headboard banging?* She hadn't even noticed. Then again, when she and Rick were close, the rest of the world failed to exist.

"Hey, if I were you, I'd be proud," Violet said. "But since I'm *me*, I'm moving into one of the empty cottages."

"I've got to take off, but I'm sorry, Vi." Rick looked at Desiree without a shred of regret in his liquid-fire eyes. "We can stay at my place so she doesn't have to move out."

"Don't sweat it," Violet said. "Zander and Zeke are going to help me move when they're done working for the day." She winked, and grabbed a few more blueberries.

I don't want to know what that wink was for.

"But don't worry. I'll still be here for your delicious, happy-humper, post-coital breakfasts every morning."

"Ohmygosh." Desiree buried her face in Rick's chest.

Rick tipped her face up, a wide grin lighting up his handsome face. "I guess we can never stop, or everyone will starve."

NO ONE STARVED over the next week and a half. In fact, everyone around Desiree and Rick probably gained ten pounds. Their ravenous appetites for each other carried over into even more elaborate breakfasts. Violet had let that slip at a bonfire last week, and Drake and the others had begun finding reasons to drop by at breakfast time. Even Mira and Hagen had joined them. Hagen had helped Desiree cook French toast, reminding her of how far her mind had strayed from her life back home.

She hadn't thought about school or teaching at all, although she missed Emery even though they'd been keeping in touch with texts and phone calls. She loved every minute of having so many people to cook for. A room full of people who felt like family made the house feel alive. She'd even begun looking up recipes again. She knew this summer was like playing house, but she couldn't help wishing it never had to end.

It was Saturday evening, and she and Rick planned to go out for another surprise date. She was used to being the planner, but she realized that as much as she loved schedules and plans, she'd been running pretty loosey-goosey all summer, taking up the slack when Violet got caught up in doing pottery or exploring the area and stealing time for moonlit walks and stargazing in the widow's walk with Rick. They'd even gone into town and listened to a band play by the beach. She wasn't a vagabond like her mother, but it felt good to let herself ride the wind a little bit.

She walked along the driveway picking flowers from the newly manicured gardens, dwindling away the time as she waited for Rick and marveling at how the yard and house were coming together. It had taken months for the gardens to become tangles of vines and weeds that had nearly suffocated all the flowers. But it had taken only a few days to make them beautiful again. It was funny how a little love could make everything better. The renovations to the house were nearly complete, and the flower boxes had kept Cosmos from climbing over the fence, although he had started digging under the fence despite the new plastic pool Rick had bought for him. What had started out as a disastrous turn of events had turned into a life-changing summer.

She carried the flowers to Violet's cottage, remembering

how, when she was a little girl, she'd dreamed about living in one, with Violet next door and her mother in the big house. *Little-girl-lost dreams.* In a sense, this summer had made that dream come true.

Desiree peered through Violet's screen door. Her sister stood by the back window, reading. She wore a black miniskirt and a tank top. Her finger trailed along the page as she read. She looked content. *Sweet* even. Cosmos was asleep on the living room couch. How could she leave them at the end of the summer?

"Hey," Desiree said.

Violet glanced up, smiling as she closed the book.

"I brought you some flowers. Can I come in?"

"Sure." She held the book against her chest.

"I can't believe I haven't been in any of the cottages before this." Desiree stepped inside, taking in the artsy batik wall hangings and the pictures Violet must have taken from their mother's studio covering bright white walls. Tie-dyed throws covered the arms and back of the white sofa and wicker chair. The setup hadn't changed from when she was a little girl. A bar still separated the living room from the kitchen, and a small eating area led to French doors, which opened to a small deck in the backyard.

"Let me get a vase." Violet grabbed a pretty, colorful glass vase from a cabinet. "The other two cottages are in good shape. Thanks for the flowers. They're beautiful."

"Did you make all these batiks and throws? They're really pretty. I'd love to buy one from you." Violet had started working with fabrics with Lizza when she was around twelve. Desiree was glad she was still making them.

"I made them, and I'll make you one, but you're not buying

it."

"Thanks." Desiree walked across the room to look at pictures on the wall more closely. "You took some of Lizza's pictures?"

"I'll put them in the shop when we need more stock. But the white walls were killing me." She put the flowers in the vase and set them on the table. "I thought you had a big date with Rick."

"I do. He's picking me up soon, but I was taking a walk and wanted to bring you the flowers."

"You look hot," Violet said.

"Thanks. I still have no idea where we're going." She'd worn the dress she was wearing the first night she and Rick had met. She caught sight of the first picture she'd painted, the one of Violet as a little girl, hanging in the dining room. "You took my painting?"

"I probably should have asked. Do you mind?" Violet crossed her arms over the book she was holding, a pensive expression on her face.

"No. I'm flattered, but I thought you hated that dress."

Violet shrugged. "I did. But you painted it." She busied herself putting the book she was reading on top of a stack of others by the couch and straightening them. "That made it special."

Desiree felt like she was going to cry, but as she and Violet grew closer, and she made new friends, and the renovations came to fruition—with a new kitchen, baths, and paint colors she and Violet had chosen together—and Rick's return to DC neared, *everything* made her feel that way.

"What were you reading?" Desiree asked, to try to force her weepiness away.

She held out the book, and Desiree scanned the title. *Running a Bed-and-Breakfast for Dummies.* "Are you thinking of staying after Lizza comes back?"

"Don't you mean *if* she comes back?" Violet plopped onto the couch.

"You have a point. I hadn't really thought about that, although I should have, given her history."

"Ya think?" Violet scoffed. "You could stay with me."

"Stay? I can't stay. I have a job—"

"Run the inn with me. Get a job here and teach in the off season."

"Vi, it's not our inn to run." As she said it, she couldn't deny that she'd had a fantasy or two about doing just that. But her fantasy included Rick staying, too, not returning to DC. "Wait. Why aren't you going stir crazy? I thought you had a hard time staying put, like Lizza."

Violet leaned forward, elbows on knees, eyes trained on the floor. "I did, but only because I never felt like I belonged anywhere."

Desiree sank down beside her. "That's how I felt around you and Lizza when you'd visit when we were little."

"She loves you, you know. She talked about you all the time. About how much you'd like this or that."

"Right. You don't have to try to make me feel better, Vi. I accepted a long time ago that she left and never looked back." Desiree pushed to her feet, her heart racing.

"She left, but she looked back, Des. You got more headspace than I did."

"I don't understand how that can be, given how little attention she's paid me over the years."

"Don't you *get* her yet?" Violet sprang to her feet, her voice escalating. "She doesn't think we need her time or attention to know she loves us. *Cosmos?* The universe? We're supposed to soak it all in."

"Yeah? Well, I guess this sponge never got the memo, because I've felt a big black hole inside me for a long time. If not for my father and Emery, I would have gone bonkers. She has *always* been my Achilles' heel."

Violet held her steady gaze. "And you've always been mine."

Desiree's jaw dropped open, stunned by Violet's confession. "Me?"

"Don't make a big thing out of it." Violet stalked into the kitchen. "This summer has been the only time I've felt like I belonged somewhere. You have the biggest fricking heart of anyone I've ever known. And even though you have that look on your face like"—her voice rose an octave—"*do you have to be crude?*" In her regular voice, she said, "For some strange reason, you love me anyway, and you're good to me. And you accept me even with my faults, and it's fricking fabulous."

Tears welled in Desiree's eyes. "You *are* fricking fabulous." She pulled Violet into a hug, ignoring how Violet's arms hung stiffly by her sides.

"Are you done yet?" Vi said flatly.

Desiree shook her head. "Not even close." She guided Violet's arms around her waist and refused to let go. "I'll take you on my date with me if you don't hug me back."

With a sigh, Violet relented. "You're so annoying."

"So are you."

"You said my careful F-word."

"Hey, Vi?" Des sniffled through happy tears.

"Yeah?"

"Shut the frick up and hug me."

Chapter Fifteen

"JUST A FEW more steps." Rick's heart beat wildly as he led Desiree down the dock, her eyes closed. Could she sense the anticipation of an evening sail in the wind? Recognize the feel of the dock beneath her feet? Did she hear the sea calling them, the way he did?

"I forgot what this was like." The words came without thought, but he *had* forgotten. He'd been so mired down with seeing and hearing his father, fearing his father's memories would slay him, that he'd lost touch with the reasons *why* his father loved sailing so much. The reasons *he* loved it.

"Surprising me? I feel like you surprise me all the time. It's wonderful." She flashed the sweet smile that melted his heart and reached for him, touching his chest with both hands. "Your heart is going crazy. Can I open my eyes?"

"Not yet." Committing this moment to memory, he reveled in the feel of her hands, the way her anticipation settled the remaining discomfort stirring inside him. He touched his lips to hers, feeling proud, and anxious, and happy all at once. "Okay, sweetheart. Open your eyes."

Her beautiful, meadow-green eyes swept over his face, and in the next breath, they glided over the boat. Her fingers curled into his shirt, and worry lines wrinkled her forehead. "Rick…"

He touched his lips to hers again. "It's okay."

"But your father, and—"

"I know. I'm okay." He told her about going on the boat with Drake when it was docked the other night, and how they'd talked about their father for two solid hours. They'd laughed and they'd cried, and by the time he'd gone to see Desiree that night, he'd known what he needed—and more importantly, what he wanted.

"I never had a reason to stop running and face what's kept me from doing the one thing my father loved most. Until you."

She opened her mouth, but as had happened so often with them, no words were necessary.

"Come on, baby." He helped her onto the boat. "Let's make your dream come true."

Half an hour later they were moving swiftly through the water, the land fading into the distance. Rick waited for the awful feelings to drag him under, but all that came was the soothing sounds of the sea washing against the boat, the rustling, slow swish of the sails, and his father's voice in the wind.

Hear that, Ricky? That's pure bliss, right there.

The sun kissed the horizon, and dozens of shades of orange, yellow, and red bloomed over the dark water. Rick gathered Desiree close, filled with a sense of peace and belonging that had been missing in his life for a very long time. He gazed into her eyes. He couldn't imagine going a day without her, much less a week at a time once they left the Cape.

"I know how hard it was for you to even talk about what happened to your father. I can't believe you actually did this for me," she said.

"*You* did this for *me*, babe. For the first time in as long as I can remember, I feel like I'm exactly where I'm supposed to be. With you, on the water. All of this."

A while later they anchored the boat and ate dinner by moonlight. Rick pulled out his phone and snapped a few pictures. She was covering her face in the first one and beaming like a princess in the next. He took a selfie of the two of them, and then another, stealing a kiss as he took it. They laughed and kissed, and he told her some of the stories his father used to make up about being a deep-sea diver and discovering treasures in far-off lands. Stories that were so outlandish, even now, as he relayed them to her, they still made him shake his head.

"There were times he'd have us in stitches, and he'd laugh so hard he couldn't finish his story." His gaze swept over the sea, and he realized he was no longer waiting for the demons to rise and swallow him.

"Are you okay?" Desiree caressed his cheek, and he covered her hand with his, holding it there.

"More than okay. Thanks to you."

"And Drake," she reminded him. It was just like her to give credit to someone else.

"Drake, this summer. *Our* summer." He held her closer, and she rested her head on his shoulder. "I miss him, Des. Out here, thinking about him? I thought I'd feel torn apart. I was so afraid of drowning in his memory that I couldn't see past the pain. But being here with you has brought all the great things about him back to life. Thank you for that."

"I think you'll always miss him," she said. "That's what love is. You ache for the people you wish you had in your life, and you ache for the ones who *are* in your life." A soft laugh escaped her lips. "We're an achy clan. But I think this is a good ache, right?"

He laughed and kissed her through their smiles. "A very good ache, babe. The best ache ever. I met this woman on the docks one night when I tried to get on the boat a few months ago. She told me that life takes us where we need to be when we need to be there, and I think she was right. Life brought us both here at the right time. I couldn't have handled this months or years ago. But now, with you, *for* you, I feel like I'm ready to move forward."

"I want that for you. I think your father would be so happy to know you've spent all this time with your family again, and doing the thing he loved so much. Do you want to say something for him? Goodbye? Something to honor his memory?"

She was so sweet, always thinking about what he needed, taking over hours at the shop without complaint when Violet failed to show up, making the grounds of her grandparents' property gorgeous, even though she knew her mother might let it all go in a few short weeks. How did he get so lucky to have connected with the one person who could make him see the beauty in life again and feel emotions he thought were lost forever?

"I'm sailing again, and I'm with the woman I'm falling head over heels for. The woman I know my father would adore." He pulled her closer and kissed her tenderly. "We are honoring him."

DESIREE KNEW NOTHING about boats, but it was clear that Rick knew everything there was to know, and watching him sail them out into the sea was like seeing poetry in motion.

The wind whipped through his hair, and his eyes shone brighter than she'd ever seen. He was a happy guy, but seeing him on the water made it clear that there was even more positivity and happiness inside him waiting to come out. She hoped she would be there to catch every joyful moment of it.

Rick had lowered the table in the rear of the boat and covered it with enormous cushions that extended the bench seats into a big bed. He brought blankets and pillows up from the cabin. She had no idea how many hours had passed, and she didn't care, as they lay kissing beneath the stars. Rick's hands moved over her body like he owned it, and he did. All of her. This amazing, strong man had conquered his greatest fear for *her*. Her own mother couldn't put her first, and Rick, after knowing her only a few short weeks, made her feel like she was his *everything*. She wanted him to know she felt the exact same way.

"I meant what I said," he told her between heated kisses. "I'm falling hard for you, baby. This is no *summer* romance."

"I know. I'm falling, too."

She tugged up on his shirt, wanting—*needing*—to feel his skin against hers. Gone was the timid girl who had blushed at the very thought of sexy lingerie and dirty words. Tonight she was his in every sense of the word. She was going to be his wildest fantasies come true, and she didn't need a dare, or a reason beyond the way her heart had come to life, to give him all of herself.

He gazed deeply into her eyes, his emotions filling the air around them with a heartbeat all its own. "I've been waiting for you my whole life, sweetheart. I'm not just falling for you. I'm falling in love with you."

Chapter Sixteen

"DO YOU THINK Des will still let us come over for breakfast after you go back to DC?" Drake asked as he and Rick carried plates of crepes and fruit out to the patio of Desiree and Violet's house, where the others were waiting.

Breakfast had become a community event. The guys had moved their running time earlier in order to make it back for the lavish morning meals Desiree prepared.

"Don't count on it," Violet said to Drake as she poured coffee into mugs. "Unless Rick has a stand-in lover to keep Des satisfied while he's gone."

"Which he *does not*." Rick was used to Violet's brash comments, but he was wrestling with his own anxiety about leaving tomorrow, and the last thing he wanted to do was to joke about Desiree and any other man.

"Hey, we have a bunch of friends who live in the Seaside community," Serena said with a tease in her eyes. "I'm sure we'll be inviting them to breakfast soon, and I hear Leanna has two hot brothers. You never know." She waggled her brows.

Rick glared at her.

"Unfortunately," Violet said, "Des's cooking ability seems to be tied to the number of orgasms she's had that morning."

"Geez, Vi," Rick snapped.

"If that's the case, you do have all those wonderful battery-operated boyfriends right down the driveway." Serena pointed in the direction of the shop. "Breakfast could be miraculous *every* morning."

Rick shook his head. How was he supposed to survive missing this?

"A few good nights with them and she may not miss Rick at all," Dean teased.

"Jerk," Rick grumbled, and headed back inside.

Desiree was setting the last of the crepes on a plate, looking hot in a peach halter-top minidress she'd bought when she'd gone shopping with Serena and Mira yesterday. The dress showed off all her curves, and drove him wild. Actually, everything about her drove him wild. They'd made love earlier, and he wanted to carry her upstairs again and stay in bed all day long, being close to the woman he loved.

He kissed her shoulder, and she held her breath, letting it out with that dreamy sigh that had first captured his heart.

"Hi," she said as she turned to face him.

He took the spatula from her hand and set it on the counter. "How's my beautiful girl?"

She shrugged, sadness rising in her eyes, crushing him to pieces. He kissed her cheek, her lips, her chin, the tip of her nose, and finally, a smile broke through the sadness, putting him back together again.

"It's only two or three weeks until you're back in Virginia, and then every weekend we'll be together." He framed her face with his hands and kissed her deeply. "I promise, sweetheart. You know I can't stay away from you."

"I never knew love could be so consuming. I already miss

you, and you haven't even left yet." She gripped his shirt. "I don't want to wake up without you. I wish you could stay longer."

He lifted her onto the counter and stood between her legs, so they were eye to eye. "I wish I could, too. I have to go back and wrap up the deal I've been working on for the past few months, and try to mediate the issues between my partners before it all blows up."

"I know." She wound her arms around his neck. "Kiss me, Rick. Kiss me like you never want to lose me, so even after you're gone I can still feel it."

"Baby," he whispered, the last sound smothered by the press of his lips.

They kissed as if they'd been lovers for fifty years, their tongues sliding and delving, taunting in ways that were so right, so hot and delicious, he got carried away and lifted her into his arms, needing to be closer to her. Their passion took over so fast and urgent, in seconds they were lost in each other.

"You own me, baby," he said between kisses. "Every bit of me. From the very first time I saw you, and with every smile, every kiss, every single touch, I've been falling deeper and deeper in love with you."

She held her breath as he spoke and released it with that sultry sigh that struck him in the center of his heart.

"Show me," she said against his lips. "*Bathroom.* Hurry!"

He made a beeline out of the kitchen and into the bathroom, loving this new eager, bold side of her as much as he adored her sweeter, more vulnerable side. They made quick work of stripping away clothes, and then she was in his arms again, and his heart rushed out.

"I love you, baby. I love you so much I can't see straight."

A slow smile crept across her face, the hazy look of lust hovering in her beautiful eyes. "I love you, too." She touched her lips to his as their bodies came together, and whispered, "Say it again. Say it so many times I hear it in my sleep."

DESIREE HAD PROMISED herself she wouldn't stew about Rick leaving tomorrow. After all, she'd be back in Virginia soon, and as he'd said, they would see each other every weekend. But a few weeks seemed like forever, and after washing up, as they carried the rest of the crepes out to the table, where his family and their friends were laughing and talking, her stomach plummeted. She'd built a life here. A life that made her tremendously happy. How could she leave? How could Rick leave his family again?

She set the plate of crepes on the table, and Rick tugged her against him and kissed her temple. *How can I go a few weeks without this? Without you?*

Violet tapped her spoon on her coffee mug. "By the look of that blush on my sister's cheeks, I'd say we're up for a second course!"

How could she leave her brash sister after they'd just found each other? Desiree put a hand on her hip, trying to keep a stern expression, but inside she was already missing her. "You'd better be quiet, or these breakfasts will stop."

Dean's finger shot up in the air. "I've got duct tape if she can't manage it on her own."

Violet glared at him; everyone else laughed.

Cosmos went paws-up on the fence, barking up a storm, and everyone turned to watch as Lizza climbed from a cab in another bright maxi dress, her thick hair billowing around her face. She looked even more radiant than she had a few weeks ago. She dropped her suitcases in the driveway and headed in their direction.

Desiree grabbed the back of a chair to steady herself as hope soared inside her. Had she come back because she felt bad and wanted to spend time with them after all? "What's she doing back so early?"

"Hey," Rick said. "That's the woman I met on the dock."

"What? When?" Desiree asked as Violet opened the gate and Cosmos bolted out. Her mother scooped him up, laughing as he smothered her in puppy kisses.

"A few months ago," Rick explained. "I told you about her. She's the one who told me life would take me where I needed to be, when I needed to be there."

"Rick...? That's Lizza. She's my mother."

Lizza set Cosmos down, and he ran around the yard barking, his tail wagging, like his long-lost friend had finally arrived. *The friend who had forgotten to tell us you even existed.* Desiree squelched that annoyance as Lizza embraced Violet.

"I thought you said you were away for the summer?" Violet's arms hung loosely at her sides, her gaze shifting to Desiree with a look Desiree couldn't read.

Lizza moved like the wind around the table, touching each person's shoulder or back or arm. "I was but...Oh, goodness. Look at this lovely gathering of gods and goddesses!" She reached over Drake's shoulder, grabbed a strawberry from the bowl of fruit, and popped it into her mouth. Her eyes moved between Rick and Desiree, sparkling with satisfaction. "Cosmos did his job. I knew he was special." Turning her attention to Drake and the others, she said, "Tell me. Who are all you lovely people?"

"I'm Serena." Serena waved from across the table and pointed to the others as she spoke. "And this is Drake, Dean, and Rick."

"It is a pleasure to meet *all* of you. I'm Lizza, Violet and Desiree's mother." She opened her arms as if she were going to bless the food. "Eat up. Fill your souls with this delicious bounty, and I will be out of your hair in no time."

The amusement in Drake's eyes turned to concern, and he shot a look at Rick.

"Lizza...?" Desiree shook her head to try to clear her confusion. "Out of our hair? You aren't staying?"

Still eyeing Rick with a look of sheer joy, Lizza said, "It appears the universe has other plans for me."

"What?" Desiree and Violet said in unison.

"I met the most amazing people while I was away," Lizza explained. "They're going on a meditation mission overseas. Visiting villages and leading—"

Violet held her palms up, silencing her. "Hold on. What do *they* have to do with you and this property?"

Lizza laughed. "Silly me. Did Rob finish the renovations?"

"Yes, but not the ones *you* wanted," Violet said gruffly.

"Then I think we should sell the house, and you ca—"

"No!" Violet and Desiree snapped.

"Maybe we should give you some privacy." Drake rose from the table.

Lizza put a hand on his shoulder, pushing him back down. "Nonsense. Eat, sweetheart."

"We busted our butts to keep your gallery and shop alive," Violet seethed, stalking toward their mother. Only she could look fierce in a bikini top and miniskirt. "Desiree worked her butt off in the gardens, too, in case you hadn't noticed. And Dean and Rick helped with the flower boxes because your dog kept going into the pool at the resort. You are *not* selling this house."

Lizza's smile faded, and she picked up Cosmos, petting him with a sad expression. "It took me weeks to teach him to climb that fence."

Desiree's hand fisted by her side and Rick tightened his hold on her. "You *taught* him to climb the fence?"

Lizza smiled brightly and shrugged. "Cosmos knew what had to be done."

Violet threw her hands up in the air. "I'm not even going to try to pick that apart. I'm staying to run the inn. If you want to go wherever your friends are going, fine. But you're *not* selling the house."

"Wait? You're staying? For real?" Desiree's pulse kicked up.

"If she doesn't sell the house, I am." Violet glared at Lizza.

Lizza set Cosmos down, and her hands flew to her heart. "I knew this would happen! I dreamed about it. This is perfect. Just brilliant!"

"So, I can run the inn?" Violet asked skeptically.

"Absolutely," Lizza said. "It was in the stars all along."

"You can't run it by yourself." Desiree's mind bounced between wanting to stay and wanting to go back to Virginia to be closer to Rick.

Serena shot up from her seat. "Desiree, you can stay! This is perfect! I'll help you guys get started and teach you how to build a rental base, like I did with the resort."

Drake grabbed the back of her shirt and tugged her back down to her seat with a chiding expression.

Rick turned Desiree in his arms, searching her eyes. "What

do you want to do, sweetheart?"

She clutched at his arms. "Be near you." Her eyes darted to Violet. "And be with Violet." She glanced at all her friends around the table and said, "And them."

"Then stay," Rick said with love in his eyes. "We can still make this work. I'll fly up and take long weekends, work remotely for some of the time."

"But—"

Rick touched his lips to hers, silencing her. "You've waited your whole life for a chance at having a relationship with Violet. Now's your chance. Love like ours doesn't change because of a few miles."

"It's in the stars," Lizza whispered loudly.

Tears welled in Desiree's eyes. Could she do this? Could she make this big a decision without feeling like she was becoming her mother? "Are you sure?"

"I've only been more sure of one thing in my life." Rick wiped her tears away. "That I couldn't let the beautiful blonde leave Indian Neck Beach without meeting her."

Chapter Seventeen

LATER THAT MORNING, after everyone else left, Desiree sat on the front porch with Cosmos, talking to Emery on the phone and trying to digest all that had happened. Lizza was leaving after she and Violet returned from their walk, and as ridiculous as it might be, Desiree felt like she was losing her all over again. The longer she sat and thought, the more upset she became about the whole situation. She didn't want to spend the rest of her life wondering why Lizza left her all those years ago, or now. She needed answers.

"Emery, are you still there?" Desiree looked at her phone to make sure she hadn't lost service. She'd explained the whole morning to her, and now, as the airwaves hung in silence between them, she realized how much she'd miss her best friend.

"Yes, but…you're *moving*? And you're in love with a man I haven't met or approved of?"

Desiree laughed. "I took your 'go for the hot Jet Ski guy' as approval. Aren't you missing the point about Lizza? I'm so mad at her."

"Are you kidding? I wish she'd get a dog to find *me* a man. But seriously, Rick will really come to the Cape to see you?

That's a long way. And how about me? Can I come see you? Can we have monthly visits? Can I stay with you next summer? I'm going to have BFF withdrawals, and you better not like Serena or Mira more than me, or I'll go all ninja crazy on your butt."

Desiree laughed. "Yes, to all of that, and nobody could ever replace you."

"And you're happy? Really, truly happy?" Emery asked.

"*So* happy. Rick is everything I could dream of and more. And I have a second chance with Violet. Everything is different here, Em. I think I'll probably teach in the off season, but this summer…Emery, I've changed. I'm *painting*, and sort of doing things spur-of-the-moment."

"It's all that sex you're having. You make me look like a virgin."

"Shut up!" Desiree laughed.

"Um, Des? You do realize that the biggest reason you're happy is leaving tomorrow, right?"

"I know," she said sadly. "But we'll figure that out."

"I don't know Rick, but if you gave him your heart, I know you chose carefully."

She spotted Violet and her mother coming up the driveway. "They're back. I have to go, but I'll call you after Rick leaves."

"Okay. Remember, when you tear Lizza a new one, she knew Cosmos would bring you and Rick together." Emery burst into laughter. "The dog!"

"Emery!"

"Sorry. Go get your answers. I'll have chocolate and tissues ready on your behalf after he leaves. Love you."

Desiree slipped her phone in her pocket and pushed to her feet. Holding tightly to Cosmos's leash, she steeled herself for a confrontation. Her stomach twisted as she walked down the driveway, meeting them by the cottages.

"These gardens, Desi." Lizza waved to the beautiful flowers along the driveway. "They're gorgeous."

"Thank you," came out forced. "I need to talk to you. I want to know why you're doing this."

"Doing what, honey?" Lizza looked at Violet, who stepped closer to Desiree.

That simple show of solidarity amped up Desiree's anger, because her mother had hurt Violet, too.

"*All* of this," Desiree said harshly. "You lied to get us here, upended our lives so you could spend a few weeks clearing your head, and now you're leaving again."

"I didn't lie to you, honey. I *was* dying inside, and your lives were upended long before you came here," Lizza said matter-of-factly. "If anything, coming here settled you both down. And I didn't plan to leave again. This trip just came up. Life is fluid."

Violet opened her mouth to speak, but Desiree cut her off, and the pointed question that was eating her alive came tumbling out. "Just frigging tell me once and for all. *Why* did you leave me?"

"What do you want me to say, Desi?" Lizza asked in a thoughtful voice. "That your father wasn't what I wanted? That you weren't what I wanted? I can't say those things, because I adore you, sweetheart, and I adore your father."

Tears spilled from Desiree's eyes. She *adored* them? She was trembling, becoming more frustrated by the second. "Then how could you leave us and never look back?"

Violet put a hand on Desiree's shoulder, drawing more tears.

Lizza stepped closer. "You want answers that make sense to

you, and all I can do is give you the truth and hope you understand. I've looked back every day of my life, and when I did, I knew you were loved and that you have always had exactly what you needed. You were where *you* needed to be. It would have been selfish of me to drag you all over the world because that's what *I* needed and who *I* am. Your father and I knew from the time you were a little girl that you needed structure and consistency. We also knew that I couldn't live that way. But I fell in love with your father from the moment I met him, and, baby girl, I fell in love with you from the moment I found out I was pregnant. I wanted to try. Your father was good and kind, and he reminded me of my own father. But that was also what drove me away. I felt suffocated."

She reached for Desiree's hand. "Don't you see, Desi? There's no *excuse* for being who we are. We're individuals, and we do the best we can. Staying would have made me miserable, which would have made us all miserable. I had to let you go in order for you to grow into the woman you are. Every time I came back to see you, I wanted to stay. But I knew I couldn't. Staying would have meant leaving again a few days, weeks, or months later, when my insides clawed at me to get moving, and that would have made you even more upset. You have a full life. The only thing you missed out on was me. And trust me, Desi, I'm not that great. But I do love you."

"But you hurt us! All of us." Desiree didn't care if she sounded like a petulant child, because that was the person her mother had hurt and left behind.

"I did," her mother admitted. "But I never meant to. I thought I knew what Violet needed, too. But I was wrong, as she's made very clear to me." She and Violet shared a silent message that told Desiree they'd just had a similar conversation.

"Girls, I'm only human. But hopefully now I've done some good to heal those wounds for both of you. You have to know you girls are my heart and soul, and you're always with me." Lizza shifted the neckline of her dress, exposing a tattoo in the shape of a heart that was half orange and half purple.

Too overwhelmed to speak, Desiree wrung her hands together. Violet turned away, but not before Desiree saw her damp eyes.

"Violet told me you were painting again, and she was doing pottery. And you have a wonderful man in your life who needed you as much as you needed him. The house looks beautiful." Lizza took Desiree's hands, smiling warmly. "Things are *good*, Desi. Violet said you're keeping the shop open. Will you keep painting?"

She nodded absently, still putting the pieces of herself back together.

"Then I named it perfectly," their mother said.

"Devi's? The supreme goddess?" Desiree asked. "Do you think of yourself that way?"

Lizza laughed. "*Please.* You know how I dislike titles. I named the shop after my girls. *Devi*, as in, Desiree and Violet."

LATER THAT EVENING, Rick came out of the rec center with a cold beer, his eyes instantly finding Desiree crouched by the fire pit, helping Hagen put his marshmallow onto a graham cracker. It was a chilly night, and she'd changed into a pair of jeans shorts with a white lace tank top beneath a loose gray sweater. He couldn't take his eyes off her. Her sweater slipped off one shoulder, and she glanced over with a seductive look in her eyes as she pulled it up. It slid right back down, and she trapped her lower lip in her teeth, knowing *exactly* what she was doing to him. He was glad his family and friends wanted to throw him a going-away party, but it was torture to give Desiree a chance to mingle when all he wanted was to be alone with her.

Serena, Drake, Violet, and Mira were talking a few feet away. Serena said something that caught Desiree's attention, and then she went right back to helping Hagen put the top graham cracker on his s'more. He was sure he should be thinking about Desiree and babies or other things that would signify how much he wanted a future with her, which he did. And maybe he'd go straight to hell, but all he could think about was getting that sticky marshmallow and chocolate all over her so he could lick it off.

Matt sidled up to Rick before he reached the others. "My boy has a thing for your girl."

Rick laughed. "Smart boy." Hagen took a bite of his s'more, and Desiree brushed crumbs from his cheek, smiling as she said something to him.

"Right about now, your heart is expanding in your chest." Matt took a sip of his drink. "And you're wondering how you'll get on that plane tomorrow morning."

"Tell me something I don't know." His mind had been a relative war zone for the past few days. He wanted to give Desiree everything, to make up for every ounce of loneliness she'd ever felt, to give her every last part of himself, the way she had given herself to him. But giving her everything meant setting aside all he'd worked for, everything he'd built, and letting down his partners.

"Okay, here's one for you." Matt spoke quietly as they neared the others. "It took me a year to finally ask Mira out, and it took me only a few weeks to ask her to marry me. I wished I hadn't wasted that year."

Rick watched Matt reach for his sister. Hagen ran over to show them his s'more, and those thoughts of a future and a family with Desiree came rushing in.

He gathered her in his arms. "I miss you already, sweetheart."

She pressed her finger to his lips. "We're not going to talk about you leaving, remember?"

He did remember, but not telling her how he felt was apparently not an option. After her mother had left, they'd talked about Desiree's plans, and though she was conflicted about choosing to stay so far away from where he would be living, he knew she was doing the right thing for herself. He'd never want to come between Desiree and Violet, and he respected her even more for having the courage to put her relationship with her sister first. He knew how badly she would miss Emery, too. But she'd faced this decision head-on, just as she had when she'd first come to Wellfleet and her mother had thrown her for a loop. She also seemed surprisingly okay with her mother's excuse for her sporadic visits, even if he wasn't. He would have liked Lizza to have stayed longer and tried to strengthen their relationship. But if Rick knew one thing, it was that some wishes would never come true.

He kissed the tips of Desiree's fingers, glad for the wishes that did.

"Uncle Rick." Hagen tugged at Rick's shorts. "We made you something as a going-away present."

"You did?" He lifted his nephew into his arms and tousled his hair. He was going to miss the little guy a lot. Soon Hagen would be too big to be picked up. "What did you make me?"

Hagen pulled a paper bag from behind his back. "Open it!"

Rick opened the bag and pulled out a small wooden sailboat, complete with little fabric sails, and his heart filled up even more. "Buddy, this is—"

"It's your boat. Me and Dad made it, and I painted it. Mom said you could take me sailing next time you visit. I didn't want you to forget, so I wrote you a note." Hagen turned the boat over in Rick's hands. "See?"

Rick read Hagen's writing on the bottom. "Take Hagen sailing." A lump formed in his throat as he lifted his eyes to his sister, who mouthed, *Love you.* Clearing his throat to try to pull himself together, he said, "I'll take you sailing next time I'm here, little man."

They passed around the boat, and Mira came over and hugged him. "He's going to miss you. *I'm* going to miss you."

"Me too, sis. But I'll be back often." He glanced at Desiree, who was talking with Drake and Serena. "Can you check on Desiree for me while I'm gone? Make sure she's okay?"

"Are you kidding? She's stuck with us. She's like family now. Plus, Serena's already made plans to help them with licensing procedures and everything else involved with running the inn. We'll be here for her, don't worry."

Dean came around the side of the rec center and hollered, "Touch football!"

"Yay!" Hagen cheered.

Serena grabbed Desiree's sleeve and tugged her toward the beach. Desiree shot a smile over her shoulder at Rick. He blew her a kiss and headed for the beach. They played girls versus boys, and spent more time tackling and laughing than playing football. Rick was enjoying the sand time with his girl, covering her in kisses as she giggled and wiggled beneath him.

When they hollered for the next play, he tried to face off with Desiree, but Hagen had beaten him to the spot in front of her, leaving Rick to square off with Violet.

"I ought to kick your butt," Violet said with a challenging stare.

"Why?"

"Because she's going to be a weepy mess after you leave, and guess who's going to be stuck cleaning up those tears?"

"Vi—"

"All kidding aside," she said. "I don't mind picking her sobbing body off the floor, but she's a heck of a lot happier than she was a month ago, and we both know that's all you."

"It's you, too, Vi. She loves you."

Her gaze softened, and just as quickly she lifted her chin and squared her shoulders. "You'd better not forget her while you're gone, or find work too *pressing* to make it back to see her. Or I *will* kick your butt."

He missed the throw on that play and made sure to beat Hagen to the right position the next time. Desiree got the ball and squealed, looking adorable as she clung to it, trying to figure out where to run.

Violet yelled, "Throw it here!" just as Rick grabbed Desiree around the waist and ran off with her.

She tossed the ball in Violet's direction, laughing as he carried her toward the dark dune. "It's *touch* football!" she insisted as he scaled the dune and headed into the long grass. "*Touch!* Not tackle. *Touch!*" she said as he straddled her waist and pinned her hands to the ground.

"I love it when you're bossy." With a quick glance over his shoulder to ensure they had no spectators, he ran his hands all over her, kissing her neck as she squirmed and giggled. "I'm all for touching, especially since you've been teasing me all night."

She ran her hand up the leg of his shorts. "I *like* teasing you."

"Baby, I hope you've had enough playtime with your friends, because I want to touch you in a way that has nothing to do with football."

He lowered his mouth to hers, shifting to the side, and pushed his hand beneath her shorts. His fingers slid over the satiny smooth material.

She trapped her lower lip again, eyes wide, cheeks flaming. "They're crotchless," she whispered.

Holy…

He looked down the dune at the beach below, where everyone was busy playing football. How was he supposed to *think*, knowing his oh so careful girl had gone full-on dirty with crotchless panties? He barely had the presence of mind to accept he couldn't make love to her right there on the dunes as he pushed to his feet, bringing Desiree up with him, taking her in a deep, passionate kiss. He swept her into his arms, thoughts of the others *gone* as he carried her through the long grass toward his cottage.

DESIREE WAS SO turned on by the time they reached Rick's cottage, she wanted to strip naked and attack him, but this was their last night together and she'd been thinking about this moment for *days*. He kicked the door closed behind them, planting his hands on either side of her head and trapping her against the door.

She'd planned a whole strip-tease, and even practiced in the mirror. But with Rick's hard body pressed against her, she was afraid her weak knees wouldn't carry her across the floor. He brushed his lips over hers, the way he'd been doing for weeks, his warm breath sailing over her skin.

"Do it again. Brush your lips over mine. I love when you do that."

He did it again, a wicked grin lifting his cheeks. "Crotchless panties, baby?" he whispered, spreading heat like wildfire to her core.

She could barely breathe. This was the first time she'd been in his cottage, and as much as she wanted to explore his place, she couldn't tear her eyes away from his.

"How am I going to make it through a single day without you?" His husky voice sent a thrum of heat beating inside her. "I'm so in love with you, baby."

He kissed her softly, a tease of a kiss.

"My girl," he whispered.

"I love you, Rick," she said between his tender kisses.

"I love you, too, sweet girl."

He lifted her into his arms and carried her into the bedroom, where he laid her on the bed. As he came down over her, the love in his eyes made her feel cherished. She wanted to memorize everything about this moment, from the electricity in the air and the feel of him against her, to the passion and adoration in his eyes. How could she have decided to stay so far away from where he would be? She already missed him, and he hadn't even left yet.

"Now that we're alone." His lips tipped up in that devastating smile that had first made her heart skip a beat, and he kissed her so tenderly, she dissolved into him. "I'm going to love you slow and steady, so you feel me inside you tomorrow, and the next day, and the next…"

Chapter Eighteen

THE MORNING MOVED too quickly, and Rick had a feeling that every minute after he left Desiree, time would suddenly crawl by. As he finished packing, he couldn't shake the heaviness in his heart. He'd fought the idea of returning to the Cape for so long, and now he couldn't stand the idea of leaving. Desiree moved through his cottage like she belonged there. Not only did she belong, but she'd become as much a part of him as the blood in his veins.

She marveled at Hagen's drawings, which were stuck to the refrigerator with magnets, and moved around the living room asking a dozen questions about his family photos. She wanted to know what he'd been thinking when he'd held Hagen as a newborn and what they were celebrating when the picture of him and his mother had been taken, the one where she had her head on his shoulder. Did he remember that very moment? She was so inquisitive, wanting to soak in every part of his life he was willing to share. That was just one of the things that made her so special. She saw *into* him, wanted to know what made him who he was, and he knew she genuinely cared about the answers.

He zipped up his suitcase, unable to take his eyes off her as she stood at the mantel gazing at another photograph. She wore one of his T-shirts, tied at the hip, and those sexy shorts from last night. Her feet were bare, and her hair was still damp from their shower. He'd loved her in bed, loved her beneath the warm spray of the shower, and he wanted to love her to the ends of the earth. He crossed the room and turned her in his arms.

"You okay, sweet girl?"

"As okay as can be expected. Violet and I will be so busy getting the inn ready now that we have a plan, I'm sure my days will be packed. Nights, though..." Her lips curved up in a sweet smile. "You and I have to burn up the FaceTime hours."

"Every single night," he promised. "And as many mornings as you can spare. You know I need to see you before I start my day. And in two weeks you'll be in my arms again, and we'll make up for every second we were apart." He'd already made the flight reservations to return for a long weekend.

"Perfect. Do you realize this is the first time all summer that I've been in your cottage?"

"Mine or yours makes no difference in my mind."

"I know, but there's so much *love* in this cottage. I swear I can feel your family *everywhere*." She picked up a picture of him and his father on the sailboat. "You have his smile, Rick. He looks just like you described. Full of energy. When I look at this picture, I can hear you two laughing."

When he looked at the picture in her hands, he wondered if their kids would look like his father.

"Why didn't we stay here at all?" she asked, drawing him from his thoughts of the future.

"I thought you'd want to be with Violet and Cosmos."

"I did, but..." She motioned toward the photographs and

the drawings Hagen had made. "I hadn't realized how big a part of you was here. When you come back, I'd really like to stay here in your world."

Could his heart get any fuller? "We'll stay wherever you want. And if you want to take a few of the pictures to your place, you can."

Her eyes lit up. "Really? You wouldn't mind? I'll be careful with them."

"Baby, my things are your things. Take whatever you want."

Mischief rose in her eyes. "Careful. I might rummage through your clothes, looking for something to sleep in that smells like you."

He kissed her, laughing. "Your cuteness gets me every time. Take my whole closet, baby."

A knock sounded at the door seconds before it pushed open, and Drake and Serena walked in.

"I told you they'd be dressed," Serena said. "Hey, girl." She went straight to Desiree and hugged her. "Are you okay?"

"What am I? Chopped liver?" Rick teased. He was glad they'd become so close. Mira, Matt, and Hagen had come to say goodbye earlier.

"You're the one who's leaving," Serena pointed out.

"She's got a point." Drake pulled him to the side of the room while the girls talked. "All kidding aside, it meant the world to me that we went in on this business venture together. I know we've put your partners out all this time, and I feel bad about that. But honestly, it was worth it. I've missed you, and I finally feel like I have my brother back."

"Me too, man." Rick embraced him. "You'll keep an eye on the girls for me? They've been through a lot with their mother, and although Violet comes across as a spitfire, you and I both know everyone needs looking after."

"Already in my plans."

AN HOUR AND a half later Rick drew Desiree into his arms in the small Provincetown airport. The events of the last few weeks played in her mind like a movie, capturing all his smiles, from the heated to the boisterous, and the way his eyes turned from amused to smoldering in the space of a second. She tucked all those and a million more wonderful memories away to draw upon later, forcing the sadness down deep. She wasn't going to make this any harder than it had to be, even if every ounce of her wanted to climb him like a tree and cling like a monkey, refusing to let him leave.

But when he gazed into her eyes, her resolve snapped. "Maybe I shouldn't stay and run the inn. I love you, Rick. I don't want to be apart. I can go back to Virginia, and we can be together next weekend."

He brushed his thumb over her cheek. "I'm so proud of you for making the decision to stay. You're my strong-willed, independent girl, and I love you for doing the right thing. This is where you belong, sweetheart. We'll see each other often. I'll make sure of it."

They called his plane, and he held her tighter, letting all the other passengers make their way through the security gate before him. He put a sliver of space between them and touched his forehead to hers.

"When I come back, everyone better be ten pounds lighter."

She laughed, even as sadness gripped her, and she snuggled against him, taking advantage of every second they were together. When they announced the boarding of his plane, he held her chin between his finger and thumb and touched his lips to hers.

"Until then, sweetheart." He kissed her softly and held her hand as he stepped away. His fingers trailed to the very tips of hers, and then he blew her a kiss and mouthed, *Love you, baby.*

He blew her another kiss from the airstrip as he walked to the plane, and she'd never been so glad for a small airport in all her life. She watched his plane take off, and with a heavy heart, she pushed through the airport doors and stopped cold at the sight of her sister standing before her, holding out a handful of tissues.

"You're gonna need them." Violet thrust them toward her.

Sobs burst from Desiree's lungs as she threw her arms around Violet.

"Seriously?" Violet sighed.

Her hand came to rest on Desiree's lower back, and that simple sort of hug drew more tears. "Why are you here?" she sobbed.

"You can let go now."

She held her tighter. "Vi?"

"What?"

"Tell me you love me."

"Geez, you're needy."

"I'm not letting go until you do."

Violet sighed again. "Fine. I love your sorry butt. Now let's go into P-town and see what kind of mischief we can get into."

Chapter Nineteen

RICK RAN AT a fast clip down the city sidewalk at just after five o'clock the next morning, the muscles in his neck and back knotted up tight. He'd paced the hardwood floors of his Georgetown home for hours, too restless to sleep. He'd thought the longing inside him would let up after he'd arrived back in DC, but the stop-and-go cab ride had grated on his nerves, and his echoing footsteps in the home he'd once considered the *find of the century* had amplified that emptiness. He'd texted with Desiree several times yesterday, and was glad Violet had kept her busy. He'd thought knowing she was okay would help, but when they'd FaceTimed before she went to sleep, seeing her beautiful face and not being able to hold her had torn him apart.

Now, as he kept pace alongside a steady flow of traffic on the city streets, surrounded by brick and concrete in all directions, he not only missed waking up with Desiree in his arms, but also waking with the pool-hopping pup licking his face, running with Drake and Dean, and eating breakfast with friends and family.

He ran an extra two miles to kill some time before heading into the office. They'd scheduled a meeting to discuss the future of their business, and Rick planned to arrive early to go over the contract for the deal he hoped to close this week.

Back home, he checked his phone first thing, happy to see a message from Desiree. He opened it and smiled as a video of her and Cosmos came to life. Her green eyes smiled back at him as Cosmos kissed her whole face. "We miss you," she said in a singsong voice. "Less than two weeks, now. Good luck with your business stuff. Love you to pieces!" She blew him a kiss and held up Cosmos's paw, making him wave, too.

He called her back, but the call went to voicemail. He wasn't big on videos, but there was nothing he wouldn't do for Desiree. He ran a hand through his sweaty hair and cleared his throat. He held up the phone, feeling funny talking to his reflection, and reminded himself not to let her know he was having more trouble with the distance between them than she was. With a smile plastered on his face, he said, "Hey there, beautiful. I missed you last night. Oh, baby, I miss you right now, but I loved the video. Kiss pool-hopper for me. I just got back from a run. Sorry for the sweat. I'd much rather get sweaty with you." *Oh man, don't go there.* "I'm going to shower and head into the office. I'll call you when I get a break. Have a great day. Love you more than you can imagine."

Long-distance relationships officially sucked.

Before showering, he printed out two pictures of Desiree he'd taken the night they'd gone sailing. In the first she had her hand over her face, because her pink cheeks were visible between her fingers, and he loved that adorably shy side of her so much the picture warmed him all over. And the second picture was the one he'd taken just after, with the wind blowing her hair away, the moonlight reflected in her eyes, and that smile. Oh, how he missed her smile. He put them with his briefcase and headed into the shower. If she couldn't be here with him, at least he could see his girl while they were apart.

DESIREE SAT AT the kitchen table pushing cereal around in her milk and petting Cosmos, who was asleep on her lap. He'd become her constant companion overnight, as if he could feel her loneliness.

Violet flew into the kitchen, wearing an ultra-mini-skirt she'd tie-dyed a few days ago and the new purple bikini top they'd bought while they were in Provincetown. "What's going on? Where is everyone?"

Desiree stared into the bowl, trying to force a smile, but it refused to come. It had been hard enough playing happy on the video for Rick and lying to Serena and Drake when she'd sent a text telling them she was going out this morning and wouldn't be making breakfast.

"Cereal."

"No kidding, sis. But *why?*"

She shrugged, set Cosmos on the floor, and carried her bowl to the sink, unable to watch the cereal get any mushier. "Just tired today. I didn't sleep very well last night."

Violet crossed her arms and narrowed her eyes. Desiree turned away. She didn't have the energy for *that* either.

"We do have *toys*," her sister suggested.

She gave her a deadpan look.

"I'm only kidding," Violet said more empathetically. She leaned her hip against the counter beside Desiree. "I know you miss him. What can I do to help?"

"I don't know. I think I made a mistake. A big mistake."

She met her sister's gaze. "I want to be here with you, but I feel like I've got this big hole inside me. I've never felt like this before, except…"

"When Lizza left," Violet said flatly.

"When you both left. Only it's different. When you guys left, I was angry *and* sad. But this…Vi, I don't even know how to explain it. I'm a grown woman, and two weeks is nothing. Soldiers and their wives go months without seeing each other. But Rick's gone for one day and my heart actually hurts like it's been manhandled."

"You're an idiot."

"Mean girl, much?"

"What? This is so simple." Violet poured herself a cup of coffee. "You *know* you can live without me. You've done it for years. But you've never been in love before, Des. Rick lights you up, inside and out. Being *in* love is totally different from loving someone. Of course you feel like you have a hole inside you."

"How would you know? You slept with the first guy you found when we got here."

Violet rolled her eyes. "I knew the guy I slept with. I'm not a total whore. He's lived here since we were kids. We used to make out while you were up in the widow's walk reading 'Little Miss Muffet.'"

"Gosh, it's like you had this whole life I was never a part of."

"I did." Violet shrugged. "Look, Des. I'm a big girl. I'll hire someone to help me run the inn. I bet Serena knows a dozen people who would be willing to work here."

"What are you saying?"

"I'm saying that I can eat cold cereal without you, but by the looks of your sappy self, you can't eat squat without him."

Desiree's heart thundered against her ribs. Could she leave Violet and go after Rick? Did that make her the worst sister in the world? "I'm not just going to leave you hanging. I'm not Lizza, and I don't want you to hate me."

"Holy cow, Des. You're as far from Lizza as anyone could be. You're going after the man you love. I'm your sister. Your blood. I'm here for you no matter what. I might miss you, but I could never hate you."

She'd waited her whole life for this connection with Violet, and her emotions erupted. She threw herself into Violet's arms. "Thank you. I really needed to hear those things."

"Great, *this* again."

Desiree laughed. "One day you'll hug me back. Until then you just have to suffer through it."

She kissed Cosmos's head, feeling a little better, and grabbed her purse and keys from the counter.

"Where are you going?"

"Out to Indian Neck. I have a lot to think about."

Chapter Twenty

RICK CHECKED HIS watch for the hundredth time since the meeting with his partners had begun, wishing he could take a break and call Desiree. It was nearly four o'clock. She would be wrapping up work for the day. Or maybe she was painting or taking Cosmos for a walk. While his partners outlined a strategic plan for the next twelve months, Rick tried to remember what about this city, and this business, had sucked him in all those years ago. Drake's voice roared through his mind. *You know why you work eighty hours a week, hundreds of miles away from us.*

Darn right he did. He'd needed the safety of distance and working too many hours in order to forget what he was running from. But Desiree had changed that. In just a few short weeks she'd reminded him of the importance of dreams, and family, and *love.* She showed him what strength really looked like, and she'd given him a reason to feel again.

And here he was, sitting in a meeting with two men who were driving him up the wall with their bickering and leaving the woman—and the family—he adored, hours and hours away. Missing *him,* and probably wondering why he was being such a stubborn fool.

He'd built this business to make his father proud.

He looked across the table, listening to one partner arguing about the bottom line and the other saying they had enough money to survive for years and to give him a break. What was he doing? If his father were alive and sitting in this room, he'd tap him on the shoulder and nod toward the door. *Come on, buddy. We've got better things to do than complain about money. Life's waiting. You're either moving forward or moving in the wrong direction.*

Rick pushed to his feet feeling lighter already.

Craig and Michael looked over, stress pinching their brows, tension riddling their tight jaws.

"Where are you going?" Craig asked.

"I'm done. I'm out. Michael, you can take over my clients. I'll send a personal note to them explaining that I'm relocating and you're taking over. That should take care of your financial obligations for the next year, at least."

"What?" Craig bolted to his feet. "You can't just leave the partnership."

"Listen, we had a good run, but I don't have it in me to do this anymore. The three of us were great friends, and look where we are now. Michael's going through the roughest time of his life and you're berating him for being human. Michael, I feel bad for you, man, but it's been months. It's time to get back on the ball. Hopefully this will help both of you. You don't need me hanging around."

They both spoke at once, and Rick held up his hands. "Guys. I'm not changing my mind. I'll have our attorneys take care of the appropriate documents this week, but right now I've got to get back to the Cape."

Rick blew out of the conference room and pulled his phone

from his pocket, feeling like he'd just been cut loose from years of prison. He stalked down the hall to his office as he called Desiree. One ring, two. *Come on, pick up.*

He pushed open his office door as the phone rang a third time, and he lifted his gaze toward the sound, nearly dropping the phone at the sight of his sweet girl standing in the middle of his office. She was fishing in her purse, and stilled, tears filling her eyes.

"Hi." Her voice cracked.

His heart raced as he took her in his arms. "Baby? What are you doing here?"

"I couldn't eat cereal," she said through tears and kisses. "I love the Cape, and I love Violet, but nothing compares to my love for you. I don't want to be all those hours away."

"You'll never have to again. I was just calling to tell you I was coming back."

"Back?" Her face clouded with confusion.

"To *you*, baby. To the Cape, where we both belong."

Chapter Twenty-One

FALL SWEPT THROUGH the Cape at breakneck speed, bringing colorful foliage and brisk air. But in the span of a few short weeks, winter bullied its way in, leaving a blanket of white over the quiet, small town. Rick and Desiree had moved in to one of the cottages on her property so she could be on site once the inn opened early next year. Rick loved having all their belongings in one place, their family photographs intermingled, her favorite candles in every room. He'd even built a special bed for Cosmos, which they kept *beside* their bed, but the little pool hopper still found his way onto theirs after they fell asleep. Rick didn't mind. He was truly blessed. He'd been given a second chance with the family he'd spent too long away from, and he went to sleep every night with the woman he adored and woke up loving her even more than he had the night before.

It was Christmas Eve, and everyone had gathered at the inn to exchange presents, except Mira and her family. They were off exploring castles for the next few weeks. Desiree's father had a business meeting out of the country, but he'd Skyped with them yesterday, which had made Desiree's day. Excited about the surprise he'd planned for Desiree, Rick pulled out his phone and sent a quick text to Serena, setting his plan into motion.

"Got a date?" Violet smirked as she sidled up to him with Cosmos trailing beside her. "I'm pretty sure everything you need is right here in this room."

She was as snarky as ever, in a pair of leather leggings and a short black sweater. But Rick really liked her, just as he had from the moment they'd met. She might be brash, and overprotective of Desiree, but he couldn't blame her. They'd gone far too long without each other.

"You've got that right," he said. "I was just checking to see if her present had been delayed."

He watched his beautiful girlfriend busily taping a picture Hagen had made to the window behind the Christmas tree, alongside several other pictures from the students in her children's art class, which she held on Wednesday afternoons. She'd been painting more often, and like her mother, all the paintings stuck to one theme. Although Lizza's theme was women, Desiree's was family. She'd painted memories of her and Violet, and pictures of her father, Rick, Mira, Hagen, and the rest of their close friends and family. She'd even painted a picture of Lizza wearing a long orange dress and standing on the front porch of the inn.

"I don't think she'll care if her gift arrives late, or *at all*. Look at her, with that goofy smile and all dressed up in that fancy little black dress. That's a woman who wants for nothing."

But Rick knew Violet was wrong. There were things Desiree wanted, and he was determined to give her all of them.

"Vi!" Serena called from across the room, waving her over.

Rick caught Desiree's eye as she peered around the Christmas tree. A shy smile curved her lips. She looked like she belonged on a holiday card, with her beautiful blond hair tumbling over her shoulders, the lights of the tree sparkling beside her, and the gold and red ribbons lining the windows, candles sparkling on the sills. Her eyes darted to Violet and Serena, then to Drake and Dean, standing by the fireplace talking. Drake's eyes had been locked on Serena in her little red dress all evening. Desiree's eyes found Rick's again, the air between them igniting. She lifted the hem of her dress, flashing thigh-high stockings and a black garter belt. She was going to be the death of him, with furtive glances one minute and bold sensuality the next. And what a perfect death it would be. How was he going to make it through the evening knowing she was all sexed up under that little black dress?

Serena called Desiree over to help her get something from the kitchen, and Desiree smoothed her dress over her thighs and walked gracefully across the room as if she hadn't just set his body on fire.

DESIREE POURED CHAMPAGNE into glasses and set them on a tray, looking around their gorgeous new kitchen. She and Violet had learned to compromise. She'd gotten the stainless-steel appliances she'd wanted, and the countertops—black granite with flecks of gold and amber—were all Violet. The maple cabinets tied it all together beautifully, the same way the Cape had bound the sisters together. She had a full new life, but she missed Emery terribly. Saying goodbye had been the hardest thing she'd done in forever. They kept in touch with FaceTime and texts, but it wasn't the same as having her best friend barge through the front door demanding breakfast or ranting about this date or that one. She had plenty of new friends, but they'd never replace Emery.

Desiree, Violet, and Serena had spent the afternoon baking cookies and making an elaborate lamb dinner while the guys had decorated. She wished Emery and her mother could have been there for the party, but Emery was spending the holidays with her brothers. She'd sent an email to Lizza, and wasn't surprised by her response. *Miss you, too, lovey. I'm always with you in spirit!*

When Violet and Serena finished arranging the hors d'oeuvres on trays, Serena said, "I think we're ready."

"I can't wait to give Rick his present." She'd painted a picture of Rick and his father on the boat, and hoped they could hang it above the fireplace in their cottage.

"Let me carry the champagne." Violet took the tray from Desiree. "Wouldn't want you to drop it when you get all googly-eyed over your Savage."

"I wouldn't." Desiree laughed, but it wasn't so far-fetched. Rick made her weak in the knees with his thoughtfulness and their late-night talks as they walked along the shore. Even now, when it was too cold to sit on the beach, they spent time around the fire pit at the resort, with Drake and the others. Rick was playing guitar more often, and Desiree would never tire of hearing him sing.

She followed the girls out of the kitchen, carrying a tray of cookies.

"Surprise!" everyone yelled, and the tray fell from her hands, crashing to the floor, and sending cookie pieces flying.

Tears flooded Desiree's eyes at the sight of Emery and Lizza standing before the tree with big red ribbons across their bodies like they had won a beauty pageant. She barreled into both of them, hugging them so tight, she thought they might break.

"You're here!" Crying and laughing, she looked over their

shoulders at Rick, who was grinning so wide, she knew he'd orchestrated the whole thing. He mouthed, *Merry Christmas. I love you*, which made her cry harder.

"Violet!" Desiree waved her over.

"Go for it, hugaboom," Violet said as she picked up the tray from the floor. "I said my hellos when they got in last night."

"You knew?"

"Someone had to help track down Lizza," Violet said.

"I think my heart just exploded. Thank you both." Desiree couldn't stop crying even as Rick introduced Emery to the others and Lizza embraced her again.

"That man, Desi," Lizza said. "He loves you to pieces."

"I know." She went to him, and he gathered her in his arms. "I don't know how to say thank you for something this wonderful."

"I promised to make all your dreams come true, and I meant it." He leaned in closer and whispered, "And thank you for my gift. I can't wait to unwrap you later."

"Shh." Her eyes darted to the others. "Violet will make a public announcement if she finds out."

Desiree's heart was full as Emery hugged each one of her friends. Dean watched every move she made, and when Emery embraced him, the sparks could be felt around the room. He'd grown a beard over the winter, and Emery had a definite thing for beards.

"Someone get the man a pair of scissors before he tears that bow off her," Violet said as she carried a broom out from the kitchen.

"Forget the scissors. You save that ribbon for later, doll," Dean said with a lascivious look in his eyes. "I can think of a few good uses for it."

"Dude, she just got here." Drake dragged Dean away.

Desiree pulled Emery and Lizza into her arms again. "Thank you both for coming."

"Your man sent us plane tickets." Emery smiled at Rick. "You now have my official approval, and you may proceed with dating him."

"How about marrying him?" Rick asked as he reached for Desiree's hand and dropped to one knee.

There was a collective gasp, and it took Desiree a second to catch up and realize this was *real*. Rick gazed up at her with so much love in his eyes it wrapped around her and brought her to her knees in front of him.

"Rick?" she whispered, tears streaming down her cheeks again.

A smile lifted his lips. "Sweetheart, you are the best thing that has *ever* happened to me. From the very first moment I saw you, I have fallen deeper in love with you. And I know my love will continue to grow with each passing day. Baby, you light up my days and heat up my nights. I want to give you everything and experience all that life has to offer with you. Babies and white picket fences, family dinners and moonlight walks. I want to see you paint pictures of our children playing on the beach, and make you blush when you're old and gray."

He wiped her tears away with the pad of his thumb, and she inched closer, until they were knee to knee.

"Will you marry me, Desiree? Be mine and let me be yours forever?"

She lunged into his arms, nearly knocking them both over. "Yes! A thousand times yes!"

Cheers rang out around them, and Cosmos yapped happily, circling them as they sealed their promises with kisses. They were passed from one friend to the other, hugged and congratulated, and then she was in Rick's arms again, gazing into his dark, loving eyes. *The eyes of my future husband.*

Cosmos circled them, and Rick scooped him up. "I owe pool hopper a world of thanks for leading me to you."

Desiree glanced at her mother, who was busy talking with Dean and Emery, and she realized her mother was right after all. With a little help from her mother, Cosmos had known what needed to be done.

The End

Ready for more Bayside fun?

Fall in love with Dean and Emery in *Sweet Passions at Bayside*!

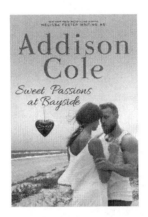

Chapter One

THERE WERE A few things worse than being stuck in traffic and needing to pee, but after driving since the crack of dawn and sitting on the same stretch of highway for the past forty minutes—which was about thirty minutes longer than her bladder could handle—Emery Andrews couldn't think of a single one. Her back teeth were floating, and if she didn't find a bathroom soon, her car would become a swimming pool. She should have thought about weekend traffic *before* hightailing it out of Oak Falls, Virginia, and heading for her new home and workplace, Summer House Inn, in Wellfleet, Massachusetts. But thinking things through wasn't Emery's forte. She was more of a just-do-it-and-worry-about-things-later type of girl, as evident in her move to the Cape.

Now, if she could only get there.

She gazed out at the long line of brake lights in front of her and picked up her phone to call her best friend, Desiree Cleary. Desiree had been like a sister to her since they were five years old, and last summer, she had fallen in love, reconnected with her half sister, Violet, *and* decided to move to the Cape and open the inn, all in the space of a few short weeks. Desiree's excitement was contagious. Every time they spoke on the phone, she raved about her new life with her fiancé, Rick Savage, and her plans for the inn, and it had sparked introspection in Emery. She realized *she* wasn't living a life she was excited by in Oak Falls—and she had no one to blame but herself. After making a poor decision right before the holidays and going out with her boss at the Oak Falls Back Care and Rehabilitation Center, where she had worked full-time as a yoga back-care specialist, she'd ended up leaving the practice. Unfortunately, she'd signed a non-compete specifically for providing the one thing that brought her the most fulfillment and could no longer practice yoga back care within a fifty-mile radius of the rehabilitation center. In the small rural town of Oak Falls, her career, and her personal life, seemed to have stalled.

She'd needed a fresh start, and when Desiree had invited her up to Wellfleet to teach yoga at the inn, she'd jumped at the chance.

Desiree answered the phone on the second ring. "Hey, Em. I can't talk. It's changeover day. I have three customers waiting to be checked in and two on hold. Call you later?"

"Wait! I'm in Orleans, trying to get there. But—"

"Orleans? Really?" There was no missing the excitement, or the hesitation, in Desiree's voice. "I thought you were coming next week. I don't have an open room until this Wednesday. Why didn't you call and let me know you were coming early?"

"Because after quitting my job and packing up my apartment, the emptiness freaked me out and I was excited to get the heck out of Oak Falls and see you!"

Emery had always been the adventurous one, while Desiree had been cautious, thinking things through to the nth degree. But along with Emery's boxed-up belongings came a big *what if*. What if she couldn't find enough clients to make a living? And as she'd sat in her empty apartment contemplating that worry, she'd realized that leaving the only place she'd ever lived, and leaving her family, wasn't going to be as easy as she'd imagined. But although she'd been sad about leaving them, her three older brothers had called her several times during her long ride up, making her glad to be moving out from under their watchful eyes. She knew if she had stayed in town for another week, they, and her other worries, would have driven her batty. She had never let *anything* stop her from doing things in the past, and she knew the only way to get over those fears was to plow full speed ahead—and plow she did!

"But with this traffic," Emery said, "I'll never get there. I'm stuck on the highway right before the rotary. Should I get a motel room until you have a vacancy?"

"Oh, Em, you'll never get one. It's peak season. Everyone's booked. But don't worry. I'm sure Vi will let you stay in her cottage." Desiree and Violet had renovated the old Victorian and the four cottages that had once been owned by their grandparents. "I'll mention it to Vi, but you might as well find someplace to hang out for a few hours until the traffic eases up.

227

Maybe you can do some shopping in Orleans," Desiree suggested. "I'm so sorry, but I really can't talk right now. Will you be okay for a few hours on your own?" Before Emery could respond Desiree said, "*Of course* you will be. You love new adventures! We'll catch up when you get here. And if you hang out in Orleans, be sure to bring me something from the Chocolate Sparrow!" Desiree blew a kiss into the phone and the line went dead.

The decadent chocolate shop had been closed when Emery had visited over the holidays, and the way Desiree talked about it, their chocolates sounded practically *orgasmic*.

I could use a few orgasms—chocolate inspired or otherwise.

She mulled over the idea of trying to make it to the chocolate shop as the cars ahead of her crawled into the rotary. Traffic was at a standstill getting off the rotary and onto the main drag in either direction—toward the Summer House Inn *and* toward the orgasmic chocolates in Orleans. She squeezed her thighs together. She'd worn her new bikini beneath her tank dress and had hoped to be lying out on the beach by now. The last thing she needed was to pee all over it. She spotted an exit on the opposite side of the rotary.

The heck with it. Desiree was always telling her about back roads the tourists didn't know about. It was time for her first Wellfleet adventure.

She squeezed by the line of cars waiting to get onto the main drag and drove halfway around the rotary to a side road. As she pulled onto it, she realized it ran in the wrong direction, back the way she'd come. She scrolled through her contacts and called the man who had become her *second* best friend, Dean Masters. She'd met Dean when Rick, who was Dean's business partner and one of his closest friends, had flown Emery in over the holidays to surprise Desiree the night he proposed. They'd hit it off right away, and they'd kept in touch after she'd returned home to Virginia. What had started as a storm of daily teasing texts about a big red ribbon she'd had tied around her body the night they'd met had turned into evening phone calls and morning wake-up messages, and eventually, into a friendship she'd come to trust and rely on.

"Hi, doll. How's it going?"

Dean's deep voice, and the endearment he'd used since the day they'd met, brought a smile, and just like that, the knot in her stomach eased. Dean had seamlessly filled the gap Desiree had left behind, binge-watching shows with Emery while they Skyped and talking until the wee hours of the morning about everything and nothing at all. They were so different, they shouldn't have clicked. While Emery barreled into situations with little thought about repercussions, Dean was a thinker, careful and methodical, like Desiree. And, like Desiree, he'd become the yang to her yin.

"Hey, big guy. *Please* tell me you can get me to the inn from"—she glanced at the road sign—"Rock Harbor Road." At the next corner, she turned off the main road and onto a residential street, hoping to find a back way to the inn or maybe one of those small-town shops Desiree was always talking about, so she could use their bathroom.

"You're in town?"

"Yes! *Please* get me to someplace with a bathroom fast. Traffic is a nightmare, and I've got to pee so bad I swear I'm going to knock on the next door I see."

"Okay, slow down," he said with a serious tone. "Before you make some stranger's day, follow my directions. Turn right onto Bridge Road."

"Um…" She looked for road signs. "I turned off the main road already, and I have no idea what street I'm on now."

"Of course you don't."

She rolled her eyes at the smirk in his voice.

"Why don't you use your GPS?"

Two weeks ago, she'd called him when she'd gotten lost coming home from a concert and he'd walked her through how to use the GPS. Even with his careful instructions, she'd gotten frustrated and nearly thrown the darn thing out the window. "You *know* I hate that thing. The stupid voice tells me what to do way too late, and I can't hear it with the radio on, and I *really* think it should have a male voice option anyway."

He laughed.

She tried to concentrate on the narrow, windy road and not on her near-bursting bladder. "Don't do that!"

"What?" He chuckled again.

She squeezed her thighs together. "*Don't laugh!* If I laugh I'll wet my pants."

He was silent for so long she checked her phone for a signal. "Hello? Dean? Are you there?"

"Sorry. I muted you."

"Why?"

"You told me not to laugh, and I'm picturing you bouncing in your seat trying not to pee, and…" His words were lost in his laughter.

And so went the next fifteen minutes as Dean figured out where she was and directed her to his house. By the time she got there she was ready to burst. She flew out of her car, tearing a path around gorgeous, overflowing gardens, and headed for Dean's front door. He came around the side yard, shirtless, carrying an enormous rock that covered his entire torso. His jaw was clenched tight. Veins bulged in his thick neck, broad chest, and massive arms as he bent his knees and set the rock at the edge of a garden.

Her breath whooshed from her lungs.

Holy mother of hotness.

She'd almost forgotten how large and powerful, how *commanding*, he was in person, and how from their very first glance, he'd made her stomach flip and tumble. His hair was the same honey-wheat color as hers, cropped so short he looked military. And *wow*, he'd kept the beard he'd grown over the winter after all. He'd told her he usually went clean-shaven over the summers, but she'd pleaded with him to keep it. She'd told him the girls would love it, and she knew she was right. He looked even tougher than usual, and coupled with his perpetually serious expression, he appeared as if he were going to snap at any moment.

The big faker.

Beneath that big, bad facade was the most patient man she'd ever met. That trait had taken her by surprise, and now she found herself swallowing hard to silence the lascivious woman inside her who was preparing for a coming-home party.

No way. Not happening. She'd dated friends before, and it never ended well. She'd long ago put Dean into the off-limits section of her brain, whether her body remembered that rule or not.

He rose to his full height of six-plus feet, spotting her. An amused look rose in his gunmetal-blue eyes, and she realized she was staring at him, with her thighs pressed together. *Aw, heck!* What could she do but laugh, which quickly sent an urgent sensation rippling through her bladder.

Dean jogged up to the front porch and threw the door

open. "Go on, doll. Down the hall to the left."

"You're my hero." She planted a quick kiss on his cheek. She'd asked him why he called her that the first weekend they'd met, and his response had been, *No reason.*

He smacked her butt as she ran through the door.

"I swear I'll pee on your floor!"

"Not the response I usually get," he called after her. "But if that's what you're into…"

She couldn't stop grinning. It was so good to see him, so good to be back near Desiree and the other friends she'd made last winter. With her bladder finally empty, she washed her hands and took a moment to check herself out in the mirror. Yup, she looked like she'd spent all day in a car. Her hair was tied in a knot and secured with a pencil she'd found in the console. Several strands had sprung free, giving her a disheveled look. She pulled out the pencil, and her hair tumbled down her back. She cupped a hand over her mouth and breathed into it.

Ugh. Coffee breath.

She opened the vanity drawer and dug around looking for toothpaste. *Floss, Band-Aids, deodorant, nail clippers, beard oil, beard balm.* She picked up the beard oil and opened the top to sniff it. *Mm. Cedar.* She read the label. Organic. *Nice.* Scented with peppermint, eucalyptus, and lavender essential oils. Looked like her second-bestie treated himself well. She put the cap back on and set the beard oil in the drawer, then rifled through another drawer and found toothpaste. She squeezed a bit on her finger and scrubbed her teeth clean.

"Hey, doll. You okay in there?" Dean called through the door.

She pulled it open, held up her finger to indicate *one second,* and gathered her hair over one shoulder as she turned the faucet

232

on and dipped her mouth under it. She rinsed her mouth and washed her hands as he watched with a curious expression.

"That's so much better. I borrowed your toothpaste."

He arched a brow. "Got a date?"

"Ha! I wish." She threw herself into his arms, hugging him so tight she could feel his heart pounding against hers. "I'm so glad to finally be here!"

"Me too." He set her on her feet. "Sorry about the dirt. I'm sure I smell pretty ripe, too." He hiked a thumb over his shoulder. "I'm landscaping out back."

She brushed the dirt from the front of her dress and dragged her eyes down his incredibly hot bod, wondering why he didn't have some chick there with him. Desiree had told her that girls hit on Dean all the time. "You smell like your beard oil, which I *might* have snooped into."

His eyes narrowed. "Snooped?"

She waved a hand dismissively. "Of course! I needed toothpaste. Anyway, I like the way it smells, and it's good to know you take care of yourself in ways other than just building these bad boys up." She ran her hands over his bulbous biceps and he gritted his teeth. She laughed and patted his cheek. "You look like you want to growl at me."

Having grown up with three older brothers, she got along better with guys than girls and had always had more guy friends than girlfriends. She'd learned at a young age that guys had a hard time holding anything back. If he wanted to growl, she'd let him growl.

"Something like that," he said under his breath.

She followed him into the living room. "Why is your stuff in there anyway and not in the master bathroom?"

"Only one bathroom in the house."

"Really? Why?"

"I don't know. Why would a single guy need more than one bathroom? More importantly, I thought you weren't coming up until next week. What happened?"

Ever since Desiree moved away and she and Dean had become friends, Emery had felt like her life was here now, too. "I felt like I was waiting for water to boil, and I was so excited to come and start my life here, and see you, Des, Vi, and Serena and everyone else, I said the heck with it!" Serena ran the administrative offices of the resort Dean co-owned with Rick and Rick's brother, Drake. "And here I am! But with the traffic, I can't get to Desiree's, and she said it could be backed up for hours. Something about changeover day?"

"With only one road on and off the Cape, it's one big traffic jam on changeover days. Saturdays are the worst, but Sundays can be a headache, too."

"Do you know a back road to her place?"

He turned, brows knitted. "I can take you over on the Jet Ski."

"Oh, fun!" Her excitement deflated as quickly as it had arrived. "But then I can't bring my stuff."

"Why don't you hang out here and help me in my yard? We'll throw something on the grill for dinner, and you can go over when the traffic clears."

"You must landscape *all* the time. Your yard looks like it belongs in a magazine."

"Thanks." He shrugged and said, "Gotta do what you love, right?"

She knew that in addition to being co-owner of the resort, Dean maintained a few clients with his own landscape business—the hospital where he used to work as a trauma nurse and the local assisted living facility, where he worked in the gardens with the residents. Emery liked to tease him about his elderly fan club. Dean was great at keeping his emotions close to his chest, which made him difficult to read sometimes, but whether they were texting or talking on the phone, his passion for his work always came through loud and clear.

"Very true." She loved what she did for a living, but lately she'd craved more than the yoga classes she'd been teaching at a gym since leaving the rehab center. She hoped one day to return to being a yoga back-care specialist and to turn her passion for yoga back care into something more meaningful. But those were plans for another time.

One major life event at a time.

To distract herself from her thoughts, she focused on Dean's cottage. She took in the hardwood floors and wood-paneled walls that ran the length of the open living room and kitchen, which were separated only by a table for two. A black cast-iron oven and cooktop and fridge complemented earth-toned granite countertops atop rustic wood cabinets. Long, rough-hewn wooden shelves held dishes and cups, giving the place the brawny feel of a bachelor pad.

"I saw glimpses of your place when we FaceTimed and Skyped, but"—*like seeing you in person again*—"experiencing it firsthand has a much stronger impact. This is incredible. So earthy and rugged. I love it." She ran her fingers over the simple oak table.

"Thanks. This is the original house built on the property. When I renovated, I wanted to preserve the rustic feel, so I used old, sun-bleached scaffold boards for the walls and floors. Check this out. It's my favorite feature." He went to the wall that faced the kitchen, unhooked something near the top and then near the bottom, and slid the entire wall *into* the living room wall, like he would a pocket door. "These are barn doors I repurposed from another property."

At least ten or fifteen feet of wall space disappeared before her eyes, opening the small kitchen to a magnificent trellis-covered patio, with potted plants overflowing with life on top of enormous rocks, like the one Dean had been carrying when she arrived. Comfortable-looking rockers and two oversized loungers had a gorgeous view of more impeccable gardens.

"Wow, Dean. I've never seen anything like this." She followed him outside, where low stone walls lined either side of the patio. A fireplace anchored one end, and she spied the telltale wooden stall of an outdoor shower just beyond. Her gaze swept along the gorgeous pavers, and she imagined how wonderful it would be to meditate there in the early mornings, when the rest of the world was asleep. She'd seen the hardscaping he'd done at the resort, but this was even more breathtaking.

They walked along a rocky path between two garden beds. She recognized some of the flowers and was happy to see roses and lavender, which she could use to steep tea. As they wound through the path surrounded by vibrant flowers, with the sun shining down on them, it felt like she'd stepped into his private paradise.

"Sort of coaxes you into thinking about a simpler lifestyle, doesn't it?" he asked.

"Definitely. If I lived here, I might never want to leave. But what landscaping are you doing? Everything already looks gorgeous."

His hand pressed against her back as he guided her around a wall of bushes. She'd forgotten how often he'd done that the weekend they'd met, and how nice it felt. Most guys just said they'd show her something and expected her to follow. Her burly buddy might look standoffish to some, but he was the most gentlemanly guy she knew.

"Thank you for letting me use your bathroom and hang out for a while." She put her arms around his waist and hugged him. His entire body felt like one giant muscle. His hand moved up her back, returning the embrace. It wasn't the rushed embrace of a man looking to get lucky—which she was all too familiar with. It was a gentle yet powerful loving embrace that spoke volumes about their close friendship, and it made her feel like she'd come home instead of having left it all behind.

"Anytime, doll," he said. "And if it'll earn me hugs, then use my bathroom as often as you'd like."

They walked around more garden beds, and nestled between a rock garden and a grassy area with lounge chairs and a small table, there was a patch of tilled earth with all sorts of weeds growing around the edges.

"This is my latest project." The edges of his lips tipped up. "Are you in? Or do you want to sit in traffic?"

"Heck, yes, I'm in. But I warn you, I have a black thumb. I can kill a plant just by looking at it."

He laughed. "I highly doubt that. I'll go grab another trowel and a couple of cold drinks. Be right back."

Helping weed his garden was the least she could do. After all, he was the one who'd convinced her to give this move a go. During one of the many nights when they were FaceTiming, she'd mentioned that she was thinking about coming up for the summer to see if she could get a seasonal yoga business off the ground, hoping it would not only be a nice change of pace for her, but that it would also bring added value to the inn for Desiree and Violet's customers. Dean had asked, *How can you succeed at anything, giving only half an effort?* She'd seen it as a *huge* step, moving away for the summer, not half an effort, but then he'd followed that question with one that had stopped her in her tracks. *Are you always afraid to commit, or are you worried you'll miss your family?* And she'd found herself retracing the last few years of her life and realizing that maybe, *just maybe*, he'd figured out what she never had. And the more she'd thought about it, the more convinced she'd become that she had been the adventurous one, but only within the safety of her small hometown. It was time to blaze a new adventure and blow that girl out of the water.

She heard a phone ring in the house, jarring her from her memories. Shrugging off those thoughts, she set to work ripping out the weeds.

To continue reading, please buy *Sweet Passions at Bayside*

Dear Readers,

The Sweet with Heat: Bayside Summers series is just one of the subseries in the Sweet with Heat big-family romance collection. You may enjoy starting with *Read, Write, Love at Seaside*, the first book in the Sweet with Heat: Seaside Summers series (free in digital format at the time of this publication). All Sweet with Heat books may be enjoyed as stand-alone novels, so jump in anytime! Characters from each subseries make appearances in future books so you never miss an engagement, wedding, or birth.

Not all future releases will have preorders. Please be sure to sign up for Addison's newsletter and follow her on Facebook so you don't miss them.

www.AddisonCole.com/Newsletter
www.facebook.com/AddisonColeAuthor

Happy reading,
Addison

More Books By The Author

Sweet with Heat: Seaside Summers
Read, Write, Love at Seaside
Dreaming at Seaside
Hearts at Seaside
Sunsets at Seaside
Secrets at Seaside
Nights at Seaside
Seized by Love at Seaside
Embraced at Seaside
Lovers at Seaside
Whispers at Seaside

Sweet with Heat: Bayside Summers
Sweet Love at Bayside
Sweet Passions at Bayside
Sweet Heat at Bayside
Sweet Escape at Bayside

Stand Alone Women's Fiction Novels
by Melissa Foster (Addison Cole's steamy alter ego)
The following titles may include some harsh language

Chasing Amanda (mystery/suspense)
Come Back to Me (mystery/suspense)
Have No Shame (historical fiction/romance)
Megan's Way (literary fiction)
Traces of Kara (psychological thriller)
Where Petals Fall (suspense)

Acknowledgments

Every time I start writing a new series, I fall in love with the writing process all over again. Creating another fictional world on Cape Cod has been such a joy! I hope you enjoyed meeting Rick, Desiree, and all their fun friends and family. I can't wait to bring you the rest of the Sweet with Heat: Bayside Summers love stories.

Heaps of gratitude goes out to Lisa Bardonski for our fun chats about Rick and Desiree. As always, I am indebted to my meticulous and talented editorial team. Thank you, Kristen, Penina, Juliette, Marlene, Lynn, Justinn, and Elaini for all you do for me and for our readers.

As always, I am grateful to my family for allowing me the time to slip away and create my fictional worlds.

Addison Cole is the sweet alter ego of *New York Times* and *USA Today* bestselling and award-winning author Melissa Foster. Addison enjoys writing humorous, and deeply emotional, contemporary romance without explicit sex scenes or harsh language. Addison spends her summers on Cape Cod, where she dreams up wonderful love stories in her house overlooking Cape Cod Bay.

Visit Addison on her website or chat with her on social media. Addison enjoys discussing her books with book clubs and reader groups and welcomes an invitation to your event.

Addison's books are available in paperback, digital, and audio formats.

www.AddisonCole.com
www.facebook.com/AddisonColeAuthor